M000191155

HARRISON • JONES

EQUAL

TIME

POINT

A NOVEL

Equal Time Point
Copyright © 2009 by **Harrison Jones**. All rights reserved.

No part of this publication may be reproduced, stored in a retrieval system or transmitted in any way by any means, electronic, mechanical, photocopy, recording or otherwise without the prior permission of the author except as provided by USA copyright law.

This novel is a work of fiction. Names, descriptions, entities, and incidents included in the story are products of the author's imagination. Any resemblance to actual persons, events, and entities is entirely coincidental.

Published by Av Lit Press

Visit the author's website at www.harrisonjones.org

Dedication

For Diane

She continues to remind me that tomorrow's
vision is not limited by today's horizon.

Acknowledgments

This project would never have left the ground without the contributions of hundreds of aviation professionals who unselfishly, and sometimes unwittingly, enriched my career and my life. We shared tears, laughter, and views of the earth rotating miles beneath us that left no doubt that God is a wonderful creator.

I am most grateful for the support and encouragement of my family and traveling companions extraordinaire: Diane, Susan, Madison, Harold, Colton, Kyle, and Cason.

I also want to thank my editors, Emily Wilson and Stephen Carradini. Your talent and patience is most appreciated.

CHAPTER ONE

The captain glanced down to see the number one engine fire light glowing red. The warning bell was so loud that it left no doubt there was a serious emergency.

"Silence the bell and declare an emergency," said the captain.

The first officer pushed the button to silence the bell and prepared to tell the tower that they had an emergency. The bell continued to ring.

"Silence the bell," the captain angrily repeated.

The bell continued to ring. He turned to yell at the incompetent copilot, but blinked his eyes when he found himself in total darkness. His heartbeat raced and he felt helpless in panic and confusion. How could this be happening? It was pitch black and he could no longer feel the familiar yoke and throttles in his hands. *Is this how it all ends?* In the darkness he could hear a voice competing with the noise of the bell. The words grew louder, and he began to understand. He recognized his wife's voice.

"Charlie, turn off the alarm clock before it wakes up the entire neighborhood!" He blinked his eyes again and found himself sitting in his bed with beads of sweat running down his

1

face and his old-fashioned wind-up alarm clock ringing on the nightstand.

He shut the alarm off and his wife said, "Thank God. Charlie, that thing could wake the dead."

"Sorry, honey, I guess I was out of it."

"What were you mumbling about anyway?"

"I don't know," he lied, "Must have been dreaming."

"Well, now that our day is off to a ringing start, why don't you shower and I'll get the coffee going."

Charlie Wells ambled barefooted into the master bath and began his morning routine. He bent to touch his toes and began his stretching exercises to work the kinks out of his six foot frame. He was only six years away from the mandatory retirement age for airline captains and not as flexible as he once was. His aching back reminded him that he was scheduled for another eight hours of ground school today, and the stiffness would only increase sitting in a classroom. He looked longingly at the Jacuzzi tub and promised himself a nice soak if he survived the day.

He shaved his slightly weathered face, ignored the gray that had infiltrated his stubble, and convinced himself that his hairline had stopped receding. The scalding shower at full blast rejuvenated him, and he emerged from the steam wrapped in a towel with the scent of coffee in the air. Following his nose to the kitchen, he found Patti pouring two cups. He wrapped his arms around her from behind and placed his chin on the top of her blond head. "Sorry about the rude awakening."

She turned and smiled with sleepy brown eyes. "Coffee's ready. Would you like Cheerios with milk, or milk with Cheerios?"

"Coffee sounds good. At the risk of being predictable, I think I'll have the Cheerios with milk."

"Charlie, you're a lot of things, but predictable isn't one of them."

"Thank you, I think."

"Did you read the entire airplane manual last night? How late were you up?"

"Not very. I was just going over some things the FAA thinks I should know for my annual training."

"If they knew how cranky you were during these three days every year, maybe they would lighten up."

"I'll be sure to mention that. Can I quote you?"

"Not if you want dinner tonight. What time will you be home?"

"I'll be in the classroom again today from eight to five, and the flight simulator tomorrow afternoon."

"Does this mean I won't have to hear Mr. Bojangles alarm the neighborhood tomorrow morning?"

"Leave my alarm clock out of this. I haven't been late in twenty-six years."

"Do you think you might be a little paranoid about it?"

"You know the airline pilot's motto, 'In God we trust, everybody else is suspect.'"

"Are you referring to the few that don't think they *are* God?"

"There is that, of course."

Charlie took pride in being punctual and arrived at the training center thirty minutes before class time, despite the morning rush hour traffic around the Atlanta airport. The facility included several multi-story red brick buildings that contained classrooms as well as the flight simulators. Each building prominently displayed the *Tri Continent Airlines* logo. Tri Con, as it was called, had evolved from the merger of several smaller carriers and initially served North America, South America, and

Europe. They now flew to Asia and Africa also, but the name had not changed.

He decided he had time for coffee and dropped his flight kit on a rack designed for that purpose outside the cafeteria. The black leather bag weighed about thirty pounds and contained aircraft manuals, charts and maps for airports and airways around the world, as well as other paraphernalia required for his flights. Pilots referred to it as their brain bag. The cafeteria was crowded with pilots and flight attendants scheduled for training, and he joined several of them waiting in line for coffee.

Someone stepped up behind him and said, "Hey Charlie, you're just the man I need to see. Let me buy you a cup."

Charlie turned to find Colt Adams grinning at him. Colt and Charlie had been classmates when Tri Con hired them twenty six years before and had been friends since.

"Colt, whenever you offer to buy I know the hammer is about to fall."

"Well, actually I was going to approach you with a proposition."

"Thank you, Colt, but you're not my type. We can still be friends, though."

"Very funny, Charlie. Seriously, I need to swap a trip. Actually, we're flying the same trip, but I need to swap days. Would you be interested?"

"What's in it for me?"

"I'll invite you to my next wedding."

"Will it be different than the other three?"

"I don't know, I haven't met her yet."

"Well, you've piqued my curiosity. When would this big swap occur?"

"This week. I'd like to fly your rotation on Tuesday and you take mine on Wednesday."

"Is this because you've alienated your crew and they no longer feed and water you?"

"No, they love me, but I need Friday off."

"You promise someone's husband isn't going to take a shot at me?"

"I promise."

"Okay, Colt, I'll check with Pattie and let you know at lunch."

"I appreciate it, buddy. Tell Pattie if I get married again she'll be invited to the wedding too."

They took their coffee with them, retrieved their brain bags, and made their way to the lobby and the elevator. Charlie shortened his stride to match that of Colt who was several inches shorter. The two friends constantly needled each other, but Charlie always enjoyed Colt's outgoing personality and quick sense of humor. Both captains were confident and easy going, which endeared them to their copilots. The elevator was packed with pilots, all of them trying to balance brain bags in one hand and coffee in the other. The second and third floor buttons had already been pushed, but predictably someone in the back said, "Ballroom please."

Someone else said, "Sorry sir, I didn't know I was crowding you." Charlie had to smile at the old joke. He'd decided long ago that pilots were the product of a depleted gene pool.

On the third floor, they walked down the corridor, and everyone disbursed into various classrooms. Charlie and Colt found the one they were assigned to and met the four other pilots attending the class. They were all first officers that Charlie and Colt had flown with at one time or another.

The copilots pretended that they were not concerned about the training session or having their knowledge and ability tested. Charlie found it amusing that they demonstrated their nonchalance in various ways. One read a newspaper, another sat with his feet propped on the table, and one appeared to be texting on his cell phone. It was just another routine day with your career on the line.

Charlie thought of the training sessions as a necessary evil. The ground school classes tested a pilot's knowledge and the four hour simulator check-ride evaluated his actual flying skills and judgment under stressful emergency conditions. He often wondered if his proficiency and motor skills would deteriorate as he grew older. Many times, when a captain quietly took an early retirement, it was not because he wanted to, but rather because he could no longer achieve the minimum standards necessary to pass the check-ride. Most pilots knew that the ultimate test, if it ever came, would be in an airplane full of people and not the simulator. Charlie had attended too many memorial services for pilots to think otherwise. He hoped he would never be tested other than in the simulator.

The instructor walked in with his arms loaded with books and stacks of papers and surveyed the room. The copilots simultaneously dropped their act and became attentive.

Phil James was considered the top ground school instructor at Tri Con, and was well-respected as the resident expert on the aircraft. He had a knack for using common logic to explain complex technical information.

He smiled. "Good morning, gentlemen. I'm glad I didn't have to come bail any of you out to get you to class today."

Colt said, "We had you on speed dial, just in case."

Phil walked to the podium and unloaded the books. When his hands were free, he pushed his glasses further up the bridge of his nose and smoothed the wisps of reddish blonde hair at the fringe of his baldness, an action he would repeat with regularity throughout the day.

The pilots dug their manuals out of the brain bags and spread them out on the tables in front of them. The classrooms were modern and comfortable with desk chairs that had armrests.

They were adjustable to rock or recline. Charlie assumed Colt would be dozing soon. He thought about the first Tri Con classroom they sat in twenty-six years before: a small, noisy room at the back of the hangar where they listened to rivet guns bang away all day, drowning out the instructor.

Phil loosened his tie and then walked around the room, distributing the outline for the day's class and explaining what he hoped to achieve. He grinned. "There will be a multiple guess written exam this afternoon, covering the aircraft's systems and procedures. The crew concept is not allowed. You cannot cooperate to graduate."

The class groaned in harmony.

By mid-morning they had analyzed the aircraft's three hydraulic systems with all their reservoirs, pumps, accumulators, and backup capability. Phil could see that their saturation point had been reached and declared, "Let's take a twenty minute break before we discuss the fuel system and how rich the Arabs are becoming. Everyone's cell phone came out immediately, and Charlie called Patti. "What would you say if I fly on Wednesday instead of Tuesday?"

"I'd say, 'Great, I'll revise your chore list to keep you busy.'"

"Hmm...maybe I'll reconsider."

"If you don't pass your check ride in the simulator, you won't have a job on Tuesday or Wednesday."

"Thanks for reminding me."

As Charlie was hanging up, Colt returned with two cups of coffee. Charlie told him that the trip swap was a done deal.

Colt said, "I wish I had known that before I bought you another cup of coffee." He took his own cell phone out and called crew scheduling to have the swap approved. The only part of the conversation that Charlie heard was when Colt said, "Yeah, yeah, I'll buy coffee when I see you on Tuesday."

He hung up the phone and said, "Man, everybody's holding me up over a simple trip swap."

"You can afford it, Colt, even with all the alimony you pay."

"Next time a woman asks me to marry her, I'm just gonna buy her a house instead."

"Good idea. You can save the lawyer's fee."

Phil came back in, signaling for class to resume. "Gentlemen, we're going to talk about the fuel system, but first I want to set the stage. Our airplane holds about 285,000 pounds of fuel, depending on the ambient temperature and the way it affects volume. That's about 42,500 gallons, at 6.7 pounds per gallon. Using a round number of three dollars per gallon, it costs Tri Con approximately $127,500 every time you say 'fill it up.' As you can imagine, the company would like for you to practice fuel conservation at every opportunity. It should be a factor in your decision-making process."

Colt spoke up. "Phil, I hear what you're saying, but cost is not my top priority in making decisions about my flights. Safety, and particularly my own, is always the first consideration."

"That's as it should be, Colt, and I'm with you, but the company wants us to emphasize the high cost of fuel and ask that you help save whenever possible. They just want you to know that when you take those three throttles in your hand, you're dealing with a lot of cost."

"I think of it as dealing with three hundred butts sitting in those seats behind me and a billion dollars in liability if they don't get home to their families, not to mention the hundred million dollar airplane and my precious butt. I'm just saying, saving fuel is not a big priority."

"You're preaching to the choir, my friend, and I agree with you one hundred percent, but let me give you a couple of examples that they have asked us to discuss. As you know, the heavier the airplane is, the more fuel it burns, and we certainly don't want to reduce passengers or cargo weight. The only weight we can control is how much fuel we load. On international flights, federal regulations require that we have enough fuel to reach the destination, plus ten percent, plus fuel to reach the alternate airport if the weather is down at the primary, plus forty-five minutes of holding fuel if there is a delay. Of course, that's the minimum required, but the company would like to stay as close to that number as possible. Any excess fuel means that we are burning fuel just to haul fuel."

Charlie said, "Phil, you realize that we are planning our flights based on what someone thinks the weather is going to be in a foreign country as much as fourteen hours after takeoff, and if the weather is bad, traffic stacks up and that ten percent contingency fuel goes away real fast. Any of us can give you examples of holding for two hours or having to go to a third alternate. Think about it: if traffic stacks up at the primary, everybody goes to the alternate, and then traffic is stacked up there too."

Colt said, "It's simple, Charlie. All you have to do is ask yourself what a pencil pusher would do in that situation."

Everyone laughed, including Phil.

"Believe me, guys, I'm on your side. As long as you get the concept, I'm a happy camper, and I know you'll always do the safe thing. If I'm sitting in the back, I hope you have lots of fuel."

One of the first officers said, "The only time you have too much fuel is when you're on fire."

"How true," said Phil. "And I would be remiss if I didn't mention the South American carrier that ran out of fuel in the holding pattern at JFK a few years ago and killed everyone on board."

"Fuel conservation in action," said Colt.

"There is one other situation the company would like for you to think about, and that is fuel dumping. If you have an emergency right after takeoff and need to return to land, you will normally be over the maximum certified landing weight for the airplane. Max takeoff weight is 625,000 pounds and max landing is 430,000. That means, in the worst case scenario, you would need to dump almost 200,000 pounds of fuel. That is certainly an option. The dump rate is 6000 pounds per minute, so you're looking at a little over thirty minutes of dump time. Another option is to make an overweight landing, which is legal in an emergency. The airplane would have to undergo an inspection but it would save a lot of fuel."

Colt said, "I've always wanted to be a test pilot and try weird things that nobody has ever actually done before."

Phil laughed. "Colt, I can tell I'm impressing you today."

"Actually I think you're one of the sharpest guys around, so we both know there are not many runways in our system that would be long enough to accommodate a 600,000 pound landing, especially if it were wet. The approach speed would have to be close to 190 knots. At that speed the brakes would definitely overheat and probably blow a few tires. There are a lot of unknowns in that equation."

"Excellent observation, Captain Adams. That's why they pay you the big bucks."

CHAPTER TWO

The Tri Con headquarters and administrative offices were located across the street from the training complex on the outer periphery of the Hartsfield-Jackson Atlanta International Airport. The most recent merger had resulted in yet another shakeup in the management ranks. Merging airplanes and routes was relatively easy compared to reconciling the difference in culture of various employee groups. Loyalties had been stretched and broken, and managers and officers had been encouraged to retire in order to make way for a younger, more energetic management team. The airline business was problematic by nature with its thin operating margins, but the new philosophy was that Tri Con would be successful by applying solutions that had worked in other industries. Independent consultants and headhunters had been retained to locate and recruit management personnel from other industries to implement Tri Con's new business model.

Allen Smallwood entered the conference room and walked quickly and confidently to stand at the head of the table. He felt no need to apologize for being ten minutes late to the meeting that he had called. He brushed an imaginary speck from the lapel of his Armani suit and let his eyes drift over the people seated at the conference table. Some of them wondered if they had been summoned to hear him speak or just to watch him model his suit. Smallwood had recently been lured away from a sports shoe manufacturer to become Tri Con's manager of cost control. His headhunter had negotiated a nice salary with incentives based on the overall reduction in Tri Con's operating cost.

The committee that he chaired today included the heads of various departments in the company that Allen had identified as potential cost targets. There were eight men and three women on the committee. Allen took a few more moments to open a bottle of water that his secretary had placed on the table for him.

He took a leisurely sip before beginning. "Ladies and gentlemen, let me begin by reminding you once again that personnel and fuel are by far the largest cost burdens on Tri Con's balance sheet. We have reduced the overall head count of employees by eight percent so far, and as we implement more elements of our plan, I feel that we can double that number. As we bring more automated check-in kiosks online, we will be able to eliminate ticket agents proportionately.

"We have reduced our flight attendant staff to the FAA minimum on each flight and cracked down on sick leave abuse, thus allowing us to furlough five hundred flight attendants.

"Beginning next month, we will be contracting with Aero Mech Inc. to perform our aircraft maintenance for Atlanta line operations, which will enable us to eliminate three hundred mechanics from our payroll. If that goes well, we will implement the process in other stations in our system. I remind you that each employee currently represents a cost of approximately $85,000 per year including salary and benefits, as well as retirement obligations. We will be exploring other options going forward, but for now I see no downside to our method. Are there any comments or issues that we need to address?"

The Atlanta terminal manager spoke up. "Allen, I do have one concern. I think the kiosks work fine for our experienced passengers to check in without having to speak to an agent at the ticket counter. However, what worries me is, if the airport shuts down for several hours because of weather, all those passengers have to be re-booked, and they can't do that at the kiosks."

Allen said, "Oh, we will always have agents; we just don't need half as many with the kiosks."

The manager said, "Will you agree that the reduced number of agents will be extremely busy?"

"Of course they will. That's called productivity."

"Then my question is, who is going to deal with the thousands of passengers that need to re-book after a shutdown?"

"Obviously, that's an exaggeration. There would never be that many."

"Actually, Allen, we board several thousand passengers an hour in Atlanta, and while we're doing that, more are coming in the door to check in. In addition to that, every time a flight lands, most of those people connect to another flight. If the airport closes for several hours, we could easily have ten to fifteen thousand passengers to re-book. People will be spending the night sleeping on the floor of the terminal."

"Well, I know that sometimes our passengers are unavoidably inconvenienced, and I can certainly understand your concern. Perhaps a focus group could offer viable solutions. Thank you for bringing it to our attention."

Allen quickly continued on.

"Now I want to make sure that we address the fuel cost issue today also. It has come to my attention that one of our flights out of San Francisco recently dumped 50,000 pounds of fuel at a cost of $22,000. That is such a total waste of funds." He turned to the flight operations manager. "How can you justify that, and what are we doing to prevent it from happening?"

The flight operations manager explained, "Well, the flight lost an engine on takeoff. They had no choice but to return for landing. It was raining, and the long runway was closed for maintenance. The captain elected to dump fuel in order to land safely. That's pretty routine, Allen."

"Well, there has to be a way to eliminate that sort of waste. That's a tremendous amount of cost."

"I've asked the ground school to emphasize fuel conservation in all their classes, so it will be a focus in the coming months."

Allen turned to the manager of in-flight service.

"Have we reduced the number of sick days the flight attendants are taking?"

"We've implemented the new policy requiring a doctor's excuse, and we're seeing some improvement. However, the numbers are mitigated by the fact that we furloughed according to seniority, and five hundred of the youngest and therefore healthiest flight attendants are no longer with us. The remaining flight attendants are older and have more health issues, requiring sick leave."

"Well, it's not like they actually do manual labor. Surely a minor health issue shouldn't keep them from serving drinks."

"We'll continue to stress the policy."

Molly Jackson had served as a flight attendant for fifteen years before accepting her position as manager of in-flight service. She thought, *Where did they find this imbecile?*

Allen concluded, "I think that wraps it up for today. I encourage each of you to continue to bring forth whatever cost-cutting measures that you can identify so that we can analyze them and improve the bottom line. I think the airline industry is long overdue to join the real world of modern business, and I want Tri

Con to lead the way. Thank you all for your diligence and cooperation."

After everyone left, Allen turned to his secretary and asked, "What do you think? Do you sense any resentment or reluctance?"

"No, sir, I think they appreciate your leadership."

"When you get last week's numbers for the average fuel burn on our flights, please bring them to me."

"Right away, Mr. Smallwood."

Allen leaned back in his chair and smiled. He had already identified ninety million dollars in cost savings and began calculating his incentive bonus in his head once again.

Charlie and Colt insisted that Phil let them buy lunch, and they enjoyed an hour of entertaining each other with funny stories and exaggerations bordering on prevarication. They also enticed Phil into telling them what emergencies would be thrown at them in the simulator the next day. Of course, they had both already interrogated several captains who had taken simulator checks recently, but you could never have too much information.

They reconvened after lunch, and Phil had them solve aircraft performance problems concerning runway length required and maximum altitude for given weights. They used the afternoon break to wake up and then began the final session.

"Gentlemen," Phil began, "we are fortunate not to have many emergencies, except in the simulator, of course. However, you must always be prepared to deal with any situation. We're going to review the general procedures for emergencies. I want to preface our discussion by quoting what our operations manual says about captain's authority.

> The captain is authorized to take any action necessary to maintain safety of flight. When immediate action is required, in an emergency situation, he may deviate from prescribed procedures, weather minimums, and federal aviation regulations in the interest of safety. Such action is authorized without air traffic control clearance.

"That's pretty straightforward, guys. The captain has complete authority to do what is necessary. All six of you have made some good points during our discussion today, and a lot of them are not covered by the book. Sometimes you don't have time to read the book, and sometimes a situation is not covered by the book. You have to use your experience, judgment, and instincts."

Colt said, "You know what they say about flying. It's hours and hours of boredom interrupted by moments of sheer terror."

"I'm sure that's true, and boredom is good. We obviously don't have time to talk about all the possible emergencies, so we're going to concentrate on evacuations, which is how a lot of emergencies conclude. I want to talk about some generalities, and then we'll go down to the mockup and look at the doors and evacuation slides and so forth.

"As you know, we carry three hundred passengers on a full flight, and when the airplane was certified, the manufacturer had to demonstrate that all three hundred people could be evacuated in ninety seconds using only half the doors. We have eight doors, so they only used four. Once the doors are armed at the departure gate, the evacuation slides deploy automatically when the door is opened. They are all dual lane slides, which means two people can slide down side by side. Please don't let anyone jump out the door onto the slide. When that happens it becomes a trampoline and they will be launched into the troposphere. The flight attendants are trained to have the people sit and slide.

"By the way, the company has reduced our flight attendant staffing to the FAA minimum. You now have only eight, and not the eleven you are accustomed to. You can do the math: one per door."

One of the first officers said, "So if one of the girls is injured, it's the same as an unusable exit?"

"That's a possibility, unless a passenger opens it," said Phil.

Colt said, "Is this covered in the fine print on the ticket?"

Phil continued. "Let's talk about crew duties. All of our international flights have at least three pilots: a captain and two first officers. One of the first officers is designated as the relief pilot.

"The relief pilot will normally proceed to the forward right door, then exit and assist from outside. Be alert for anyone who might trampoline into the air and come down on top of you.

"The first officer will normally proceed to the forward left door, exit there, and assist from outside. In both cases you should assemble the people a safe distance from the airplane. We don't want to have someone mowed down by a fire truck.

"The captain will normally proceed to the forward doors and assist from inside. When everyone is off, he will make his way to the rear of the airplane if possible, make sure everyone has evacuated, exit the rear, and assume command outside."

Colt said, "Wait a minute, I want to be one of the guys that leaves first, screaming, 'Follow me!'"

"Ah, command is lonely, Colt." Phil said. "Of course, the slides also serve us in a ditching situation, and when we get downstairs I'll go over how to detach them and use them as rafts. First we're going to play, 'Bet your job' by taking the written exam."

17

The next forty five minutes were spent whining about the trick questions and making excuses for the few that they answered incorrectly. The low score in the class was ninety-three.

They rode the elevator down and went to the lower corner of the building. The aircraft mockup was designed as a replica of a section of the passenger compartment, complete with real seats and emergency equipment. Phil demonstrated how to arm and disarm the door and then opened it to reveal a fully deployed escape slide angled into the basement below. He explained how the slide was automatically inflated with nitrogen when the door was armed and opened.

"I want to talk about ditching, but first I should tell you that there has never been a mid-ocean ditching by an air carrier passenger jet. Airplanes have gone into the water, but it has always been on takeoff or landing and very near land. The manufacturer recommends landing with the landing gear up and full flaps. They say that the airplane will stay afloat for an extended period of time if the integrity of the fuselage is maintained. The wing tanks should provide buoyancy, and the doors should remain above the water level. If however, the fuselage is damaged and water starts entering, then all bets are off.

"The crew duties are similar for ditching and evacuation. The one exception is that the relief pilot goes to the over wing area and launches a raft instead of assisting at the front door. The passengers actually exit onto the wing and the slide raft deploys outboard of the wing engine. The first officer goes to the forward left door and launches a raft. He also takes the emergency radio beacon with him. The captain's duties are the same; he proceeds to the rear of the airplane, making sure everyone is off, and then boards a raft, taking the emergency medical kit with him."

Charlie said, "Do the flight attendants at the rear doors know to wait for the captain before leaving in the raft?"

"No one has ever asked that question, but it's a very good point. I'll have to ask the flight attendant instructors and let you know."

"I'm telling you," Colt said, "The copilots are getting the best of this deal."

Everyone laughed.

"If you'll look at the top of the slide there is a cover that's marked 'Open here for ditching.' Inside, there is a lanyard that detaches the raft from the airplane when it's pulled."

"Can we put a note inside reminding them not to leave the captain?"

One of the first officers said, "Don't worry, Colt, I'll come back and get you."

"Yeah, right. I don't trust anybody who is junior to me on the seniority list with an opportunity to move up a number."

Phil said, "Once you release the raft from the door, it will still be tethered to the aircraft with a line. After everyone has boarded, you can release the snap hook and move away. There is also a hook knife located next to the attach point, that you can use to cut the line if necessary. The raft capacity is fifty people. There are inflated boarding stations on either side in the event people need to board from the water. Remember that survival time in cold water can be very limited."

One of the first officers asked, "Are we supposed to do all this in the dark?"

"Hopefully the emergency lights above each door will illuminate the evacuation area. Each raft also has battery-operated lights that automatically come on when the slide deploys. The battery packs should last at least thirty minutes."

"With my luck the lights will attract sharks," said the first officer.

Colt said, "If you have a lawyer in your raft, the sharks will leave you alone out of professional courtesy."

"By the way," Phil said, "The captain is authorized to perform marriages and funerals at sea. The marriages are temporary but the funerals are permanent."

"Phil, you're as sick as these people I have to travel with," Charlie said.

"Hey Phil," Colt asked, "Do you know how many pilots it takes to replace a light bulb?"

"No, how many?"

"Just one, he holds the bulb up and the world revolves around him."

"Let me finish up here so I can get rid of you idiots." Everyone laughed.

"Once you are safely away from the airplane, you will find a survival pack in each raft. The pack will contain the following items:

- A repair kit to fix holes in the raft
- A hand pump to keep the raft inflated
- A paddle
- A small bucket to catch rainwater and to bail water from the raft
- A flare pistol
- A signal mirror
- A flashlight
- A whistle
- A compass
- Dye marker to make the water around you visible to rescue personnel
- A desalination kit to make seawater drinkable
- A fishing kit
- A first aid kit
- Seasick pills
- A limited supply of energy bars
- A survival book

Colt asked, "Where's the Jiffy Johnny?"

"You're going to have to get creative there. However, there is a canopy to keep the sun and rain off of you."

"I'll designate one of the boarding stations as the *loo*. The ladies can't complain about the lid being up or down."

"Sounds like a plan. Gentlemen, that's all I have. I know you'll all do well in the simulator tomorrow. You have my number if I can be of help. Fly safe."

Everyone shook Phil's hand and thanked him. Recurrent ground school was over for another year.

CHAPTER THREE

The Cavu Lounge was located between two major hotels near the airport. It had served as the local gathering place for airline employees for more than thirty years. The lounge derived its name from the aviation weather acronym CAVU, which indicated *ceiling and visibility unlimited*. It was ironic that many patrons left the Cavu with somewhat limited visibility after a few hours of drinking beer and shooting pool.

Raymond Slackman had arrived at the bar around four-thirty after his day shift at the airport. He had not bothered to change clothes after work, and his shirt with the Tri Con maintenance logo smelled of jet fuel mixed with beer. He had already lost forty dollars playing pool and spent another twenty on beer. He stood on his tiptoes and leaned across the table to make a shot on the eight ball. He knew his opponents left these types of shots for him because he was too short to reach them. He blew the shot when the cue ball fell into the pocket and the eight hit the rail. His opponent looked down at him and laughed as he picked up the money on the table. Ray twisted the hair of his full beard in his fingers and thought, *Go ahead and laugh, big guy. I'll find a way to get even. I always do.* He glanced at the clock and noticed that it was now after seven.

He found a stool at the bar and called to the bartender, "Hey Annie, how 'bout some food? I'm starving over here."

"I thought you were on a liquid diet or something, Ray."

"Nah, just thirsty after a hard day."

"You know what's on the menu. What can I get you?"

"How 'bout a burger cooked rare with everything on it? Maybe some fries."

"You got it, Ray. Coming right up."

After putting the burger order in, she came over with napkins and utensils.

She asked, "What are you going to do next month? You got something lined up?"

"Not really," he answered.

"A lot of the guys are going to work for Aero Mech. Have you thought about that?"

"Those guys are taking a thirty percent pay cut and working with no benefits. Doesn't sound like a good deal to me."

"Didn't you transfer here from Dallas? Have you still got folks there?"

"Believe me, I'm not going back to Dallas. My wife divorced me and stayed there when Tri Con forced me to transfer after they merged with the airline I worked for. Wait till she and her sleazy lawyer find out the company has kicked me in the teeth again, and her half of the pay check doesn't show up."

Over the last hour or so, Ray's speech had become slurred, and his eyes were heavy.

"You've had some tough breaks, Ray, but you're still young. You'll bounce back."

"Yeah, after giving Tri Con eight years of my life and busting up a marriage to keep my job with them, this is my reward."

"Let me check on your burger. You'll feel better if you eat."

"I'll feel better when Tri Con finds out what it's like to get kicked in the head. What goes around comes around. All they care about is their precious bottom line." He thought, *Don't you worry about me, girl. Old Ray's got a plan.*

Annie went to check on his order and came back with his food and a bottle of ketchup.

"Get me another draft to go with this."

"Sure, Ray, you driving home?"

"Yeah, I'm okay. It's not far."

"Go easy on the beer then. You've got enough problems without an accident or a DUI."

"Yeah, I might lose my job with Tri Con."

She noticed that Ray had unfolded a piece of paper and laid it on the bar to look at.

"You got a love letter there, Ray?"

"Yeah, this is my love letter to Tri Con. I'm going to help them out with their bottom line before I leave."

Four new customers sat down at the other end of the bar, and Annie went to take care of them. She knew the bar would get busy now and stay busy until after the shift change at midnight. She served the new guys and noticed Ray get up and walk unsteadily toward the restroom. He had finished his food, and when she cleaned away the empty dishes, she saw the paper still lying on the bar. When she picked it up so she could wipe down the bar, she saw that he had made handwritten notes on it. Her curiosity got the best of her, and she read the top of the page: Tri Con Maintenance Manual—electrical wiring schematic—fuel dump valves.

Molly Jackson made it a habit to be at her desk no later than seven a.m. on Monday mornings. As manager of in-flight service, she would have to deal with every problem involving a flight attendant that had occurred since Friday. Her normal routine was to go through the stack of incident reports and delegate as many as possible to her four assistants. She settled her lanky frame into the executive chair at her desk and leaned forward to place her purse into the bottom drawer. Red curly hair fell across her face, and she brushed it back into place before kicking her high heels off and concealing them under the desk. She leaned back in the chair and closed her green eyes for a moment before attacking the reports. Molly had been admired as a flight attendant because of her ability to deal with the most irate passengers and leave them smiling. At the age of thirty-nine, she was much younger than many of the flight attendants that she supervised, but they did not resent the high standards that she set, and she was respected for her sense of fairness.

When her secretary arrived at seven-forty-five, Molly was only halfway through the stack. It was going to be a hectic day.

"Good morning, Janie. How was your weekend?"

"Morning, boss. It was pretty quiet, although the tooth fairy paid a visit to my six-year-old. Looks like it was a busy weekend at Tri Con, if all those are incident reports."

"Indeed they are. You can take the ones I've reviewed and distribute them to the assistants to be handled."

"Any good ones in there?"

"You'll like the one on top. A lady passenger told one of the flight attendants that her meal was not fit for a pig, so the flight attendant replied that she would try to find one that was."

Janie laughed, "That's a good one. I think I like her."

"Good. Would you like to tell her that she will be on probation for the next three months?"

25

"No thanks, boss. I'm just here to type and get coffee."

"In that case, could we have the latter first?" Molly giggled. "If you ask me if it's fit for a pig, you'll be on probation too."

"Wow, even the tooth fairy has a better sense of humor than you."

Molly laughed. "See if you can find some doughnuts to go with the coffee, and we'll pig out."

A few minutes later Janie returned with the coffee and a pink message slip.

"Mr. Smallwood's secretary called to inform us that he would like you to visit his office as soon as possible to discuss an urgent matter."

"Like I need another urgent matter."

Janie said, "Everything is urgent with him. All the secretaries call him Mr. Smallbrain."

"You have a warped mind. I've decided you must be a flight attendant trapped in a secretary's body."

"Well, I have spilled coffee on you a few times, but I think my body is better than most of your flight attendants'."

"Sad but true. Give me the coffee before you spill it on me. I'll go see what Smallbrain wants."

Molly was kept waiting for ten minutes before the secretary escorted her into Smallwood's office.

"Molly, it's great to see you. Thanks for coming over."

"What's urgent, Allen? I've got a busy day."

"I'll get right to the point then. I'm going to Madrid on Wednesday evening, and I would like for you to accompany me. I have convinced Tri Con that we can save a lot of money if we outsource some of the functions that our full-time employees perform there. We're negotiating with a Spanish company to provide maintenance and baggage services for us at considerably less cost."

"Allen, I know very little about mechanics or bag smashers."

"Of course not, neither do I for that matter. But I do know what they cost us. The reason I want you to be there is because we're considering establishing a flight attendant base at Madrid and staffing it with local employees. Their pay scales are much lower than in the United States, and they do not expect benefits or retirement."

"Allen, do you have any concept of the can of worms that would create?"

"In what way?"

"The effect it would have on morale for one thing. We are still in a service business, at least to this point. Employees with low morale do not provide good service."

"I've taken that into consideration of course, but the cost savings are so great that we have to explore the possibility."

"Speaking of cost, have you factored the expense of training? Those flight attendants would have to meet our standards."

He said, "Yes, yes, there would be an initial cost, but we would recoup that easily over time."

"I think the turnover rate of those employees might be very high, and we would be constantly training new ones."

"In that case, we could always tweak things if need be. Look, I've already talked to the vice president of finance, and he suggested that you accompany me. Of course when we get back you can submit a written report through me with whatever conclusions you have."

Molly replied, "I have to tell you, I have serious reservations about this. It might be beneficial for you and I to have an in-depth discussion about the duties of a flight attendant."

"Of course, I would very much like to do that. In fact, you could fill me in with that information during our trip."

"I'll have to talk to my boss about this, Allen."

"Actually, it's already approved. You should have a memo and an itinerary on your desk shortly. I know it's short notice, Molly, and I hope you don't think me presumptuous, but it will be a very productive trip for Tri Con."

Molly walked back to her office with a sense of dread. She could imagine a long flight and being regaled with tales of Allen's past heroics in the sports shoe industry.

CHAPTER FOUR

On Wednesday morning, Charlie began preparing for his evening flight to Madrid. He was happy that Colt had taken the flight on Tuesday, and he had enjoyed an extra day off with Pattie. After the mental gymnastics of the proficiency check in the flight simulator, he had been glad to turn his attention to no-brainer stuff like cutting grass and washing Pattie's car. He checked his itinerary and confirmed that Tri Con Flight Eleven was scheduled to depart at six p.m., which meant that his report time would be at four-thirty, an hour and a half before. He removed all the training materials from his brain bag, made sure he still had the required items for his regular line flights, checked to see that his uniform had been cleaned, and then took Pattie out for a nice lunch.

Ray Slackman had ham sandwiches and potato chips for lunch. He and the other mechanics on day shift took their lunch at eleven and ate in the break area provided for them. They sat in plastic chairs at three long wooden tables surrounded by vending machines. The mood was somber as they discussed their pending releases from Tri Con and what their futures might hold. At noon the shift foreman came in with afternoon assignments.

"Ray, I want you to do the service check on ship 826. It's due into the gate in about ten minutes. Check the log book and let me know if the crew has any squawks that you might need help with. If not, just do the service check and sign it off. It's not scheduled out until six o'clock, but if it has issues let's take care of them early."

He handed Ray several sheets of paper, which made up the routine list of items to be checked. Each item had a block to be marked and initialed by a licensed mechanic before the aircraft could be released back into service. The service check was normally a gravy job, just a matter of checking to see if things were working properly and signing them off. Ray was happy to get the easy task, but it was also the opportunity he had been waiting for. He needed an airplane all to himself for a couple of hours. He thought, *It's time for the payoff Tri Con.*

He went to his locker and retrieved the copy of the wiring diagram he had been studying and placed it on the clipboard along with the service checklist. He found his tool pouch and strapped it around his waist, then went out to meet the inbound flight.

The hot August sun had driven the temperature into the nineties but it was at least ten degrees warmer on the concrete ramp. Ray waited with the team of baggage handlers who would begin unloading luggage as soon as the aircraft arrived, and the engines were shut down. The bag smashers, or ramp rats as they were called, rested in the shade of the jet way that the passengers would use to disembark. They all looked up when they heard the huge three-engine jet turn into the ramp. Flight numbers meant very little to mechanics, and Ray looked at the permanent number painted on the nose wheel door to see that this was indeed ship 826.

Each of the ramp personnel had specific duties to perform for aircraft arrival. Two of them trotted out to watch the wingtips and insure clearance from the various equipment on the ramp. Another performed parking marshal duties to guide the captain to the proper stopping point, while others stood ready to chock the wheels and plug in the ground electrical power and air conditioning. When the captain shut down the engines, they all swarmed the cargo compartments. It looked like a pit stop at an auto race.

Ray watched as everything happened at once and thought that it was like watching a well-orchestrated ballet that was efficiently performed hundreds of times a day. He walked over to the nose wheel and plugged a headset into the interphone receptacle.

He pushed the microphone button and said, "Cockpit, maintenance."

One of the cockpit crew answered, "Hello, maintenance."

"You guys break anything?"

"No, sir, she's the queen of the fleet. No problems at all."

"Okay, thank you, sir, and have a good one."

Ray thought once again how aviation got in your blood and how much he was going to miss being a part of the ballet. It hurt to know that all his training and expertise would be wasted, and he would no longer be a member of the fraternity. It angered him even more that the Tri Con management didn't understand aviation or people and that money was the only thing that influenced them.

He walked around the airplane and began checking off items on his list. He saw that the red and green position lights were working on the wingtips. The white position lights on the tail were working, the brake wear indicators on the landing gear were in good shape, and the tires looked good. He had already signed off the rotating red anti-collision lights on the top and bottom of the fuselage when the airplane was taxiing in. He climbed the stairs on the jet way and waited at the door until the passengers had all left. He found the lead flight attendant and asked if there were any problems in the cabin. She asked him to check out a coffeemaker, but everything else was good. He checked all the cabin lights and inspected the evacuation slide packs on all the doors. He found the inflation pressure on each one to be sufficient.

At last everyone was gone, and he went into the cockpit and began once again checking off items on his list. He extended the landing lights and turned them on. He could see the bright lights reflected in the windows of the terminal. He completed another page and a half of items in the cockpit and then opened the aircraft logbook and turned to a fresh page. He filled in the date and aircraft number, and then wrote in the first item box, "Aircraft service check completed, all items satisfactory." In the signature block he signed, Raymond Slackman.

Ray pulled the inbound flight's log sheet, leaving the carbon copy in the book, and then went back outside. He looked around under the gate area until he found a tall stepladder and dragged it out to the airplane. He placed the ladder under the center of the fuselage just below the front of the wing and climbed up to open the access door to the accessory compartment. Once inside, he sat on the floor, surrounded by aluminum racks of electronic equipment and black boxes with little colored lights blinking on them. He took out his copy of the wiring schematic and quickly found the panel he wanted. There was a multitude of wiring bundles from the forward fuselage that connected at this point with the wiring that ran out into the wing area. The connections were made with screw-on plugs that were secured with twisted steel safety wire to prevent them from vibrating loose. He read the placards on the panel until he found one that was labeled, "aft inboard main tank fuel transfer pump," and another that read, "left and right wing fuel dump valves." He took the tools he needed from his tool pouch and found the two wires that would accomplish what he wanted. Each of the thousands of wires on the airplane had unique numbers stamped on them every few inches to identify them. He consulted the wiring schematic one more time to be sure, and then cut the wire that powered the fuel pump. Using a red, insulated connector, he spliced it to the one that powered the dump valves open. He sat back and admired his work, *A nice million dollar splice. This pump will power up about four hours after takeoff, and if Tri Con hasn't paid old Ray to tell them which circuit breakers to open, fuel will dump in the ocean and bye-bye airplane. We'll see who the sharpest mechanic at Tri Con is, and just try to take alimony out of this payday.*

He gathered his tools and the schematic and climbed out of the accessory compartment. As he stepped onto the ladder someone called out, "Hey, Ray, you taking a nap in there?"

Ray looked down and saw one of the other mechanics passing underneath the airplane.

"Hey, Billy, that's a great idea, but I was just checking the equipment cooling fans."

"Man it's hot enough, they better be cooling good."

"You got that right, dude."

"I'm looking forward to cooling at the Cavu in a couple hours."

"Me too, Billy. I'll see you there."

CHAPTER FIVE

At three o'clock the Atlanta terminal manager was notified by his secretary that the check-in kiosk software had developed another glitch. The two dozen automated machines allowed passengers to stand in line to check themselves in rather than standing in line for a ticket agent to check them in. The kiosks were advertised as a wonderful convenience to save customers time, and some of them believed it because the TV said so. Of course, the malfunction occurred just in time for the afternoon international push. The lines at the international ticket counter began backing up immediately, and passengers were already fuming and worried that they would miss their flights. The manager authorized overtime for the day shift agents and had the shift supervisors start asking for volunteers to stay over at time and a half pay rates. He longed for the good old days when he could staff the ticket counter with enough people to provide the service the passengers deserved. He walked out to the ticket counter to see how bad the situation was. There were at least ten unmanned check-in positions because he didn't have the personnel to staff them. He signed on to a computer at one of the unused positions and checked the afternoon bookings. Fortunately it was an average Wednesday, and the loads were not extremely heavy. Hopefully he could get enough overtime volunteers to man the empty positions and expedite matters somewhat. Even so, he might have to delay a few flights in order to get everyone checked in, through security, and then out to the gates.

He was logging off the computer when the agent working the position next to him said, "I think we got a crisis developing at the handicap counter."

He looked down to the end of the counter and saw a line of wheelchairs at the handicapped check-in position and an agent looking for help that wasn't going to come anytime soon.

He walked down to the position and asked the agent, "Did we injure these people or did they show up in this condition?"

"I don't know, boss, I just stepped over to check in one and when I looked up there was a line."

"You'll be happy to know we're getting five more kiosks next week."

"Wonderful."

"I'll see if I can get a supervisor to help you out."

"Good luck. I see three of the four already working a position."

"In that case, I guess you're stuck with me."

"I appreciate whatever you can do."

The manager stepped through an opening in the counter and along the line of wheelchairs.

"Can I have your attention please? Does anyone have a flight departing within the hour?"

A middle-aged man had just pushed another wheelchair into the line, and he spoke up.

"Sir, we're all traveling together. Everyone is booked on Tri Con Eleven to Madrid."

"Okay, that will make things easier. How many people are in your party?"

"Nineteen altogether, eighteen will need assistance plus myself."

"Very well. If you could make sure everyone has his or her passport and ticket available, we'll move you right along. I'll call for skycaps to help you through security and out to the boarding area. You have plenty of time."

"Thank you very much. Our group is attending the International Conference on Handicapped Discrimination. I appreciate your help."

"Glad to be of assistance, sir."

He walked back to the agent at the computer.

"You're not going to believe this. They're traveling to Madrid as a group to oppose discrimination against handicapped people."

"Good. If they want to be treated equal, they can get in line with everyone else."

The manager chuckled.

"You wish. If you'll check tickets and enter them in the computer, I'll check passports and handle the bag tags. Is the flight booked full?"

"Nah, we've only got a hundred and ninety-five revenue passengers booked and two company employees riding free."

The next wheelchair rolled up and the gentleman produced his ticket. The agent looked at it and said, "I'm sorry sir, but I have to ask you to select another seat, if you don't mind."

"I certainly do mind. I want to sit in the seat I bought."

"I apologize again, sir, but that is an exit row, and safety regulations prohibit handicapped persons from occupying that seat."

"There's also a regulation that prohibits discrimination against handicapped persons. Have you read that one?"

"Yes, sir; it makes an exception for the exit rows."

"Well, I'm not moving, because I'm sitting next to my friend here." He indicated the man in the wheelchair behind him.

"He can't sit there either, sir. I'm sorry. How about if I give you two gentlemen a row of seats all to yourselves just a little further back?"

"I guess we have no choice, but I will definitely look into this. You may hear about it later from your manager."

The agent looked at the manager and got a big smile.

"I appreciate your cooperation, sir, and I'm sorry for the inconvenience."

Molly Jackson walked into the terminal at four o'clock and approached one of the check-in kiosks. There was a red tag hanging on the machine that announced, "System out of service, please proceed to the ticket counter."

Molly had already had a long day. She had been in the office at seven-thirty with her rolling bag packed for the Madrid trip, and she had worked through lunch in order to make sure that everything was covered for the two days she would be out of town. From the kiosk, she could see several hundred passengers already in line at the international counter. She headed that way, and when she got closer she saw the terminal manager working the handicapped counter. When she approached, he saw her and smiled.

"Can I help you ma'am?"

"I was told to see a Mr. Kiosk in order to lodge a complaint."

He laughed.

"You're in the right place, just get in line."

"Can I do anything to help?"

"Can you stay for a week or so?"

"Actually, I'm on the Madrid flight."

He said sarcastically, "Oh great, Molly, go and enjoy your vacation, we'll stay here and deal with this."

"Unfortunately, it's work."

"Well, I think this position is under control. If you meet me down at one of the unmanned computers, I'll check you in and get you out of here."

Molly walked around the long line of people and found him at the end of the counter. He already had the computer online and had completed her check-in except for her baggage. He printed out the bag tag and attached it to her rolling bag.

Before they could log off the computer, the next person in line rushed over and said, "Hurry, I'm going to miss my flight."

Molly said, "Don't worry, sir, we'll take care of you."

She handed his ticket to the manager and asked, "How many bags can we check for you today?"

"Just one, thank you."

The manager was amazed at Molly's ability to calm people and take charge.

She smiled at the passenger and said, "We've got a rookie on the computer here but I think he's got it figured out. Let's have a look at your passport and you'll be on your way." She looked at the passport and handed it back. "Thank you very much, Mr. Jamison, and have a great flight. We're glad to have you with us today."

As the man turned to walk away, she waved to the next person in line and told the manager, "You catch on pretty fast. You might have a future in this business."

He laughed.

"Molly, you don't know what you're getting into here."

The next passenger rushed over and Molly took the lady's ticket.

"Oh my goodness, you almost won the free flight. Your ticket number is only one digit different than the winner."

The lady looked shocked.

"You've got to be kidding, was I really that close?"

"Let me take that bag for you, and don't worry, we've got a great flight planned for you even if it's not free."

The manager kept pounding away at the keyboard and never looked up, but he was smiling inside. He knew he was witnessing a master at work.

During the next half hour he and Molly checked in more passengers than any other position on the counter and had a great time doing it. It had been a long time since he had seen so many passengers smiling and happy. When the afternoon shift agents came in, they took over the position for them. He walked Molly downstairs to the ramp level and arranged a ride for her out to the international concourse.

The long row of wheelchairs finally made it to the security checkpoint and began clearing. They couldn't pass through the metal detector in a wheelchair, so they had to be hand-searched before being allowed to pass. This created another scene and an in-depth discussion about discrimination and constitutional rights of individuals. Even so, progress was being made until the gentleman who had been forced to change seats advanced to the head of the line. When his carry-on bag was searched, the security agent informed him, "You can only have three ounces of liquid, and this bottle of aftershave alone exceeds that. You'll have to dispose of it, plus the cologne."

"I will not. That's expensive stuff, and I won't waste it."

"That's the rule. I can't do anything about it."

"Why is that a rule?"

"The rule prevents liquid explosive from getting aboard the aircraft."

"You think three ounces of explosive could blow up the airplane?"

"That's the rule."

"Can I take three ounces aboard?"

"Yes, you may. If you pour all but three ounces out, you can take it with you."

"Well, I have eighteen people in my party. So you're telling me we can take three ounces apiece?"

"That's the rule."

"So between us we could take fifty-four ounces of liquid explosive aboard with no problem? If three ounces is dangerous, imagine what we could do with fifty-four."

The agent signaled a supervisor, who came over and invited the entire group of handicapped passengers to a private area where they would be educated in the finer points of airport security. The lecture and interrogation lasted for forty-five minutes, and was followed by each person partially disrobing to be introduced to the bomb-sniffing dog, who did not discriminate as to what or where he sniffed.

Charlie rode the employee bus from the parking lot to the international concourse. He had invited Pattie to come along on the trip and enjoy a day in Madrid, but she told him she was holding out for Paris. In reality, she had committed to spend some time with her sister and didn't want to disappoint her, which he could understand. He smiled when he thought about the fact that she never let his status as an airline captain go to his head. She had helped him pack his bag and when he put his black uniform on with the gold stripes on the sleeves, gold wings on the chest, and gold leaves on the bill of his cap she said, "I like your costume. Are you going to a party? You must be pretending to be an admiral or something." He was not likely to get a big ego with Pattie around.

When Charlie stepped off the bus, carrying his brain bag, and pulling his rolling travel bag, he could see that his flight was parked at the gate. He was sometimes still amazed that something that big could actually get off the ground. The white fuselage with blue trim was two thirds as long as a football field. The silver aluminum of the belly and wings were gleaming in the sun, and the bold blue letters of *Tri Continent Airlines* stood out high on the forward section of the airplane. The tail stood six stories high with the blue triangular Tri Con logo emblazoned on it. He realized how much he was looking forward to a normal flight after all the contrived situations in the simulator and the imagined problems in the classroom.

CHAPTER SIX

The Tri Con international flight attendant lounge was crowded with flight attendants of all shapes and sizes. The men and women ranged in age from twenty-something to sixty-something. Each of them wore the sky blue uniform that identified them as Tri Con cabin crew. Most of the ladies chose the pantsuit uniform option but a few still preferred the traditional skirt and jacket. The international trips were the most desirable working conditions because they provided the most flying hours per day and thus the most days off per month. Plus, the layovers were in world-class cities. Therefore the most senior flight attendants were likely to be found on those trips. There was one exception to that premise, and it involved the position of lead flight attendant. The lead flight attendant on each flight was in charge and decided how and when the meal services, movies, and duty free sales would be conducted. The lead was also responsible for dealing with whatever problems presented themselves during the trip and the associated paperwork. The position required certification by attending special training classes and passing a written exam. Until recently, the hassle and grief of the position had been rewarded with a premium in addition to the regular hourly flight attendant pay. When Tri Con reduced the premium to a mere pittance, the senior flight attendants dropped out of the program. Now the lead was likely to be a junior flight attendant that endured the hassle in order to fly a nice international trip: another unintended ripple effect of cost control.

Britt Fowler rolled her travel bag into the lounge and parked it in the corner. She then moved to a bank of employee computers along the wall and entered her employee number and password. She pulled up the sign-in screen, electronically declared herself present, and prepared to perform her duties as lead flight attendant on Tri Con Flight Eleven to Madrid. She noted that she beat the sign-in deadline by fourteen minutes. She next went to her mailbox and retrieved various bulletins and revisions to the *In-Flight Manual* that each attendant was required to carry. Finally, she rolled her travel bag into the designated briefing room for the Madrid flight and stowed it out of the way. She looked at herself in the full-length wall mirror and was happy to see that her uniform skirt was only slightly wrinkled so far. The gym membership was paying the dividends she had hoped for, and she thought, *Not bad for a twenty-nine-year-old divorcee.* She ran her fingers through her medium length blonde hair and congratulated herself once again for choosing a style that required little care during her constant travel. Britt sat down at the head of the conference table and began entering the revisions to her manual while she waited for the rest of the crew.

Charlie walked along the side of the concourse until he reached the door to flight operations. He wanted to put his fingers in his ears to protect them from the scream of a taxiing jet, but his hands were full of bags. He thought that the combination of jet noise and high altitude pressurization on his ears would probably render him deaf before retirement. He entered the security code, opened the door to a rush of air-conditioned air, and realized that it was hot as well as noisy on the ramp. When he walked by the crew scheduling counter, someone called out, "Hey Charlie, Colt was in here yesterday and said you were buying coffee today in recognition of services provided for a trip swap."

"Did he tell you about the Easter Bunny too?"

"You mean you didn't request the swap?"

"No, he did. I'm just doing him a favor."

"That conniving scoundrel, just wait till he gets his schedule next month."

Charlie laughed and made his way to his mailbox. Among the bulletins, revisions, and advertisements, he found an envelope with a note.

"Charlie, give this to the crew schedulers with my best wishes." Inside the envelope was a ten dollar bill and a note that said, "Too much coffee is bad for you...Love, Colt." Charlie laughed again and thought that Colt's legend would last long after his retirement.

After signing in for the trip and delivering Colt's note, Charlie took his bags to the pilots' briefing room. Both first officers were already there and working on the flight plan. Robby Jenner had flown copilot for Charlie several times before, and he stood up to shake hands.

"Hey Robby, good to see you again. How are you?"

"Good, Charlie, looking forward to flying with you again."

"Let's make it uneventful."

"Sounds good to me."

The other first officer stood up too.

"Nice to meet you, Captain Wells. I'm Tony Johnson. I was just telling Robby that this is only my second international trip, but I'll try to keep it uneventful too."

"Glad to have you with us, Tony. Just call me Charlie. We'll try not to teach you any bad habits. Just relax, take your time, and speak right up if you have any questions. Robby and I were new to the operation once upon a time too."

"I really appreciate that, Charlie. I'll do my best to keep up."

Charlie said, "I'll fly us to Madrid, gentlemen, and you two can fight over who flies us home."

Robby said, "I've had several landings this month, Charlie, so if it's okay with you, Tony can fly the leg home."

"Sure, that's great. Tony, you're gonna love the big beast."

Robby said, "So, Tony, you'll be relief going over, and I'll do it coming back."

"Okay, I do the pre-flight walk around tonight, right?"

"Yeah, and I'll help you do the flight plan time and fuel estimates after takeoff if you need it."

"Sounds like a plan."

Charlie said, "Well, let's get to it, guys. Does the airplane have any write-ups?"

"Nothing on the carryover list, so it looks good."

"Have you got the weather reports there, Robby?"

"Yes sir. No problems for departure: scattered thunderstorms over the northeast United States and southern Canada, a warm front stretching west to east from mid-Atlantic to Portugal, and marginal approach weather for Madrid. The forecast for arrival time is a ceiling of 300 overcast and visibility one mile in light rain and fog."

"Sounds like a good day to sleep in Spain. What's the fuel load?"

"Total is 195,000 pounds. Trip fuel to Madrid is 145,000, contingency is 14,500. Barcelona is the alternate and we have 15,000 to get there with almost two hours of holding fuel."

Charlie said, "That doesn't sound too bad. I'll talk to dispatch in a few minutes and see if that warm front is going to affect Madrid or Barcelona. We may add more fuel."

"You can check my numbers, Charlie, but I think we can only add 11,000 pounds and still be at max landing weight for arrival."

"Okay, Robby, thanks. Good work. What's the flight plan look like?"

"Standard stuff. Up the east coast, eight hours and eleven minutes en route, coast out over southern Newfoundland, coast in north of Lisbon."

"What could be simpler than that?" Charlie smiled.

Robby and Tony laughed.

Charlie sat down and picked up the phone on the table.

"I'm going to talk to dispatch and meteorology while you guys work on the plotting chart for the North Atlantic, then we'll go over to the flight attendant briefing room and impress our traveling companions."

The flight attendant briefing room was now crowded with the chattering Madrid crew. Britt Fowler was waiting for the last girl to show up before beginning her briefing. She continued revising her manual. She listened to all the gossip and giggling and felt like a hostess at someone's fortieth high school reunion. The youngest person in the room besides herself must be on the far side of mid-fifties. The politically correct description would be experienced. Most of the senior flight attendants were nice enough, but Britt knew that they would ignore her leadership position and do as they pleased if she allowed it. The Fowlers were an old Atlanta family, and Britt had grown up enjoying the gentle ways and courteous manner of southern tradition. However, she knew how to deal with people who had experienced the misfortune of being born in less civilized parts of the country or the world, for that matter.

Britt looked at the crew list to see who the missing person could be and saw that it was Bertie Martin. Bertie had been with the airline for well over thirty years and for the last twenty, since the government had forced the demise of weight restrictions in employment, she had been known as Big Bertha, for obvious and apparent reasons. Britt looked around the room and wondered why some of the other women were not known as Big Alice and Big Mary. The diversity and individuality of the flight attendants was something that Britt enjoyed, but she sometimes wondered if age and physical abilities would affect performance in an emergency. She picked up the phone and was about to dial crew scheduling when the room darkened. She looked up to see the door filled with Big Bertha, gasping for breath.

Britt smiled sweetly and said, "Miss Martin, how happy we are that you have graced us with your presence."

"I signed in on time, Britt, and you're going to be glad that I stayed in the lounge and heard some news."

"Well, please don't keep us in suspense. Whatever could the headline be, and how will it affect us as human beings and servants of Tri Con?"

"Don't be a smarty pants, Britt." She began to catch her breath. "Ladies, check your shoes for scuffmarks and your pantyhose for runs. Mama Molly is on our flight tonight."

Alice Elon asked, "Molly Jackson is on our flight?"

"Miss manager of in-flight in the flesh, and she's traveling with that twerp Allen Smallwood, the guy who took away lead pay and furloughed all the junior flight attendants."

Mary Dobson asked, "Isn't he married? Are they having an affair?"

Shelia Graham said, "Who cares? Let's tell it as the truth and see if the rumor beats us to Spain."

Laughter erupted, but no one discounted the idea.

Nancy Hammond remarked, "That guy has got to be a cheapskate. Since they fly free, this is probably his idea of dinner and a movie."

Nancy was well known for her sarcasm and irreverent sense of humor.

Everyone wanted to get in on the fun, and Pam Arnold, Nancy's best friend and partner in mischief, said, "Well, it must be working; they're spending the night together."

Candace Whitten, who usually had very little to say, added, "It will make a long night for all of us."

Britt looked through the papers on the table and found the passenger list.

"Well, look at this, the lovely couple are seated at 4A and 4B in business class. Do I have volunteers to serve in business tonight?"

Silence. Everyone looked down at the table or at the floor.

Britt said, "I, of course, have to work up front, and I'm sure Nancy and Pam will make us all proud as they assist me in serving our vocational mentors. In fact, they will probably be so impressed, the lead pay and furloughed flight attendants will be reinstated to their original glory before we are halfway across the Atlantic. The rest of you cowards can slink away to the rear cabin and serve the common masses."

Pam said, "Come on, Britt, I think I'm coming down with something. I don't feel like dancing for these bozos tonight."

"Pam, I've always admired your social grace and your wonderful ability to portray the unique Tri Con image. I'm sure you'll represent the entire seniority list in the most sterling and exemplary manner."

"Bull, like crap you do."

"Be a sport, Pam. You can have first break right after the evening meal service. Now here are the players, ladies. We have one hundred ninety-five paying passengers plus the lovely couple in 4A and 4B. We have one unaccompanied minor, a ten-year-old girl seated in the mid-section. Bertie, I want you to meet her in the gatehouse, take her to her seat, and then be responsible for her. In addition, we have twenty-one assist on and assist off."

Nancy said, "Twenty-one! Was there a disaster I didn't hear about, or did they empty a nursing home?"

"I don't know, but I want to start boarding them early. We don't get paid until the door closes, so keep the aisles clear while they carry these people in and strap them down."

Nancy said, "You can bet at least one of them is going to pee in his seat before the night is over."

"Probably. Keep the aerosol air freshener handy. They're all seated back there with you cowards, so enjoy."

Pam said, "Hey, serving the prima donna management aristocrats might not be so bad after all."

"Speak for yourself, Pam," Nancy said.

There was a knock at the door, and Alice reached over from her seat and opened it to see the three pilots standing there.

Britt said, "Good evening captain, welcome to the party."

Charlie said, "This is a motley crew if I ever saw one." He had flown with most of the girls before.

Britt stood up and offered her hand.

"I'm Britt Fowler, I'm the lead tonight."

"Nice to meet you, Britt, I'm Charlie Wells. At what point do you think you lost control of your crew?"

"I'm not sure they're controllable, I just try to keep them from hurting themselves."

They laughed, and Charlie introduced Robby and Tony. He and Britt exchanged a written list of names for their respective crew.

Charlie addressed the group. "I won't take a lot of your time but I want to give you some information about the flight. I spoke with the security coordinator a few minutes ago, and he is not aware of any problems beyond the ongoing awareness levels that we're all accustomed to. If you think something is suspicious, by all means let us know right away.

"The flying time tonight is eight hours and eleven minutes, and if that changes significantly we'll let you know. There is a possibility of holding at Madrid, and we'll keep you up-to-date on that as we get the weather reports en route. Looks like a decent ride tonight, maybe some brief bumps about two to three hours after takeoff as we fly around some thunderstorms, but I think we can avoid most of that. Britt, will you be done with the meal service by then?"

"I think we will. We only have 197 passengers booked, and we'll begin the service early so people can sleep if they choose."

"Good deal. The weather in Madrid is forecasted to be wet in the morning and then clearing in the afternoon, so it should be good for sleeping and shopping. Ladies, you're always welcome in the cockpit if you want to get away from the crowd, and we appreciate you checking on us to see if we're still awake. Let us know if we can be of assistance."

Britt said, "Thank you, Charlie. I'll keep the food and coffee coming all night, and I'll be working in business class if you need anything."

"Thank you. The airplane is at the gate, and I don't know of anything that might delay us, so we'll see you up there in a few minutes."

As Charlie turned to leave, he almost ran into Molly Jackson.

"Hello, Charlie. Are you flying me to Madrid tonight?"

"Well, if it isn't the famous Ms. Jackson. Did you decide to come down from the ivory tower and earn an honest living?"

The girls in the room liked that a lot.

"I wish. Unfortunately I'm traveling on business. I just came down to introduce myself, so these ladies wouldn't think I was spying on them. I always hated it when a supervisor showed up on my flight unannounced. It always made me want to go into the bathroom and see if my pantyhose had a run or some other grievous infraction."

Britt smiled and covered her mouth to keep from laughing. She was impressed with the tall redhead and her impeccable appearance.

Charlie said, "It's great to see you, Molly. I hope we get a chance to visit. If you get bored back there, have Britt bring you up to see us."

"I'll take you up on that."

Molly stepped into the room and said, "You must be Britt Fowler. I'm Molly."

"Nice to meet you, Molly. We've just finished our briefing and were about to head up to the gate."

"Well, I'm glad I caught you before you left. I just wanted to let you know that this is not a check ride. I know your job is hard enough without tiptoeing around some self-righteous pencil pusher. In fact, if you're shorthanded, let me know. I can spill drinks with the best of them."

"Thank you very much. I won't hesitate."

"I'll get out of the way and let you work, Britt. Nice to meet you."

Molly smiled at the other girls and left.

Nancy said, "All right, hold the rumor. She's much too nice to be socializing with someone with a cost fetish."

They began gathering bags, purses, and paperwork, then lined up at the restroom before going to the airplane.

CHAPTER SEVEN

The three pilots walked through the jet way, with their rolling bags rumbling in harmony. As they walked into the airplane, Robby turned to Tony and said, "The first thing you have to remember is enter the airplane and turn left."

Tony chuckled.

"Yeah, that's the same as the domestic flights I've been flying for five years. At least I'll get one thing right."

They walked through the business class section, and Charlie said, "The second thing we have to do is get some air conditioning going. It's hot in here."

"I'll take care of it, Charlie. That will be the first flight attendant complaint of the night," Robby replied.

They approached the cockpit and began the familiar routine. The copilots waited outside and allowed the captain to enter the cramped space alone to stow his bags and build his nest. Charlie would never actually admit how much he loved his work place. The electronic hum and unique smell of the flight deck somehow provided an inner peace, and the practiced routines that efficiently accomplished every task gave him a feeling of satisfaction that would be hard to describe. The competitive humor and sarcasm of flight crews that relieved the boredom and sometimes tension, created a camaraderie that an outsider would never understand. He placed his brain bag in its slot to the left of his seat and then stretched a moment before assuming his place for the next ten hours. When he was comfortable, he automatically began flipping switches.

As soon as Charlie was in his seat, Robby began the same ritual on the right side of the cockpit. When Robby was situated, Tony stowed his gear and then asked, "You guys need anything before I go outside to count the wings and engines?"

"Make sure they're flying in tight formation," Charlie answered.

There were fifty-three items on the cockpit preliminary checklist. Charlie and Robby would do them from memory, then read the checklist later to confirm everything was accomplished. They both checked their oxygen masks for pressure and flow. Charlie checked to see that the parking brake was released and flipped the seat belt sign on. Then he began loading the flight plan into the flight management computer. Robby started the auxiliary power unit in order to begin cooling the airplane. The APU was actually a small jet engine located in the tail that provided electricity and pneumatic pressure for air conditioning and engine start. Soon cool air was flowing and the creature comforts were improving.

There were as many items on the exterior walk around check as in the cockpit. Tony slowly made his way around the airplane looking for anything unusual or out of place. He checked the landing gear, wheel wells, engines, and all the flight controls. When he got back to the cockpit, Charlie asked, "Does it look airworthy, Tony?"

"Yes, sir, the only thing I need to check is the center access compartment door. I'm not sure it's closed all the way."

Robby checked the door alerts and said, "You're right the light is on."

Tony asked, "Can I borrow one of the radios?"

"Take your choice," Charlie said.

Tony dialed a frequency into the radio and transmitted, "Maintenance, Eleven."

"Go ahead, Eleven."

"Evening guys, we need someone to check our center access compartment door. We're showing a light on it."

"No problem, sir, I'll get somebody out there with a ladder to check it out for you."

Charlie said, "Thank you, Tony. Good catch. Did the girls show up yet?"

"Yeah, Big Bertha asked if we could cool it down back there."

"Why didn't we think of that?"

Britt stowed her bag, went into the center galley, and began checking supplies. She counted the meals in the racks, then picked up the phone and called the aft galley.

Alice answered, "Thanks for calling Tri Con, how may I direct your call?"

"Cute, Alice. I'm ten meals short up here. Did they load them back there?"

"No, we actually have a few extras, though."

"I don't think my business class people want to eat the garbage you serve back there. Do you need anything?"

"We could use some garbage bags and another case of bottled water."

"I'll work on it. I'm going to start boarding in about five minutes. Send me somebody to help."

"Okay, thanks Britt."

Britt went to the cockpit.

"Could one of you guys call operations and tell them we need ten business meals, some garbage bags, and two cases of bottled water?"

Charlie said, "We've got you covered, Britt."

"Can I get you guys anything before we get busy?"

They all ordered beverages.

Britt went into the jet way, picked up the phone, and called the gate.

"We're ready. Send them."

The gate agent picked up the PA microphone.

"Ladies and gentlemen, we will begin general boarding for Tri Con Flight Eleven in just a few minutes. At this time we will pre-board those passengers needing special assistance. Please have your boarding card available as you approach the doorway. Once again, we are only boarding passengers who need special assistance at this time."

At least thirty people stood up and clogged the boarding area, then had to be moved to allow the twenty-one wheelchairs to pass into the jet way. The eighteen from the ticket counter had been joined by three more from connecting flights.

Molly Jackson sat in the gate area facing the window. She could see Charlie and Robby in their white shirts with the gold epaulets on the shoulders as they performed their chores in the cockpit. Her secretary had just informed her, via cell phone, that everything was under control. She also requested a souvenir from

Spain. Molly wondered where Allen Smallwood could be and hoped he didn't show up. Unfortunately, she saw him strolling down the concourse in his Armani suit and carrying a hang up bag over his shoulder. She considered trying to sneak away, but he saw her and waved. He sat down beside her and said, "Molly, we have got to improve our efficiency at the ticket counter. The process consumes entirely too much time."

She somehow knew that he would never mention the broken kiosks or the fact that he had implemented the process.

She said, "That's not my area of expertise, Allen, but perhaps a focus group could offer suggestions."

"I think that might be productive. Would you be willing to participate?"

"My plate is pretty full, but you could probably recruit some of the ticket agents to serve."

"Hmm. Is the flight on time?"

She looked at her watch. "I'll have to get back to you in about forty minutes."

He looked puzzled and then smiled.

"I see your point."

Molly saw Bertie Martin come out of the jet way and approach the agent. They walked over to where a middle-aged couple sat with a little girl. Bertie sat down and talked to the little girl for a few minutes, then they stood up and the parents each hugged the little girl. Bertie pinned a round metal emblem onto the girl's shirt to identify her as an unaccompanied minor, and they held hands and chatted away as they went down the jet way. The little girl had her backpack on her shoulders and carried a teddy bear in her other hand.

Britt saw the wheelchairs line up in the jet way. She watched as the agents transferred each passenger to a special narrow chair with wheels that could be rolled down the aisle of the cabin. As each passenger was transferred, a tag was applied to his wheelchair, and then a bag smasher folded the chair and took it outside to be loaded in the cargo bins. The process seemed to develop a rhythm of its own, and the agents were soon doing two at a time. She did not envy their task, because some of the handicapped passengers must weigh well over two hundred pounds. Eventually, however, all twenty-one of them were strapped into their seats at the rear of the cabin. Next, Big Bertha brought the unaccompanied minor in and gave Britt the special paperwork indicating her seat number and who would be authorized to take custody of her in Madrid.

When general boarding began, the business class passengers appeared first, and Britt greeted each one at the door and directed them to their seat. Nancy and Pat helped them stow their carry-on bags and took beverage orders. They also took their jackets and hang-up bags to the coat closet at the front of the cabin. The parade continued as the tourist class passengers boarded. Britt looked at her watch and concluded that she would have the cabin prepared for an on-time departure at six o'clock. She went to the public address panel and pushed the proper buttons to start the prerecorded "welcome aboard" announcement, which included the rules for carry-on items. At the conclusion it repeated the same announcement in Spanish.

Charlie said, "Looks like we might actually get out of here on time tonight. Did you get the ATIS yet, Robby?"

"Just about to do that right now, boss."

ATIS was the acronym for *automatic terminal information service* and involved a continuous recorded message that could be monitored at any time, thus relieving the air traffic controller from having to repeat the information to each airplane.

Robby adjusted the volume on the overhead speaker and dialed the ATIS frequency into the radio. "Atlanta information Bravo. Atlanta weather, wind 030 at 8, visibility greater than 12, sky 25,000 scattered, temperature 89, dew point 58, altimeter 30.12. Atlanta departing Runways Eight Right and Nine Left. Advise on initial contact you have information Bravo."

Robby copied all the information onto his scratch pad. He and Charlie both adjusted their altimeters to the barometric pressure of 30.12 inches of mercury and confirmed the airport elevation at 1020 feet above sea level. Charlie inserted a temperature of eighty-nine degrees Fahrenheit into the flight management computer.

Robby handed Charlie a piece of paper and said, "I've copied the clearance, and it's as filed, so we're good to go."

From the interphone someone said, "Cockpit, maintenance."

Charlie answered, "Go ahead, maintenance."

"Yes, sir, I buttoned up the access door, did the light go out?"

"Yeah, it's out. Thanks a lot."

"Did you put it in the book?"

"No, we didn't write it up. The logbook is clean, thanks."

Charlie said, "Let's run the checklist, and we'll be ready."

Tony picked up the laminated page and began calling out the long list of challenges. After each challenge, Charlie looked at or touched the item being checked and gave the proper response. After the last item, Tony said, "Checklist complete."

It was usually during the reading of the checklist that it occurred to them that every word uttered in the cockpit was recorded.

✈

Molly spoke to Britt when she and Allen came through the door.

"Having fun yet, Britt?"

"Absolutely, it's like the circus is in town."

Allen handed her his hang up bag and said, "You can take care of this."

Molly rolled her eyes, and they moved up the aisle to row four. Allen took the window seat without asking Molly if she had a preference and immediately pushed the attendant call button, causing a tone to sound and a little white light to illuminate above his seat. Nancy heard the tone and walked down the aisle until she found the seat with the whine light illuminated. She smiled at Molly and asked Allen, "Can I get something for you sir?"

"A martini, no olive."

"Yes, sir. Can I get you something Miss Jackson?"

"A bottled water would be great, if it's not too much trouble."

Allen took his cell phone out and placed a call.

Britt walked to the front of the cabin with the hang-up bag. Nancy was mixing a martini.

"That guy is a world-class jerk."

"You must have met Mr. Smallwood. I've been given the privilege of hanging his bag."

"Don't hang it yet, I want to put some lipstick on a couple of his shirt collars. We'll see if his wife thinks he's a jerk too."

"Nancy, only you would think of that."

"Nah, Pam does it too."

Britt checked her watch and saw that it was ten minutes until six. Everything was under control.

Ray Slackman sat at the bar in the Cavu lounge. At ten till six he finished his fourth beer and asked Annie for one in a bottle. He laid some money on the bar. "Are you leaving early Ray?"

"I'm just going to get some fresh air. I'll be back."

He walked out the door and across the hot parking lot to his pickup truck. After opening all the windows in hopes that a breath of wind might cool it a degree or two, he dug his portable scanner out of the console and turned it on. He had programmed the proper aircraft frequencies into the little radio so that he could follow the progress of Flight Eleven on its departure.   He selected manual and chose the first frequency in the sequence, which was Tri Con ramp control. Hopefully the flight would push back on time and his beer would last while he enjoyed the action. All he really needed was the actual takeoff time so that he could determine when to make his first phone call. While he waited, he went over his elaborate plan once again in his mind.

Ray had removed three working cell phones from the lost and found in baggage claim. The phones could not be traced to him, and he would use them to place three strategically timed phone calls to Tri Con. The first would be to make his demands and give them time to gather his money. After the flight was over the ocean, he would place the second call to reveal the flight number and how to deliver his payoff. Once he received the money, he would make the last call and tell them which circuit breakers to open to prevent the fuel dump. He thought, *Maybe I'll just forget about the last call. That would be a nice payback.*

The plan was fool proof, and he was very proud of himself. He could sense a feeling of power and control that he had never experienced before. Ray felt ten feet tall.

CHAPTER EIGHT

At five till six, the Tri Con gate agent walked in the door with a handful of papers. He made his way up the aisle in business class to the cockpit.

"Captain, we're all set. Are you ready?"

He handed the papers to Charlie.

"Is it too late to sick out?" Charlie asked.

The agent laughed as Charlie signed the dispatch release and handed it back to him.

Robby said, "We've been thrown out of better places than this."

The agent laughed again and said, "You've got the final weight data there, and it shows 197 total on board. Do you have everything you need?"

Charlie said, "Yeah, that will do it. We'll see you in a few days."

"Have a good one, gentlemen. I'll close you right up."

The agent walked back to the passenger entrance door and asked Britt, "Are you all set?"

"We're good. Thanks for getting us out on time."

He walked into the jet way, and Britt pushed the button to roll the big door down from its concealed position in the ceiling.

Once it was closed, she armed it, picked up the phone, and pushed the all call button. There was a flight attendant stationed at each of the eight doors. Britt was standing at the forward door on the left side of the airplane, and her station was referred to as the one left door. One by one the other seven flight attendants reported that their doors were armed. She pushed the cockpit call button, and Tony answered.

"The cabin is ready for push back, guys."

"Thanks, Britt."

She heard the loud warning bell on the jet way as it moved away from the airplane.

Now that the flight was ready for departure, the mood in the cockpit became more serious. The light banter and humor was replaced with professional concentration and attention to detail. The multi-tasking began as the airplane was pushed back, engines were started, checklists were accomplished, and communications with the tug driver and ramp control were maintained.

With the flight attendants moving about the cabin, Charlie was careful to slowly taxi the airplane through the congested ramp area. More checklists were accomplished, and when they approached the south ramp exit, Robby called ground control for clearance.

"Ground, Tri Con Eleven, we're coming up on six-south for taxi. We have Bravo."

"Tri Con Eleven, good evening. Right turn on Mike, you'll follow the Boeing coming out of five-south and you can taxi to Runway Nine Left."

"Right on Mike, follow the Boeing, Runway Nine Left. Tri Con Eleven."

As they joined taxiway Mike, they could see a long line of airplanes waiting for takeoff.

Charlie said, "Tony, you might as well let Britt know she's got plenty of time. Looks like at least twenty minutes."

✈

Britt heard the call signal from the cockpit and picked up the interphone.

"This is Britt. What's up guys?"

"Hey Britt, it's Tony. Charlie says it's gonna be awhile."

"Do we have time to do the over water video before takeoff?"

"Looks like at least twenty minutes."

"Okay, that's plenty. Thanks Tony. Can you give me a five minute warning?"

"Sure thing, I'll let you know."

Britt called the flight attendants in the back cabin.

"Tri Con, we do chicken right."

"Give it a rest, Alice. We've got twenty minutes, so I'm going to do both safety demos before takeoff."

"Okay, I'll let everyone know."

Britt punched up the regular safety video, and it started its spiel about seat belts, oxygen masks, and emergency exits. Next she pushed the buttons for the over water demonstration. It explained the life vest and emergency exits, including the slide rafts. At the conclusion, she made sure one of the flight attendants passed by each seat in case anyone had a question. No one ever did.

Shortly after the video concluded, the PA came alive again.

"Ladies and gentlemen, good evening from the flight deck. My name is Charlie Wells, and I'm your captain tonight. I just wanted to say welcome on behalf of the flight deck crew and give you some information about our flight. Once we are airborne, the flying time is scheduled for eight hours and eleven minutes. We anticipate an on time arrival in Madrid, and with the six-hour time zone difference, the current time in Spain is twelve minutes after midnight. It will take us a few more minutes to make our way to the runway, as there are several airplanes ahead of us for departure. However, our schedule takes this taxi time into account, and it will not delay our arrival. The weather along our route of flight is good for the most part, and we expect a smooth ride. The forecast for our arrival is calling for cloudy skies with light rain and a pleasant temperature of seventy-four degrees. We have eight cabin crew members tonight to provide hospitality for you; however, their primary responsibility is your safety. I ask that you give them your full cooperation on matters concerning cabin safety, and if you have any questions about the aircraft or safety matters, please just ask. Thank you once again for choosing to come along with us tonight. We're very happy to have each of you aboard."

Molly thought, *Good for you, Charlie. Maybe Mr. Smallbrain here will realize flight attendants are not just serving drinks.*

Molly was also impressed that when Charlie concluded his announcement, Britt immediately repeated it in fluent Spanish.

Allen asked, "What do you think the dinner menu will be?"

Molly picked up the menu that Britt had given them a few minutes before and handed it to him, wondering once again what planet he was from. Her only hope was that he would drink himself to sleep and leave her alone. Molly reclined her seat a few inches and picked up the in-flight magazine to browse. The business class seats were upholstered in soft leather and were very comfortable. The armrest held a panel that allowed multiple adjustments for the seat. It could be reclined almost horizontal for sleeping, and the footrest and lumbar could be manipulated separately. Each seat had its own entertainment center for movies or games and even a selection called Air Show that allowed the passenger to follow the airplane's progress along the route of flight. It also displayed the altitude, air speed, and time of arrival. Were it not for her traveling companion, Molly might enjoy the luxurious comforts.

Ray Slackman had become very uncomfortable sitting in the hot pickup truck. He had heard Flight Eleven push back on the ramp frequency, and he had monitored ground control until he heard them receive instructions to proceed to the runway. Now he had no way to know how many airplanes were ahead of them or how long it would be before they received takeoff clearance. The tower frequency was babbling away on the scanner, and his warm beer had been consumed. He wondered if he had time to run back into the Cavu for a fresh one before Flight Eleven reached the runway.

Once they were established on the taxiway, Charlie scanned the overhead panel and then set up the flight instruments for departure. Now there was nothing to do but slowly move up in line as the other airplanes took off. Charlie was careful to stay far enough behind the airplane in front of them to prevent their exhaust fumes from entering the air conditioning inlets and polluting the cabin. He stayed slightly to the right side of the pavement so the prevailing wind would also help that situation. When they advanced to number five in line for departure he said, "Tony, let's sit them down."

Tony called the cabin.

"Britt, we've got about five minutes. Let us know when you're ready."

"Okay, I'll call you back."

She kept the phone in her hand and selected PA.

"Ladies and Gentlemen, in preparation for takeoff, please place your seat backs and tray tables in the up and locked position, and if you have carry-on articles, please place them under the seat in front of you."

Nancy and Pam had already begun walking through the cabin, checking seat backs and tray tables. One by one everyone checked in and reported ready to go. Britt stuck her head in the cockpit and said, "We're all set, guys. I'll lock the door for you."

Charlie called for the before takeoff checklist, and the items were quickly accomplished by the time they were number two in line. They had changed to the tower frequency, and when the airplane in front of them began rolling down the runway, the controller said, "Tri Con Eleven, taxi into position and hold Runway Nine Left."

"Tri Con Eleven position and hold," Robby replied.

Charlie moved them onto the runway and lined up on the white centerline stripe. He discussed the normal departure procedure with the two copilots and explained what he would do if anything unusual occurred. He included the possibility of dumping fuel and returning for landing.

They didn't have to wait long for clearance. "Tri Con Eleven, wind 040 at 10, fly heading zero-nine-five, Runway Nine Left, cleared for takeoff."

They began rolling, and Charlie cleared his mind of everything except the task at hand. The rumbling noise and vibration of the wheels rolling on concrete faded away as they lifted off and climbed to the east. When the wheels tucked into the fuselage and the doors streamlined, the noise level on the flight deck dropped to almost silence momentarily, leaving only the hum of electronics and the whisper of the slipstream on the windshield.

He narrowed his focus and refused to be distracted by the constant radio chatter. Listening for his call sign primarily, he subconsciously tried to keep up with the other airplanes on the frequency enough to know where they were. His eyes rapidly scanned the instrument panel with only occasional glances out the windshield for situational awareness. Robby and Tony continued to read and respond to checklist, adding to the background noise.

The hectic departure sequence continued until they were handed off to Atlanta Air Route Traffic Control. "Atlanta center, Tri Con Eleven with you out of twelve point six, climbing to fourteen."

"Tri Con Eleven, good evening. Radar contact, you're cleared direct Greenwood, climb and maintain flight level two-three-zero."

Charlie engaged the autopilot and programmed Greenwood, South Carolina, into the NAV computer. He slid his seat back slightly and relaxed for a moment and then began surveying the aircraft systems. When he scanned the overhead panel, he noted that they had over sixty thousand pounds of fuel in the center aux tank. The wing tanks would remain full until all the center aux fuel had been used. That meant that he would not have to worry about imbalance in the wing tanks causing aircraft trim problems.

The weather ahead looked smooth, and he reached up and turned the seat belt light off and said, "Get up off of it ladies."

CHAPTER NINE

When the tone sounded in the cabin and the girls saw that the seat belt signs were off, they got up and began placing meals into the ovens. Beverage carts were loaded, and they prepared to do a beverage service prior to serving dinner. From experience, they had learned not to roll the cart into the aisle right away, because a line would form at the lavatories immediately after the seat belt light went off. The cart blocking the way would create a logistical nightmare.

Bertie swam upstream against the flow of people heading to the aft lavatories, even though she was wider than the beverage cart, so that she could check on her unaccompanied minor. The little girl was sitting in her seat holding her teddy bear.

"Mandy, are you okay, sweetie?"

"Yes ma'am, but I'm hungry."

"Me too, sweetie. Would you like to go for a walk?"

"Okay."

Bertie took the little girl and her teddy bear to the rear galley. She sat her down on the flight attendant folding seat and gave her several choices of beverage. She chose orange juice. Then she scavenged the galley for snacks and came up with pretzels, peanuts, and cookies.

"You're not allergic to peanuts, are you, Mandy?"

"No ma'am, I like peanuts."

"Good, you just stay here and enjoy your snack. In a little while we'll have a nice dinner for you. Do you like chicken?"

"Sure do."

Nancy had already responded to Allen's whine light twice more. When he pushed the button again, she told Pam, "Go pour a beer on him. I'm not going."

Pam had been serious earlier when she said she was coming down with something. As soon as the airplane began pressurizing after takeoff, her sinuses had opened up and she had already used half a box of tissue. Her nose was red and her patience was thin. As she left the galley, she saw Molly going into the lavatory. When she approached 4A, Allen was alone.

She sneezed into her hand and then reached above his head and reset the call light. "What can I do for you Mr. Smallman?"

"Smallwood."

"I beg your pardon."

"My name is Smallwood."

"I'm sorry. What can I do for you?"

"I'd like you to take this martini back and bring me one without the olive. I ordered it with no olive."

Pam took a tissue out and sneezed into it. "Right away Mr. Smallman."

"Smallwood."

"Of course."

She took the martini back to the galley and told Nancy, "He doesn't like olives."

"I know."

Pam stuck her fingers into the Martini and removed the olive. Nancy smiled at her and handed her the jar of olives. Pam poured several ounces of olive juice into the martini and stirred it with her finger. Nancy held her hand up for a high five, and Pam smiled innocently as she went to serve the drink.

She sneezed as she approached 4A and said, "I think you will find this one to your satisfaction, Mr. Smallman."

She smiled and walked away before he could correct her. She passed Molly in the aisle. Molly sat down and fastened her seat belt.

"Molly, one of your flight attendants has been walking through the cabin sneezing. It doesn't create a very good ambience for the passengers."

"I know, but I admire her for not taking a costly sick leave. Don't you agree?"

He looked thoughtful and then said, "This is one of the best martinis I've ever had. I'm going to ask how she mixed it."

When Pam returned to the galley, Nancy was preparing meal trays. "Mr. Smallman seems to be moody and uptight. What would you prescribe for that condition, nurse Nancy?"

"Perhaps a few drops of clear liquid laxative would improve his demeanor."

"Let's see how he tolerates olive juice first. You better not let Britt know about our medicinal prowess, either."

"Don't worry, too bad we're out of extra strength Ambien."

Ray had developed a headache sitting in the hot truck. He needed another beer. At last he heard Flight Eleven receive takeoff clearance from the tower and wrote down the time. He switched frequencies and listened as they talked to departure control and were finally handed off to Atlanta Center. Convinced that things were going as planned, he calculated that he would make his first call at eight-thirty.

Now he had two hours to kill and a second agenda in mind. He had decided to pursue a relationship with Annie. She was taller than him and a few years older, but she seemed to understand him, and he was sure that he had impressed her. He adjusted the mirror in the truck so he could comb his beard.

He returned to his favorite bar stool, but an hour and four beers later, he still had not used the opening line he had practiced. Annie was devoting all her attention to a tall mechanic wearing an Aero Mech uniform, sitting a few stools away. Every time she laughed at one of his dumb jokes, Ray became angrier. He switched to scotch and soda and began thinking about payback for both of them. When he heard her agree to meet the guy after work, he stormed out of the bar in a rage.

He found Annie's red Mustang convertible and gouged his truck key down the entire length of the driver's side. He walked to his truck, but another thought occurred to him. He went back to the Mustang, took out his pocket knife and cut a three foot slit in the fabric roof. Still not happy, he cut the valve stem of the front tire and listened to the air hiss out as he walked away smiling. *Let your boyfriend fix that.*

He turned his thoughts back to the night's business as he drove away. Glancing at the clock on the trucks radio, he saw that it was after eight. He would find a quiet place to make his first call. He laughed as he thought, *Hello Tri Con, guess who this is.*

Ray didn't hesitate when the light turned yellow. Easy decision, stomp on it. He barreled through the intersection with other driver's horns blaring and returned the gestures they directed at him. Less than a block later, the blue lights lit him up. He pulled into the parking lot of a gas station and got his driver's license out.

"Sir, did you realize the light was red?"

"I thought I could make it."

The cop was not a rookie. "Would you mind stepping out of the truck, please?"

Ray opened the door as the truck started to roll. He jammed it into park. "Sorry about that."

"Can I see your license, sir?"

Ray handed it to him. *Just give me the ticket, Gomer. I'll be rich tomorrow.*

"Sir, I'm going to ask you to take a sobriety test. Do you have any objection to that?"

"Yeah, I have objections to that. All I did was run a red light."

Another police car had rolled up and the other cop stood with his door open.

"Have you been drinking tonight, sir?"

"A couple of beers, but I don't need a sobriety test."

"That's your decision, sir. Please turn around and place your hands behind your back."

"What! You can't arrest me for running a red light." The other cop walked up to assist.

"I'm arresting you for suspicion of DUI. We can add resisting arrest if you want."

"You can't do that. I pay your salary, mister. Give me the ticket and go have a doughnut."

"Sir, put your hands behind your back please."

The airplane was climbing through clear skies now, and they were able to relax as the workload lessened. Robby turned in his seat to talk to Tony about the relief pilot duties. They divided the available flight time by three and declared that each of them would receive a two hour and twenty four minute rest break. A

Business Class seat was reserved for that purpose. Next, they turned their attention to what was called the howgozit chart. It was essential to be able to compare the actual time of arrival and fuel remaining with the estimated time and fuel at any point during the flight. Based on their actual takeoff time, they calculated the numbers for twenty six different points on the flight plan. At each of the points, they would compare the numbers and determine howgozit.

"I'm going to take last break," said Charlie, "You guys can decide the other two."

"Relief usually goes first," Robby said. "Is that okay with you, Tony?"

The interphone chime sounded, and Tony answered.

"It's Britt. Do you guys want to eat now or later?"

Charlie and Robby both chose later.

"The other guys are going to wait, but I'll be back to take my break in a few minutes. I'll eat then if it's okay."

"No problem. Would you like beef or chicken?"

"Beef would be great."

"I'll have it ready for you."

Tony checked his calculations one last time, then handed the clipboard to Robby. He began his break a few minutes late, but finished his meal quickly, reclined the seat, and fell asleep.

One hour and twenty-one minutes after takeoff, Tri Con Eleven passed over Robbinsville, Pennsylvania, near Philadelphia. Robby checked the howgozit and declared that they were two minutes late and eight hundred pounds short on fuel, well within the comfort zone.

Britt was happy that the meal service seemed to be going well. Everyone had been served, and so far there were no complaints. Tony finished his meal in record time and now was covered up to his chin with a Tri Con blanket. She looked forward to her own break, but remembered she had promised Pat she could go first. Even Allen Smallwood seemed to be content and was well into his first movie as he finished his chicken dinner. Nancy and Pam were doing a good job, but she wondered what they were whispering about in the galley.

In the aft cabin, things were going a little slower, but they were making progress. The passengers who had been served first were now finished with their meal and making their trek to the lavatory, thus causing Alice and Bertie to push the meal cart back and forth to allow them to get by. Mary and Shelia had stopped serving twice in order to assist some of the handicapped to the loo. Several of them were not mobile enough to make the trip, even with assistance, and the flight attendants working the aft cabin had each guessed a time and placed a dollar into a galley drawer. The pot would be collected at the time of the first urinary accident. The time that Alice had guessed was growing near, and she was closely watching a double amputee that she had served four beers. She was considering comping him another.

Bertie fixed a special tray for Mandy with extra portions and promised her an ice cream sundae from business class later. Mandy was concentrating on her Game Boy now and was well occupied for the moment.

Molly Jackson had finished dinner and retrieved the laptop from her briefcase in order to work on her monthly reports. Earlier, Allen had related a lengthy story about how he had hired illegal Mexicans to staff the production line at the shoe factory, and she had highly recommended the feature length film he now watched. She wondered if any of the flight attendants had Ambien.

✈

The flight benefited from a forty knot following wind and sped rapidly to the east as the sun dipped lower in the sky behind them. The air was clear and smooth, and Charlie and Robby chatted and enjoyed the view.

"Tri Con Eleven, contact New York Center on 132.85."

"Three-two point eight-five, Tri Con Eleven, so long."

"Good evening New York, Tri Con Eleven with you level at three-three-zero."

"Tri Con Eleven, New York, good evening sir. How's the ride?"

"It's been real smooth so far. Have you had any reports?"

"Yes sir, you can expect some light to moderate at three-three-zero once you pass JFK."

"Thanks for the warning."

Charlie had been watching flashes of lightning in the distance for the last hundred miles or so. "I guess the forecast was right about the scattered thunderstorms."

He turned on the radar, extended the range, and adjusted the antenna tilt down slightly. The screen painted a line of thunderstorms extending to the northeast of JFK. They were separated by forty miles or so, and each one featured a red center of heavy rain surrounded by a larger area of green or yellow indicating lighter precipitation. He transferred the image to the NAV screen to see exactly where the storms were in relation to their planned course. "Looks like they're scattered along the beach. We should be able to deviate a little to the right and miss them. We'll wait till we get closer."

The lights on the ground were beginning to define cities that were not apparent in sunlight from thirty-three thousand feet. The clouds beneath them were scattered to broken now, but a few minutes later Charlie could clearly see Manhattan and New York Harbor as they approached.

"Why don't you play tour guide and tell the people about the Big Apple?"

Robby punched the PA button and gave the announcement that he had repeated a hundred times before. "I hope I didn't wake Tony."

"Yeah, there are a lot of reasons why nobody likes first break. Let's see if they'll let us go right for a little while."

"New York, Tri Con Eleven, we'd like to deviate right to miss the boomers up ahead."

"Tri Con Eleven, deviate right of course as necessary, let me know when you can go direct Boston."

"Tri Con Eleven, will do, thank you, sir."

Charlie selected a heading twenty degrees to the right and pulled the knob that changed the autopilot mode from nav to heading. The interphone chime sounded and Robby answered, "I asked you not to call me at work."

Britt said, "You and Alice should team up and do a nightclub act. Are you gentlemen ready to dine?"

He looked at Charlie and got a thumbs-up. They had already perused the menu and made selections.

"Yes ma'am, one beef and one chicken."

"How about beverages?"

"Do you have a nice Chardonnay?"

"Of course. Would you like a couple of tequila shooters to go with it?"

"Maybe later when the boss goes on break. For now, just a couple of bottled waters."

"Give me a few minutes, I'll call you back."

Charlie turned another five degrees to the right and watched Mother Nature's light show with the cloud-to-cloud lightning over Long Island.

"Tri Con Eleven, traffic at one o'clock, two-zero miles, a Boeing 747 at flight level three-one-zero."

"We're looking."

Charlie reached up and turned on the bright white fuselage lights, and as they looked ahead, they saw another bright set of lights illuminate on the 747. The twenty miles was already less than ten with a closure rate of over a thousand miles per hour between the two airplanes.

"We have the traffic in sight, Tri Con Eleven."

"Roger, sir."

"He must be deviating too," said Charlie.

They confirmed the other aircraft's altitude on their TCAS indicator and watched him disappear under the nose. Robby wrote down the time and fuel abeam JFK and announced that they were making time and fuel. They were now one minute late and only down six hundred pounds of fuel.

The interphone chime sounded again and Britt gave the password to enter the cockpit. Robby pushed the unlock button, and when the door opened, they could smell hot food. Britt and Pam brought the trays in, and Charlie placed the aircraft logbook on his lap and set the food tray on it. He had learned long ago that the trays often had food on the bottom where they had been stacked on top of each other. The logbook saved embarrassment and cleaning bills.

Pam asked, "Was that really New York a few minutes ago, or are you guys making stuff up?"

Robby said, "We're not positive, but it sounded good, don't you think?"

"If I didn't know you, Robby, I would probably believe it."

Britt asked, "Are we on time so far?"

Charlie said, "We're one minute late, but we're working on it."

"Tri Con Eleven, contact Boston Center 134.55."

"Three-four point five-five, Tri Con Eleven, good night ya'll."

Robby enjoyed calling New Yorkers ya'll.

"Boston Center, Tri Con Eleven at three-three-zero, deviating east of course for weather."

"Tri Con Eleven, Boston, radar contact, deviations approved, let me know when you can come back to the left."

"Will do, sir."

Charlie said, "That's Providence, Rhode Island, over there."

Pam said, "How do you know?"

"Because it says PVD on my navigation screen."

"Sounds like men's underwear to me."

"That's BVD."

"I thought you said it was Providence."

"You're right, we're lost."

"I thought so."

Britt said, "This sounds like Abbott and Costello doing their 'Who's on first' routine. I'm getting dizzy. Let me know when to pick up the trays."

Pam said, "I'm leaving too. When you finish dinner, try to find out where we are."

Allen had turned his video screen to the Air Show and asked Molly, "Are these guys lost? Why are we over New York if we're going to Spain? Why didn't we just go straight east across the Atlantic?"

"New York is east of Atlanta, Allen."

"Well, I'm not sure, but I think a straight line is the shortest distance between two points."

"You can't draw a straight line on a round ball, Allen."

He paused to think about that and looked out the window.

"Look, they just turned on the outside lights. That doesn't make any sense at thirty three thousand feet."

CHAPTER TEN

Ray stood at the bars of the holding cell and looked at the clock above the desk sergeant. It was already after nine. He yelled, "I want my phone call! You have to give me a phone call! I've got important business tonight. Give me my cell phone back. My lawyer's going to straighten you people out."

The sergeant looked up, "You need to keep it down, Mr. Slackman. There are several cases ahead of you here. Just sober up a little while you wait. We'll get to you, and you'll get your phone call."

"Don't tell me to hold it down! It's a free country, in case you didn't know. I don't need to sober up."

"That's not what your sobriety test said. Dude, you might be the high score of the week.

Charlie said, "Looks like we're clear of the weather. Robby, tell them we can come left."

"Boston, Tri Con Eleven, we can go on course anytime."

"Tri Con Eleven, thank you sir. You are cleared present position direct Tusky. Contact Moncton center on 128.45. Have a good one."

"Tri Con Eleven, so long."

"Moncton Center, Tri Con Eleven going direct Tusky at three-three-zero."

"Tri Con One-One, Moncton, radar contact, flight level three-three zero, good evening, sir."

"Evening."

They were now entering Nova Scotia, and the Canadian controllers were much more proper with radio technique and phraseology. Each digit was pronounced individually. It was a little overkill for Americans, but it left less room for error with the Germans, Italians, and Ethiopians, who did not always speak perfect English.

Alice opened the galley drawer and removed the five one-dollar bills, then began looking for the aerosol air freshener.

Shelia said, "You know that wasn't fair, Alice. How many beers did you give that poor man?"

"Enough that we're both happy. You want to go double or nothing on that poor woman you gave the liter bottle of water to?"

"She looked dehydrated."

"Better luck next time. Don't be a poor loser. It doesn't become you."

Britt and Pam were just finishing their dinner when the cockpit interphone sounded again. Pam answered, "Tri Con dial-a-date."

Robby said, "You wish, Pam. It's time to wake up sleeping beauty."

"He's kinda cute. We're gonna keep him back here with us."

"No, you're not, and you can lay out my slippers and pajamas because I have next break."

"Robby, you probably haven't seen pajamas since second grade."

"Second grade was the best three years of my life."

"Why am I not surprised?"

She walked back to the crew rest seat and gently shook Tony's shoulder until he opened his eyes.

"Duty calls, sleeping beauty."

He smiled and gave her a thumbs-up. Tony folded the blanket and left it on the seat with the pillow. He found an empty lavatory and splashed water on his face, then went to the galley where Britt fixed him a cup of hot coffee to take to the cockpit with him. She followed him, and when he entered, she waited for him to hand her the empty meal trays that were sitting on the relief pilot's seat. She offered hot fudge ice cream sundaes, and Charlie and Tony both placed their orders.

Charlie said, "Robby, before you leave I'm going to visit the lavatory. Hold on to the handlebars till I get back."

Charlie left the cockpit, and Robby briefed Tony.

"We're going direct Tusky now, and the ETA and fuel look good. You'll need to call Gander shortly and copy our oceanic clearance. We're still at three-three zero and talking to Moncton."

"I got the picture, Robby. Thanks."

When Charlie returned and strapped in, Robby slid the seat back.

"Just use my brain bag. The flight plan is on this clipboard, and the plotting chart and plotter are on the other one."

Robby stood up and they danced past each other. Tony sat down, fastened the seat belt, and hit the button to move the seat forward.

Charlie said, "Sleep tight, Robby."

"Thanks, boss. Give me a wake-up call about ten minutes early."

"You can count on it."

Robby left and Charlie asked, "Did you sleep well, Tony?"

"Yeah, for a little while. It's pretty noisy back there."

"I know. Second and third break are much better. Let's get the oceanic clearance before we get to Tusky. There's a special clearance delivery frequency on the flight plan for Gander."

Gander control, located in Newfoundland, was the controlling agency for the western half of the North Atlantic.

Tony found the frequency and dialed it into the number two radio. Charlie reminded him that they were touchy about proper radio procedures. The frequency was crowded, and they listened as several other flights received clearance. Tony waited patiently with his pencil poised over his scratch pad. Finally there was a break and Tony jumped in.

"Gander clearance, Tri Con One-One, request oceanic clearance, highest possible is three-five-zero."

Gander always wanted to know the maximum altitude capability in case they needed to change the flight level. Tony knew they were too heavy to climb above thirty five thousand feet. He copied the clearance from the controller and found that there were no changes from the flight plan. He read it back for confirmation.

"Tri Con One-One, read back is correct, have a good evening."

"Nice job Tony. You might want to double check the latitudes and longitudes on the plotting chart to see if we marked all of them correctly."

Tony checked them and said, "It looks good. The equal time airports are St. Johns in Newfoundland and Lisbon in Portugal with the equal time point at about 032 west."

"Right, I made a fix in the flight plan and named it ETP. It'll show up on the nav screen when we get close."

Tony dialed the number one high frequency radio to 8906 and dreaded having to try to talk through the static and noise once they began the over water portion of the flight.

"Tri Con One-One, contact Gander Center on one-three-five decimal two-six, over."

"One-three-five decimal two-six, Tri Con One-One, good evening."

They were entering their last sector before beginning the Atlantic crossing. Charlie scanned the panels again and saw that the center fuel tanks were almost empty.

When Allen began another story about his exploits and accomplishments in the sports shoe industry, Molly excused herself and went to the forward galley. Throughout the cabin people were reclining their seats and getting comfortable for the night. She hoped Allen would follow suit if she left him alone for a little while.

Pam had gone on break, but Molly found Britt and Nancy making ice cream sundaes. Britt said, "Hi Molly, having trouble getting to sleep?"

"No, I'm just bored, I guess. Did someone request extra dessert?"

"These are for the pilots. They're not as irritating as most, so we decided to give them a treat."

Molly laughed, "Charlie's a good guy. I flew with him quite a bit when I was on the line."

"Do you ever miss it?"

"Actually, I do. Back then when I went home I didn't think much about Tri Con until it was time to go back to work. Now it's an everyday hassle. Are you taking those to the cockpit?"

"I am. Would you like to come along and say hello to Charlie?"

"Sure, let me carry one of those for you."

Tony answered the phone and then pushed the unlock button for the door. Britt came in, followed by the tall redhead he had seen in the briefing room. Britt said, "I brought a visitor. I thought you two might enjoy talking to a grown-up for a change."

Charlie said, "Hey, Molly, welcome." He picked up the logbook on the relief pilot's seat and said, "Have a seat and visit for a while."

"Thanks, Charlie. You sure I'm not interrupting anything?"

"Of course not, we're just sitting here watching the autopilot work. Britt, is everyone sleeping back there?"

"Pretty much. We'll wake them for breakfast in a few hours."

"What's the story on all those handicapped folks?"

"They're all members of an anti-discrimination organization."

"Does it present any special problems for you?"

"Two of them peed in their seats, but other than that, no problem."

"I'm sure you handled it with a maximum of delicacy and decorum."

"Alice and Shelia quietly administered air freshener. We'll have the seat cushions changed in Madrid."

Charlie asked, "Molly, do they cover that in flight attendant training?"

"I don't think so. Sounds like Britt has it figured out, though."

Britt said, "I better get back to see what disaster occurs next."

She carefully locked the door as she left.

"Tri Con One-One, contact Gander Radio, frequency eight-nine-zero-six at Color, radar service is terminated, over."

"Gander Radio on eight-nine-zero-six at Color, Tri Con One-One."

Molly asked, "What's Color?"

"It's just a navigation fix on the coast of Newfoundland. We're about to begin the crossing, and they won't be able to see us on radar any longer."

The airplane rolled into a slight turn as they crossed Color and Tony turned the volume up on the HF radio. "Let's see if I remember how to do this."

The high frequency, long range radios were necessary for the ocean crossing, but they were temperamental and subject to atmospheric interference. The signals sometimes carried for thousands of miles and created overlap with several airplanes transmitting at once.

"Gander Radio, Tri Con One-One, position on 8906, over."

"Tri Con One-One Gander, go ahead."

"Tri Con One-One, Color at 0336, flight level three-three-zero, estimating 47 North, 050 west at 0349, 47 north, 040 west next, SELCAL is bravo kilo alpha foxtrot, over."

The selective calling feature allowed air traffic control to transmit a special signal to their airplane only which would cause a blue light to flash and a bell to ding. This relieved Tony from having to monitor the scratchy radio constantly.

Gander read the position report back, confirming that it was correct, and punched up their SELCAL code, transmitting it. The bell dinged, the blue light flashed, and Tony turned the volume back down. He sighed and said, "That one was pretty easy."

Charlie said, "Wait till we get a couple hundred miles out. The HF radio can be a real pain."

Molly asked, "What were all those numbers about?"

"There are no navigation stations and no airways over the ocean. Gander designs what they call North Atlantic Tracks each day based on the winds and weather. The tracks are sixty miles apart, and they can stack airplanes onto them in altitude increments of a thousand feet from 29,000 up to 41,000. The numbers that you heard were latitude longitude fixes that define our track. You can look at our plotting chart here and see the track that we drew. We use GPS to follow the track. We have to give a position report at each fix so they can keep us separated from other airplanes."

"Could you give me that in English?"

"Sure, do you see the magenta line on the big screen in the middle of the instrument panel?"

"Oh yeah, I do."

"If that little symbol that has wings on it stays on the magenta line, everybody is happy."

"That's a much better explanation Charlie."

"Any kid with a Game Boy could do it."

Tony checked the howgozit at Color and declared, "We're three minutes ahead, and we've manufactured nine hundred pounds of fuel."

Molly said, "That's even better. I was just glad we were on the purple line."

They continued to enjoy their ice cream and thirteen minutes later, Tony made the position report at the first oceanic fix. The reports after that would be at ten degree intervals of longitude and almost an hour apart. The center tank fuel had been expended and the engines were now consuming from the main wing tanks. The electronic controller that scheduled fuel pumps on and off to transfer and maintain balance in the auto mode had woken up the main tank pumps; however, it would only use the forward transfer pumps as long as they were immersed in fuel. The aft inboard sections of the tanks were larger, deeper, and contained the aft inboard transfer pumps.

Molly and Charlie reminisced about old times and related funny stories to Tony. Several of them featured Colt Adams, who Tony had not had the pleasure of meeting. Molly told them about one of her flight attendants who had the misfortune of encountering a self-important gentleman in the first class cabin on one of her flights. He had become incensed over some issue that no one even remembered and she was unable to assuage his concerns. He began to loudly ask over and over, "Do you know who I am? Do you have any idea who I am?"

She calmly picked up the PA and announced, "Ladies and gentlemen, we have a passenger sitting in 3B that does not know who he is. If anyone knows who he is would you please come forward and identify him?"

Molly said that she summoned the girl into the office in order to personally reprimand her, but in the course of chewing her out, they both started laughing so hard they couldn't stop. She did not, however, tell her that she had received eight e-mails from frequent flyers who had witnessed the incident, commending the girl for putting the man in his place.

Molly finally decided that she should at least attempt a nap, and retired to the cabin. It was after ten o'clock by her body clock, and it had been a very long day. She blessedly found Allen asleep and hoped he would stay in that condition. The flight attendants were taking turns with rest breaks. Bertie was taking hers in the seat beside Mandy and watching her sleep with her teddy bear.

Britt had not taken her break but was sitting in her folding seat at the 1L door and reading a magazine.

Two hundred miles offshore, there was very little to do and even less to see. Charlie and Tony were keeping each other awake by talking about their families and their careers. The sky was clear above with visible stars and no moon. Below, the Atlantic was dark and could not be seen at all. The HF radio frequency was crowded with the litany of position reports from aircraft, some nearby and some thousands of miles away. They had turned the volume down and relied on the SELCAL to alert them if Gander called. They were no longer in range of land-based VHF radio; however, they tuned one radio to 121.5, the international emergency frequency, and the other to 123.45, the air-to-air frequency. Occasionally aircraft would converse with each other on the air-to-air frequency for turbulence reports and sometimes just to pass the time. They turned on the overhead lights in the cockpit, which destroyed night vision, but there was nothing to see outside anyway.

Charlie was considering calling the galley for coffee when he heard the SELCAL ding and saw the blue light begin to flash. Tony increased the volume and could hear at least three aircrafts transmitting at once in different parts of the northern hemisphere. In a slightly louder, overriding voice he heard, "Tri Con One-One, Gander, over."

"Gander, Tri Con One-One, go ahead."

"Tri Con One-One, Gander, Climb and maintain flight level three-five-zero. Cross 47 north, 040 west at flight level three-five-zero. Report reaching, over."

He looked at Charlie, who gave him a thumbs-up.

"Gander, Tri Con One-One, out of flight level three-three-zero climbing to flight level three-five-zero. We'll report reaching."

Charlie typed the new altitude into the computer and dialed it up on the altitude select panel to enable it. The throttles slowly moved forward, the nose pitched up and the airplane began to climb at about a thousand feet per minute. Charlie scanned the TCAS (traffic collision avoidance system) screen and saw no other aircraft in the area to worry about. He watched the rate of climb decrease as they approached the new altitude and settle on zero as they leveled out.

"Looks like the wind is about the same, so it shouldn't affect our next ETA, Tony."

Tony fought his way onto the frequency again and reported, "Gander, Tri Con One-One is level at flight level three-five-zero, over."

Among several other voices, he heard, "Tri Con One-One, Gander, roger level at flight level three-five-zero."

When the airplane pitched up to climb, fuel in the main tanks gravitated to the rear. The forward transfer pump became uncovered and the controller sent a signal to the aft pump to do its thing. The signal was routed instead to the dump valves. They opened immediately and began spilling fuel into the night at six thousand pounds per minute. A little less than a minute later, the airplane leveled and the forward pump was once again immersed in jet fuel. The controller recognized the situation and signaled the aft pump back to sleep, thus closing the dump valves.

Once they were safely cruising at the new altitude, Charlie scanned the panels once again. He saw nothing out of the ordinary, and called the galley to request coffee. Britt was glad to have something to break the boredom, and a few minutes later she entered the cockpit with two hot cups.

"Britt, I thought you would be on break by now," Charlie said.

"I'm planning a nap in a little while, before we start the breakfast service. How about you, Charlie?"

"Yeah, I'll let you know when to wake Robby."

Ray paced his cell and complained until his cellmates threatened to shut him up. He watched the clock on the wall and calculated the flight time over and over. At ten o'clock, he knew the million dollars was gone. There would not be enough time to go through his elaborate scenario. He watched as other prisoners were charged and released with a court date. The paper work dragged on and on.

If they released him in the next thirty minutes, and he could get to one of his stolen cell phones, he might be able to warn Tri Con and give them the information to avert the disaster. His only other option would be to confess to the sabotage and have the police call Tri Con. That option was quickly rejected. Another five minutes ticked away.

CHAPTER ELEVEN

Radioman Third Class Brian Davis was sleeping like a baby. He was stretched out beneath the sheets of his bottom rack in the forward berthing compartment. The gentle roll and pitch of the ship had put him out like a light less than two hours ago. Now someone was shaking his shoulder and saying, "Roll out of there, Davis, it's eleven thirty."

Brian's personal living space aboard the ship was seven feet long and two feet high. That was the length of his bed and the distance to the one stacked above him. The sailors referred to it as their rack, similar to the ancient torture device. He opened his eyes and in the dim light of the berthing compartment he could barely see the picture of his girlfriend taped to the rack above his. He was beginning the last year of his four-year US Navy enlistment and wondered once again if he could survive the sporadic sleep patterns of shipboard life. He rolled out of the rack on his knees and then stood up on the swaying deck. Brian had grown up in California and had the sun-bleached blond hair to prove it. He had met his current girlfriend on Virginia Beach, near the amphibious base in Norfolk. He went to his locker and dug out a pair of bellbottom dungarees and a blue work shirt with his third class petty officer insignia. If he hurried he could stop by the mess deck for mid-rats, the light snacks rationed by the ship's cook for the late shift change, before reporting to the radio room at eleven forty five to begin his midnight to four a.m. watch.

When he remembered that his best friend, Bobby Creel, had the eight to midnight watch, he took his time. He grabbed a couple of doughnuts and a cup of coffee and decided to take the outside route to the ship's bridge. There was a fifteen-knot breeze blowing when he stepped through the open hatch and onto the main deck, but only because that was the speed of the little ship. The *USS Karuk* was an ocean-going fleet tug named for an American Indian tribe. The ship was a little over two hundred feet long and was staffed with a crew of eighty-five sailors. The *Karuk* was en route from Norfolk to the Azores, and would later join the sixth fleet in the Mediterranean, where they would be available to not only tow ships, but to also perform salvage and rescue missions.

Brian could see that they were still in the grips of the warm front that stretched across the Atlantic, and visibility was restricted. The radar antenna on the mast was spinning and searching the fog for other ships. He was only a couple of minutes late to the radio room, located at the rear of the ship's bridge.

"Glad you could make it, Brian. I thought you were leaving me stranded up here all night."

"Shut up, I brought you a doughnut."

"I'll eat it on the way to my rack."

"Yeah right, Bobby, like you're not going to chow on the mid-rats till they're all gone."

"Is Cookie down there? He owes me a favor."

"Nah, just the mess cooks, but they've put out a good spread."

"I'll check it out."

"That's what I thought. What's going on up here?"

94

"Not much, just some routine messages from fleet on Satcom. I picked up BBC for a while, but that's about it. I'm out of here, buddy."

Brian went through the standard communication checks required at each watch change and made sure the VHF and HF radios were on guard and tuned to the emergency frequencies. He made the corresponding logbook entries and then turned the speakers up so he could walk out onto the bridge and speak to Lieutenant Strickland, who was the mid-watch Officer of the Deck.

"Where are we, Lieutenant?"

"How would I know, Brian? I haven't had my coffee yet."

Brian laughed. "I need to send a position report to fleet at midnight."

"Yeah, I know. We'll figure it out. Let's take a look."

They walked over to the navigation computer and watched the digital readout as it slowly changed. It seemed to be in rhythm with the rise and fall of the deck.

The lieutenant said, "Looks like we finally made it to forty degrees west. You'll be basking on the beach in beautiful Santa Maria in a couple of days: the most beautiful island of the Azores. I'll get an exact fix on the hour for you to transmit to fleet, although I doubt if they really care where we are."

Charlie was still enjoying his coffee and Britt had remained in the cockpit to talk and relieve the boredom. His break time had arrived but he didn't want to be rude by asking Britt to leave to wake Robby.

They were approaching forty west, and he decided to wait until Tony made his position report before taking his break.

Tony said, "Here we go again." He waited for a lull on the frequency and then took his turn.

"Gander, Tri Con One-One, position."

"Tri Con One-One, Gander, go ahead."

Tony reported their time and altitude at longitude forty west and gave them the estimate for the next reporting point at longitude thirty west.

Gander read the report back correctly and added, "Contact Santa Maria on five-five-nine-eight at 030 west, over."

"Santa Maria frequency 5598 at 030 west, Tri Con One-One."

Tony turned his attention to the howgozit and made the calculations.

"I think I screwed something up, Charlie."

Charlie answered. "I, of course, have never made a mistake."

Britt said, "Captain, my captain."

Tony looked puzzled.

"We lost a minute, probably due to the climb, but we lost over five thousand pounds of fuel. I must have done something wrong."

Charlie took the chart and looked it over.

"I don't see it, Tony. Are you sure the figures at the last fix are correct?"

"I think so."

Charlie did some quick calculations in his head, computing the total time since takeoff versus the total fuel burn.

"We may have a problem, maybe a bad fuel quantity indicator."

He pulled the fuel system up on the diagnostic screen.

"Let's add up the individual tanks."

The two main wing tanks contained fuel and were balanced, as were the two wing tip tanks. They also noted that a small amount of fuel was contained in the aft balance tank. This small tank was located in the aft fuselage and used to trim the center of gravity of the airplane. It presently contained almost 3000 pounds. The numbers added up to what Tony had calculated on the howgozit.

"If we had a bad indicator, the tanks would show an imbalance, and that's not the case."

Charlie clicked the autopilot off and flew manually for a minute.

"The trim is good so the fuel is actually balanced. We may have a leak, Tony." He turned to Britt. "Get Robby up, please."

They continued to analyze the problem and could not find a fault in the system. The fuel flow to the engines looked normal.

"Maybe it was a transient problem, Tony, and we still have plenty of fuel. Let's do a five minute burn check and see what we come up with."

Tony hacked the time and noted the total fuel on board.

Charlie said, "We haven't reached the equal time point yet, but we might be closer to Lajes in the Azores than St. John's in Newfoundland. Make Lajes a fix and check the distance."

Tony did the appropriate typing and saw that Lajes was more than seven hundred miles to the southeast.

"We're still closer to Canada, Charlie."

"Okay, just for drill, compute a new equal time point between Lajes and St. Johns. We'll forget about Lisbon for now."

Britt shook Robby's shoulder, and he came awake.

"Robby, it's time to get up, and Charlie says we may have some sort of fuel problem. He wants you to come back to the cockpit right away."

97

"What kind of fuel problem?"

"I don't know. He didn't seem panicked but he wants you to come right up there."

"Okay, thanks, Britt."

Robby threw the blanket off and looked for his shoes in the dim light of the cabin. All the passengers were sleeping quietly. He laced up his shoes and put his iPod in his pocket, then made his way forward.

When Robby entered the cockpit, Britt went with him. Robby asked, "What's up, boss?"

"Maybe nothing. We can't find five thousand pounds of fuel. Go ahead and change seats, and then you can double check our numbers."

Tony unbuckled and slid the seat back. He and Robby changed places, and Robby picked up the clipboard. After a moment he said, "I don't see a mathematical error. Maybe we should do a five-minute burn check."

"We just did that, the estimated fuel at thirty west is normal except we're still five thousand pounds short. It doesn't appear to be getting worse."

"Beats me, Charlie, but it had to go somewhere."

"We made Lajes the ETP airport instead of Lisbon. In about five minutes, Lajes will be the emergency divert airport. Tony has already loaded it in the secondary flight plan."

Robby double checked Tony's work and said, "Yeah, that looks good. I'll get the charts for Lajes out just in case." He looked at the approach plates and said, "You're not going to believe this, guys. There's a note that says 'Caution, cattle in vicinity of airport.' There's also a 3500-foot hill beside the runway. The good news is it's a nice long piece of concrete."

Charlie said, "Let's hope we don't have the pleasure of making a visit. Let's do the numbers for another five-minute check. Britt, I'd like for you to hang around if you don't mind."

The fuel level in the main tanks continued to decrease, and the forward transfer pump in the right wing became momentarily uncovered as the autopilot made a slight course correction to the left. The electronic controller did its job and fuel began pouring out over the Atlantic. A few seconds later the wings rolled level and the system reconfigured back to normal once again.

Charlie watched the little airplane symbol track down the magenta line, making small wind corrections to stay on course. They waited for the five minutes to tick away and then recalculated the fuel burn.

"Charlie, we lost almost another thousand pounds," Robby declared.

"Okay, we know we have a problem now. Britt, I don't want to alarm anyone, but there is the possibility that we might have to divert to the Azores. What I want you to do is wake everyone up and begin the breakfast service early. Tell the flight attendants what's happening, but don't tell the passengers yet. Also, don't get the serving carts out, run the meals out by hand so we can leave the aisles clear in case you have to prepare for landing quickly. I don't really care if anyone eats, I just want everyone awake."

"That's what I'll do, Charlie. If we go there, how long until we land?"

Charlie checked the fix page and saw Lajes was less than six hundred and fifty miles away. "About one hour, Britt, but I'll give you plenty of warning."

He turned to Tony.

"I want you to go to the aft cabin and look at the wings. If we have a leak, it's going to leave a trail. I'll turn on the wing illumination lights so you can see."

Tony held the door for Britt and then followed her into the cabin. He walked all the way to the rear galley and peered out the round window in the door. He could see the trailing edge of the wing in the glow of the lights. The lights were designed to illuminate the wings so that they could be checked for ice accumulation, but they served very well for the present situation. Tony looked very closely at both wings and could see nothing at all out of the ordinary. The strobe lights, flashing a steady cadence at each wingtip, provided a comforting feeling of normality. As he walked forward the cabin lights came up and passengers began to stir.

When he reached the forward galley, the three flight attendants were gathered and Britt was explaining the situation to them. She asked, "Anything new, Tony?"

"No, everything looks normal, but Charlie won't take any chances. If we lose any more fuel, there's a good possibility that we will land in Lajes or Lisbon."

As Tony entered the cockpit, Britt was announcing breakfast on the PA.

Molly was already awake and thought it strange to make a loud PA and wake everyone up. She had always found it effective to just start serving and people could eat or sleep as they chose. When she saw Nancy running meals out by hand, she knew something was up. Allen raised his head up off the pillow, mumbled something, and plopped back down. Molly walked to the forward galley and looked at Britt with a questioning expression.

Britt said, "We may have to divert. Charlie wants everybody awake."

"That sounds ominous."

"He thinks we may have a fuel problem."

"That's never good. How can I help?"

Charlie's intuition was working full force.

"Guys, we need a contingency plan. If we divert, we obviously can't descend on the track. There may be other airplanes below us. The standard track exit procedure is to turn ninety degrees, offset thirty miles to put us halfway between our track and the next one, and then parallel the track to descend. If we do that, I'll turn right to put us closer to Lajes. When we start down, I'll descend to at least twenty eight thousand feet. That'll put us below the lowest track, and we can proceed direct to Lajes. Tony, you handle the radios. Forget about Gander. Try to reach Santa Maria. We'll be in their airspace anyway, if we divert. Hopefully we won't do any of that, but just in case, I want you to know what I plan to do."

Robby said, "I pulled up the weather and Lajes is not great. They have a ceiling of three hundred feet and visibility at one and a half miles. I guess that warm front is still hanging around."

"If we have to go there it won't matter. We'll declare an emergency and bust minimums if we have to."

"I'm with you, boss."

Charlie turned to the approach plates for Lajes and started familiarizing himself with the airport.

Tony said, "Oh man! Look at the fuel totalizer."

The digits on the instrument were unwinding faster than any of them had ever seen. Charlie punched up the fuel system diagnostic page again and immediately saw two green symbols, one on each wing, representing an open dump valve. He rolled the airplane into a right turn, selected a heading ninety degrees from the track course, and said, "Get on the radio, Tony. Robby, punch the fuel dump switch and see if you can close those valves. Get the book out and see what you can do."

Britt was walking down the aisle with a hot tray and almost tripped when the airplane abruptly rolled to the right. She regained her balance and heard the tone indicating that the seat belt light had been turned on. She turned and hurried back to the galley.

"Girls, put everything away." She picked up the interphone and called the aft galley.

"That'll be six dollars and thirty cents, drive to the window please."

"Knock it off, Alice, we've got a problem. Button everything up and tell everyone to prepare for landing. I think we're doing the divert I told you about."

"Okay, we'll be ready. Let us know what's going on."

Britt picked up the PA.

"Ladies and gentlemen, the captain has illuminated the seat belt light indicating the possibility of turbulence in the area. Please check to see that your seat belt is securely fastened. Cabin service will be terminated temporarily. Thank you."

Pam and Nancy began their trek down the aisle checking everyone's seat belt. Britt could see Alice and Shelia doing the same duty in the aft cabin. As she moved through the aisle, the airplane rolled to the left and pitched forward slightly. She felt the familiar pressure change in her ears and knew they were descending.

Brian Davis propped his feet up and balanced his coffee against the pitch and roll of the ship. It never occurred to anyone that the ship was pitching or rolling; it was just a part of their being. He was debating whether he should shave before the arrival in the Azores. Most of the crew considered it a waste of razor blades unless they were in port. He had become bored with the BBC and turned it off. There had been no communications with other ships at all, and he knew they were far from the normal shipping lanes. Still, it was nice to have the radar searching their path for collision dangers. He had read all the electronics magazines stashed in the radio shack and looked forward to replenishing the supply when they hit port.

With the lack of anything better to do, he looked through the codebook for aircraft frequencies, just to possibly hear a human voice not connected with the US Navy. He found the list for Santa Maria oceanic radio and started scanning the HF band. There were ten frequencies listed for Santa Maria, but he remembered what he had been taught in radio school. Follow the sun to find a HF frequency that works efficiently. When the sun is high, use the higher frequencies, when the sun is low, use the lower frequencies. He started with the lower frequencies and hit pay dirt on 5598. He listened to the bored voices of a few pilots making position reports at thirty west and twenty west and heard the word *Dirma* a couple of times, although he had no clue where that was. He noticed that the airplanes used basically the same format for position reports that ships used.

It was irritating that operators stepped all over each other on the frequency but he knew it was because of the long range of HF. Transmissions were commonly covered up by other transmissions. It was annoying, and he had heard nothing but position reports anyway. He was about to turn it off when he heard, "Santa Maria, Tri Con One-One, exiting track uniform, I say again Tri Con One-One, exiting track uniform, diverting to Lajes, over."

He heard no response from Santa Maria, but he knew that didn't mean they were not replying. At sea level he might not receive them. He decided to stay with it a little longer. He wondered why an airplane might be diverting. Perhaps it was a hijacking. A few minutes later he heard a weaker transmission, "Santa Maria, Santa Maria, Tri Con One-One, off track uniform to the south, diverting direct Lajes, do you read, over."

Britt hurried over to the interphone handset when the cockpit call tone sounded. "Britt, it's Tony, we're diverting. Charlie wants you to close everything up and strap in. I'll make a PA and call you back in a few minutes."

"Okay, Tony."

Tony pushed the PA switch.

"Ladies and gentlemen, this is First Officer Johnson. I have some unfortunate news to pass along. We've developed a mechanical situation that will require a change of destination for our flight this morning. We are presently proceeding directly to Lajes in the Azores Islands and will be touching down within the hour. We regret that our normal schedule will be interrupted, but with your safety in mind, it will be necessary. Once we're on the ground we will keep you informed as to the length of the delay. Thank you."

Britt repeated the information in Spanish and then added that everyone should remain seated with their seatbelts fastened.

Allen Smallwood was incensed.

"Molly, heads are going to roll. I have important meetings this morning in Madrid and someone is going to answer for this. How could they possibly decide to land in the Azores? Tri Con doesn't even serve the Azores. We will have to pay through the nose to have the aircraft serviced and fueled. I'll bet you that this will somehow result in extra pay for those pilots. Well, I'll see that doesn't happen." He pushed the flight attendant call button.

Pam happened to be approaching his seat from behind and immediately punched off the whine light, "What do you want, Mr. Smallman?"

He ignored the stupid woman's mistake.

"I want you to go to the cockpit and tell the captain that I have important business in Madrid, and I will not be delayed. You can inform him that I am an important member of Tri Con management, and I demand that he continue to Madrid."

"Mr. Smallman, the captain is very busy right now, and I will not distract him. I'm sure he will grant you an audience at some future time, and you will be able to voice your concerns. Fasten your seatbelt like a good boy."

She walked away before he could reply. Molly covered her mouth with her hand and coughed so she wouldn't giggle.

After Charlie made the ninety-degree turn, he typed a thirty-mile offset into the navigation computer and saw a new magenta line form parallel to the original track. It only took three minutes to cover the thirty miles, and as they approached the magenta line, he rolled the airplane left to intercept and pushed the nose over to begin the descent. The speed quickly increased to the red line as the throttles came back to idle.

"I can't close the valves, Charlie. I've tried everything, and it's dumping fast."

"Okay, the system is designed with a standpipe level at twenty thousand pounds to prevent inadvertently dumping it all. It should stop at that point and we'll have over an hour of fuel. We can make Lajes with no problem."

Tony said, "I can't raise Santa Maria. I don't know if I'm getting covered by someone else or if they just can't hear me."

"Keep trying. We're going there anyway, no matter what. When we get closer you can get them on VHF. I'm going to level at twenty eight thousand feet and that should give us a VHF range of well over a hundred miles."

At twenty-eight thousand feet, Charlie leveled the nose and turned to the right to proceed direct to Lajes. He noted the distance along the new magenta line to Lajes at five hundred and seventy miles.

The tension was thick in Robby's voice. "Charlie, we just blew by twenty thousand pounds. The standpipe level didn't stop the dump. We've got about three minutes of fuel left."

Molly ignored Allen's whining and ranting. She had an empty feeling in the pit of her stomach. Thousands of hours strolling the aisles of jet airplanes had produced the innate ability to realize when things were not going well. Britt had told her that Charlie was concerned about a fuel problem. She knew the only serious problem with fuel was not having enough. She glanced at her watch and calculated that they were in a very vulnerable portion of the flight. Running out of fuel was second only to an in-flight fire on the list of mid-flight nightmares. She saw Allen reach for the flight attendant call button. He was shocked when Molly grabbed his hand.

"Shut up, Allen. Nobody wants to hear it."

Pattie Wells had enjoyed a most pleasant evening with her sister. They had visited a restaurant for a wonderful dinner and a few glasses of wine and caught up on all the latest gossip. Each vented their frustrations with life and then laughed when they realized just how little they could find to complain about. Pattie returned home after nine o'clock and enjoyed another glass of wine while she read a few chapters of the novel that Charlie had finished and recommended. At ten, she watched the local news and prepared for bed. The telephone startled her when it rang. The last thing she wanted to hear was a late night telephone call while Charlie was flying. She was relieved to hear her sister's voice.

"I just wanted to make sure you made it home safely, Pattie."

They talked a few minutes and agreed that they would get together more often. Pattie set the sleep timer on the TV in case she fell asleep before the news ended and crawled beneath the covers. When she reached to turn off the lamp beside the bed, she noticed that Charlie had forgotten to pack his beloved alarm clock. She smiled and thought about how apprehensive he was about oversleeping and how she would tease him about the early stages of Alzheimer's. She checked to make sure the antique wasn't armed and dangerous. She was sound asleep two hours later when the clock rang a five-second alarm and went suddenly silent. Pattie sat up in bed and cursed the little mechanical nemesis.

✈

Brian Davis cursed when he turned in his swivel chair, bumped his elbow, and spilled coffee into his lap. Through the open door to the bridge, he heard Lieutenant Strickland say, "Hey Davis, hold it down in there. Profanity is the product of a weak intellect."

Brian dabbed at the stain and wondered if his other set of dungarees were back from the ship's laundry. He stood to stretch, and as he did the VHF speaker came alive. "Mayday! Mayday! Tri Con One-One, any station on guard, mayday!"

Brian grabbed the mic, and when no one else responded he said, "Tri Con calling mayday, this is *USS Karuk* on guard, state your mayday, over."

"*Karuk*, Tri Con One-One, we have a fuel exhaustion emergency, present position, north 4443.7, west 03429.8, one zero thousand feet, two hundred and eight souls on board, over."

"Loud and clear Tri Con, copy N4443.7/W03429.8 two hundred and eight souls. How can we assist, over?"

The response came back weak and broken, "*Karuk*, Tri—on—One, headi—ro, four—ven miles—ect—."

"Tri Con One-One, *Karuk*, over."

"Tri Con One-One, *Karuk*, over."

Brian had endured many days and nights guarding the emergency frequencies at sea and had never heard an actual mayday. He ran to the door and called, "Lieutenant, we have a mayday."

"What kind of mayday?"

"An airliner out of fuel."

"Where?"

Brian handed Lieutenant Strickland the message he had copied.

"I'll plot this position. Get fleet on satcom and relay the mayday."

Brian went back into the radio room and typed the message into the data link and transmitted it via satellite to Navy Comfleet. He tried to raise Tri Con on guard frequency again with no luck. The gravity of two hundred and eight people dying hit him, and he sat down and stared at the VHF receiver.

The lieutenant came in and said, "They're well over two hundred miles east and a little north of our position. Any more transmissions?"

"No sir, I think they went down."

"God help them, Brian. I hope someone can get to them. We're at least eighteen hours from that position."

Santa Maria control was located near the town of Ponta Delgada on the island of Sao Miguel in the Azores. This night the entire island was shrouded with fog and mist. The supervisor dialed the familiar number from memory and waited for an answer.

"Gander Control, Laroue speaking."

"Hey Bill, it's Jose at Santa Maria, we're looking for Tri Con Eleven, did you guys send him over on 5598?"

"Yeah, we copied you on his position at forty west."

"We got that but we never got him. He's ten minutes past the ETA for thirty west."

"Probably having radio trouble. You want me to try a relay for you?"

"No, I'll try to get one of my flights to raise him on air-to-air. Hang on a second Bill…oh man, we have a problem. I just got a data link. Tri Con Eleven transmitted a low fuel mayday on VHF guard. Some Navy ship picked it up. He must have been low altitude if no one else heard it. We'll scramble on it and get somebody out there."

"Let me know what you hear, Jose."

Thirty minutes later Brian Davis received a satcom from fleet and printed it out. "Lieutenant, we received a priority from fleet."

He handed the message to the lieutenant and watched him read. The officer walked over to the plotting table and drew a line on a chart.

"Helmsman, come left two-zero degrees, new course steady zero-seven-five."

"Steady zero-seven-five, aye, sir."

"Make turns for all ahead flank speed."

"All ahead flank, aye, sir."

The engine order telegraph rang as it was selected to flank speed and signaled the engine room to increase the propeller shaft turns to make maximum speed. The ship had been at all ahead full for a week, and Brian thought the electrician on the propulsion switchboard probably just fell off his stool.

The lieutenant turned to Brian.

"I can't believe we're the closest surface vessel to their position. Someone has to call the captain's quarters and explain to him why his ship is heading a new direction and why he probably won't see the Azores anytime soon. With your communications training, Davis, I'm confident you'll do a fine job."

"Come on, Strick, last time I woke him up he sulked for a week."

Someone behind them said, "What are you clowns doing up here?"

The lieutenant recognized the gruff voice and turned to face the captain. "We just changed course and increased speed, sir."

"That's why I'm standing here in my underwear asking questions, Lieutenant Strickland."

Charlie had to make some quick decisions. They had long since placed the fuel system in the manual mode and tried to manipulate valves and pumps to stop the loss of fuel. With only three minutes left, Charlie would try anything.

"Robby, close all the cross feed and transfer valves. Trap that three thousand pounds in the aft balance tank and see if you can feed the center engine only with it."

Robby pushed light switches and watched the fuel screen. The plan seemed to be working. Charlie pulled the number two throttle to idle and said, "That should keep number two running for maybe thirty minutes. That won't get us where we want to go, but at least we will have some control."

With the center engine at idle, the airplane began to slow. Charlie let the speed bleed off to two hundred and fifty knots and then eased the nose down to maintain that speed. They began a shallow descent. Robby said, "We're down to nothing in the mains."

As he was talking, the number three engine slowly unwound and flamed out, causing lights to illuminate all over the cockpit. The generator stopped making electricity, the hydraulic pump stopped making pressure, the turbine stopped providing air pressure for air conditioning and pressurization, and warning lights and computer messages announced it all. The airplane tried to turn right, and Charlie pushed the left rudder and added rudder trim to stop it.

"Tony, there's no hope of making land, brief the flight attendants. Tell them to prepare for an emergency water landing. We'll be forced to ditch the airplane in approximately fifteen minutes. If we can, we'll send you back there to help, but don't have them count on it."

The number one engine unwound and stopped, causing another multitude of lights and messages. Charlie removed the rudder trim he had used a few minutes before, now that the thrust was once again symmetrical. He left the center engine at idle and eased the nose over more. They were now at two hundred and fifty knots and descending at two thousand feet per minute. Simple math indicated that they had fourteen minutes plus whatever time the center engine would buy them. Charlie planned to use the engine to control the landing rather than to extend the range.

Tony talked to Britt and then began transmitting on the HF radio. He got no response from Santa Maria, although he could hear other airplanes transmitting, all at the same time. Charlie ordered Robby and Tony into crew life vests. The crew vests were red so that crewmembers could be easily recognized, as opposed to the passengers', which were yellow. He had Robby take the controls, and he reached into the back of his seat and found his vest and put it on.

In the back of his mind, Charlie could hear Phil James saying, "There has never been a mid-ocean ditching by an air carrier passenger jet."

Phil would have lots to talk about from now on, and people would listen much more closely. Robby had the procedures manual out now and was reading aloud the ditching procedures and crew duties. Charlie confirmed that he planned to configure with full flaps for the slowest possible touchdown speed and that he would leave the landing gear up to prevent the rapid deceleration the wheels would cause by being underwater.

When Robby completed the review of the ditching procedures, they were descending through eighteen thousand feet. Since they had no clue what the local barometric pressure was, they left their barometric altimeters set at standard pressure. Charlie reminded them that, uncorrected, the altimeter would be in error. Once they descended below twenty five hundred feet, the electronic altimeter would become active and give them an accurate readout of their height above the water. They would depend solely on it.

The fuel seemed to be feeding the center engine without a problem, but if it failed they would have no electricity and no hydraulics; the plane would become a huge glider. Charlie ordered the ADG to be deployed. The *air driven generator* was a contraption that deployed under the nose and used the slipstream to drive a windmill propeller that operated a small generator and a hydraulic pump. Charlie tried to remember everything that it operated, but gave up and concentrated on flying.

The airplane slowly descended into the spider web like wisp of the upper cloud layer, and then they were totally enveloped in the gray mass of condensation. Charlie knew if they lost their instruments, they would be doomed. Hopefully the ADG would provide insurance for that. They had no way to know how far above the water the lower clouds were.

"Tony, we're passing twelve thousand feet. Try the VHF guard frequency and see if anyone will answer. We need to at least transmit our position to someone."

There were three airplanes within VHF range. Two of them were talking to each other on air-to-air and had turned the emergency frequency volume down out of habit. The third had forgotten to change to guard after leaving Gander's VHF range.

Tony transmitted and was relieved to hear, "Tri Con calling mayday, this is *USS Karuk* on guard, state your mayday, over."

At least someone would know their position. After transmitting their situation to the ship, Tony gave their heading and distance from Lajes also, but received no response.

"Tony, you better go back and do whatever you can in the cabin. Find a seat at the over wing exits and deploy the rafts there after touchdown. We've got less than ten minutes. I'll give a brace command on the PA about thirty seconds before splash. Good luck."

Britt was stunned. She was shocked to hear the word ditch. She was paralyzed momentarily and then sprang into action, trying to remember everything from the training classes. She briefed the other flight attendants, telling them to secure everything that was not tied down and then strap in tight at their exit door. She made a PA and heard gasps as the passengers realized what she was saying. There were a few screams and then a lot of sobbing. She briefly explained the exit procedure and the raft operation that everyone had ignored during the video before takeoff. She told them to reach under their seat and remove the yellow life vest. She had a flight attendant in each section of the cabin to demonstrate how to put the vest on and adjust it.

Once everyone had a vest on, she told them not to inflate the vest inside the aircraft. She explained that the vest had dual inflation tubes inflated by tiny CO_2 bottles, and that pulling one of the red tabs would inflate the tube. Several pops were heard as people pulled the tab and inflated the vest after she just told them not to do it. She did not have time to explain how to inflate the vest manually if necessary or how to turn the battery operated light on. Next she quickly explained the brace position and how to lean forward and lock their arms underneath their knees with a pillow on their lap. The girls made a quick pass through the cabin to insure that everyone had a vest on, and then started throwing loose items, including carry-on items, into the lavatories and closing the door.

Nancy grabbed as many items as she could that people had stored under their seats and piled them in the john. Allen Smallwood sat staring straight ahead in stark fear. His vest was inflated, forcing his head high on his neck, and he hugged a laptop computer to his chest like a security blanket. When Nancy tried to take the computer, a brief wrestling match ensued. He began protesting and making demands. As she ripped the computer from his grip she said, "Shut up, I'm trying to save your butt, not kiss it."

By the time Tony came into the cabin, most of the preparations were complete. Britt asked him if they would have electricity to open the doors after landing. He thought about it and knew the engine-driven generators would be gone and the ADG would be underwater. He took her to the forward door and explained that the system would revert to standby mode and the doors would open by using pneumatic pressure from an emergency air bottle at each location. They checked the pressure of the bottle at the forward door and found it normal. He reminded her that he would be at the over wing exits to deploy the rafts. Two flight attendants would also be there to man the doors and assist. Britt had assigned Bertie to the two-right door. Bertie had already moved Mandy to a seat next to the door where she sat hugging her teddy bear, surrounded by pillows and blankets that Bertie had gathered and used as cushions around her.

When Molly volunteered her help, Britt sent her to the rear doors to assist with the twenty-one handicapped. They both knew there was very little chance that all of those passengers would make it out. They would be very fortunate to have time to physically drag a few of them to the door. It might be a moot point, because no one might survive.

They had all just set down and fastened their shoulder harnesses when Robby's voice came over the speakers.

"Brace! Brace! Thirty seconds."

Charlie slowed to two hundred and thirty knots as they passed ten thousand feet. The rate of descent decreased to fifteen hundred feet per minute, buying them a little more time. He checked the fuel and saw that the center engine should continue to run long enough to help control the landing but he could not be sure.

His mind had raced through a hundred possibilities during the descent, but there were no options. He could feel the dampness of his hands on the yoke and removed them one at a time to rub on his pants leg. He tried to clear his mind. The situation was dire, but it was also simple. No decisions left to make. That did not stop him from sweating.

When they passed twenty five hundred feet, they were still in cloud but the radio altimeter popped into view to give him an accurate display of their height above the water.

At one thousand feet they could still not see anything except cloud in the windshield, but Charlie could not wait any longer.

"Slats extend, Robby."

Robby moved the handle, and they felt the slats on the front of the wing extend, creating extra lift and allowing them to slow.

"Flaps fifteen."

The airplane tried to balloon as the flaps created even more lift. Charlie pushed the nose forward enough to keep them level.

"Flaps thirty-five."

They continued to slow.

Charlie added power from the center engine. The thrust from the engine mounted high on the tail, and above the airplane's center of gravity, tried to push the nose down. Charlie corrected with elevator and stabilizer trim.

"Flaps fifty."

A loud horn began to sound and an electronic voice said, "Landing gear, too low. Landing gear, too low."

The warning was designed to prevent accidentally landing with the wheels up and there was no button to silence it. The checklist had not mentioned this, and it took them by surprise. If he had realized it earlier, he would have found the circuit breakers and pulled them to disable it, but there was no time now. Charlie let the airplane slow to one hundred and forty knots, which translated to over one hundred and sixty miles per hour, but that was as slow as they could safely fly. Charlie lowered the nose and adjusted the thrust, and they began slowly descending the last thousand feet, hoping that they would see the water before they impacted it. He extended the landing lights and turned them on, creating a bright white world as the beams reflected off the clouds. He wanted to smash the horn and electronic voice, but it kept blaring away. There was nothing he could do about it.

He slowed the rate of descent to one hundred feet per minute and had resigned himself to a blind landing when, at two hundred feet, the white windshield began to show shades of gray, and then dark water appeared as the landing lights created a long bright tunnel between the base of the clouds and the water.

"Give the brace signal, Robby.

CHAPTER TWELVE

Lieutenant Todd Gray stared out the windshield of the P3 Orion aircraft. The US Navy patrol airplane was normally used as a submarine hunter, but tonight Todd and his crew had been scrambled from the Naval Air Station at Rota, Spain, in response to Tri Con Eleven's mayday. The P3 was a slow, turboprop-driven craft, but it had excellent range and endurance. It was not unusual, with its four engines, to stay aloft for twelve to fourteen hours on patrol.

Todd looked at the cloud deck below them and hoped it would clear before they reached the search area. They had been airborne more than two hours and were passing north of Lajes on the way to the last known position of the missing aircraft. He checked the weather at Lajes and was not optimistic. The P3 cruised at twenty three thousand feet and bucked a forty knot headwind. The only good news was that the sun would be up soon. With nothing better to do, Todd decided to gather information.

"*Karuk*, Navy Search Eight, on guard, over."

"Navy Eight, *Karuk*, go ahead."

"*Karuk*, have you received anything more from Tri Con?"

"Negative Navy Eight. We're on guard, but no joy."

"What's the ceiling and visibility at your position?"

"Our mast is practically in the soup and visibility is probably less than a mile."

"You're full of good news, *Karuk*. What's your time en route to the search area?"

"Approximately one five hours."

"Did you try raising the anchor?"

At three-thirty in the morning, the Tri Con flight control center in Atlanta was a beehive of activity. The vice president of flight operations had been summoned from his warm bed and was joined by the chief pilot. They were now gathered in the conference room with the dispatcher for Flight Eleven, the meteorologist on duty, the vice president of technical operations, and one of Molly Jackson's assistants, Jenny Kramer. The FAA had been notified, and soon a safety inspector would arrive to start gathering all the official documentation for the flight.

Tom Hanes, the VP of flight operations said, "So all we know at this point is that they didn't report at thirty west, and then the Navy received a mayday."

Chuck Latimer, the chief pilot answered, "That's it Tom, but I think it's pretty clear they're down. The radios were working when they talked to the Navy ship, and they haven't been heard from since. We're getting our information second hand from Santa Maria radio, but it seems accurate so far."

"Okay, the first thing I want to do is take care of the crew members' families. Let's get personal representatives out to their homes before they hear it on the news. Chuck, get the pilots' addresses and phone numbers, and Jenny, you do the same for the flight attendants.

He turned to the vice president of technical operations.

"Jake, start gathering every piece of paper we have on ship 826. Let's have a look at the logbook pages for the last month and see if we made any mistakes. Even paperwork errors will be huge with the FAA. Anybody have other ideas?"

Jenny Kramer said, "Don't forget, Molly Jackson and Allen Smallwood were on there. Should we send someone to be with their family?"

"Absolutely. Make it happen."

"Molly's mother is the only relative she has that I know of, and she lives in Birmingham."

"Like I said, make it happen. Call the Birmingham station manager and wake him up. He can send someone or go himself."

Pattie had tossed and turned for more than an hour after Charlie's antique alarm had mysteriously awakened her. She had finally given up, dressed in an old pair of sweats, and decided to read more of the novel. By the time the phone beside her recliner rang, her intuition had already been active for quite some time. Still, she let it ring three times before she picked it up, looked at the caller ID, and saw "Mobile Caller."

"Mrs. Wells, this is Jenny Kramer with Tri Con. I'm so sorry to wake you. There has been an incident with your husband's flight, and we would like to fill you in on what we know. We would like to talk to you in person if that's all right."

"What happened?"

"It would be easier if we talked in person, Mrs. Wells."

"I want to know now."

"Yes, ma'am. Myself and one of the assistant chief pilots are in your driveway, if we could come in please."

Pattie turned on lights as she walked through the house. She had never once doubted Charlie, and she refused to accept that anything could happen to him now.

Charlie added thrust and skimmed just beneath the clouds. The water looked dark and murky, but relatively smooth. He had envisioned giant rolling swells and white-capped waves, but was relieved to see very little chop and no visible swell at all. He turned slightly to the right to land into what little wind there was and began to slowly drift down. He told Robby to be ready to cut the fuel to the engine as soon as they touched down. He didn't want to go scooting along the ocean surface like a swamp buggy with a big fan mounted on it. The visibility was very restricted and the water passing beneath them was dizzying. Charlie tried to focus on a point as far away as possible and concentrated on the instruments to guide him as well. It was extremely difficult to force himself to continue slowly descending, but he knew the engine could stop at any moment or a ship could appear in the windshield with no way to avoid it. The inevitable had arrived, and he was sick of hearing "Landing gear too low," and the loud horn.

The radio altimeter appeared to be accurate and as the airplane approached the surface, a new electronic voice joined the chorus.

"Fifty...forty...thirty," the altimeter called out the height above touchdown. "Twenty...ten..."

There was a slight discrepancy because when the wheels should be touching down there was no landing gear, but Charlie held the nose up in a normal landing attitude. He suddenly felt a jolting impact as the tail struck the surface. A huge plume of water erupted over the stabilizer, and the airplane decelerated at a dangerous rate, heaving them forward against their shoulder harnesses. The nose fell rapidly out of control and Robby cut the fuel to the engine. Lights flashed all over the cockpit as systems lost power and shut down, leaving only battery power. When the nose fell, the big ADG hanging down underneath dug into the sea. The cockpit plowed through the water and the spray blinded their view. The plume over the tail kicked the rudder off center and the ADG became the new rudder, slewing the airplane around and causing it to slide sideways across the surface. It seemed to go on forever and Charlie held his breath, praying that the airplane wouldn't start breaking up. The bright landing lights were gone and it was pitch-black outside the windshield. The electronic voices and the blaring horn were replaced with a roar that sounded like surf and the tsunami caused by the airplane displacing salty water.

After what seemed like an eternity, they felt the cockpit lift and the airplane decelerated to a stop. The glow of a thousand instrument lights and computer LEDs were gone and the silence was eerie. The only illumination left was the dome light operated by the batteries of the emergency lighting system, and Charlie knew they would not provide power very long.

"Robby, are you okay?"

"I think so. How many Gs did we pull?"

"I don't know, but let's get out of here."

They both reached down and pushed the button to move their seats back and realized at the same time there was no power to move it. Robby unstrapped and crawled over the pedestal. Charlie found the manual release for his seat, slid it back, and released his belts. They could hear shouts and screams emanating from the cabin, and Charlie thought he heard Britt yelling.

Robby reached the rear of the cockpit first and immediately realized they had not accomplished one of the important items on the emergency checklist. The cockpit door should have been secured in the open position. He unlocked it and turned the handle. The door would not move. The crew coat closet had collapsed and jammed the door. He could see hats and jackets and crew bags under the rubble. He also saw several pieces of orange day glow material and knew he was looking at the remains of the emergency locator beacon. He jerked and pulled the door but it would not budge.

His voice pitched higher.

"Charlie, we're trapped! We have to go out the windows."

Two of the side cockpit windows were designed to open and be used for emergency escape.

"Hang on, Robby."

Charlie fumbled behind the captain's seat in the dim glow and found the crash axe. He passed it to Robby.

"The new security door is bulletproof. Work on the hinges."

Charlie stepped back to give him room, and Robby began hacking at the door. They heard a loud whoosh of air when the emergency bottle assist opened the forward left entrance door. A split second later, another whoosh signaled the inflation of the slide raft. At least somebody was alive and functioning on the other side of the barrier. Fueled by adrenaline, Robby demolished the hinges and tugged the battered door into the cockpit.

They immediately saw that the forward galley had broken loose and slammed into the outer wall of the cockpit, collapsing the coat closet inside. The ovens, drawers, and a pile of food trays were blocking the exit at the forward right door. Soft drink and beer cans had been punctured and could be heard spewing in the wreckage.

Britt was in shock when the airplane finally stopped. She had been slammed back and forth by the deceleration forces and the belts of the shoulder harness had dug into her skin. The screams of the passengers after hitting the water were horrifying, and she had watched the galley break free, tilt forward, and collapse the wall. Nancy was somewhere in that pile of rubble.

When she was sure the wild ride had ended, she moved her arms and legs. She found them reluctantly working. She popped the quick release on her harness and stood to look out the little round window in the door. When she did not see fire or smoke, she reached up and pulled the emergency release on the bulkhead next to the door. The pneumatic bottle whooshed and the huge door moved in and then up into the ceiling. When the door had moved about a foot, the big yellow slide pack began to fall out of its cover on the door. The bottle on the pack fired before the door finished its travel and the slide unfolded and inflated into the cool night air. A row of small white lights illuminated on either side of the big, yellow monster, and she could see that the downward angle was very shallow. Looking out, she could see water just two feet below the door's threshold. The only lights in the airplane were the emergency lights operated by battery packs. She turned to the wall beside her seat and removed the flashlight so she could begin moving people out.

As she shined the light on the floor to release the raft and prepare it for boarding, someone yelled, "Get out of the way! Get out of my way!"

The man bounded over her and into the night. He hit the slide about ten feet out and bounced into the air, then disappeared. She could hear him screaming and thrashing around in the water.

The man's panic had galvanized others into action, and they were moving forward. She quickly found the lanyard to release the slide, and it fell to the water, still attached to the doorframe with a webbed line. She pulled the raft up close and tied the line to keep it in place just as the first passengers stepped into the exit area.

She waved the flashlight and yelled, "Sit and then step into the raft. Do not jump."

She continued to yell the instructions, and soon had two people at once exiting into the raft if not orderly, at least without total panic. She heard a loud banging noise that didn't make sense, and suddenly Robby and then Charlie appeared. She had never been so glad to see someone.

Robby began throwing debris aside and clearing the way to the other door. At the bottom of the pile he found Nancy still strapped into her seat. She was not moving. Charlie stepped in, and they gently removed her and felt for a pulse. It was weak, but it was there, and she was taking shallow breaths. One of her ankles was turned at an unnatural angle, and she had a lump on her forehead. Charlie stepped into the aisle and started yelling commands, and soon had the people stopped long enough to load Nancy into the raft, followed by Britt. He watched as Britt inflated one of the tubes on Nancy's red vest and then one of her own. He released the line and pushed them into the darkness.

Robby pulled the handle to open the other door and deploy the slide raft. When he had a boarding process going and the business class cabin was emptying, Charlie began making his way aft. The overhead emergency lights illuminated the cabin with a dim glow that created shadows between each row of seats. He followed the long line of white emergency track lights embedded in the floor and wished he had brought a flashlight. He carefully checked each row of seats, but he found no one at all as he hurried aft, wondering how long the airplane would float.

At the rear of business class, the ceiling panels had collapsed, blocking the passage. He fought his way through the debris and found the area around the two-left and right doors abandoned. The exit area around the right door was totally blocked with ceiling panels and air conditioning ducts. A water line in the galley had broken and flooded the floor. The left door was open and the raft was gone. He continued aft and saw a line of passengers pushing, shoving, and screaming to reach the over wing exits. He began yelling commands to calm down. When they saw a uniform and a red vest, they began to listen, and the chaos subsided somewhat. After he had their attention, he reassured them, and a more orderly evacuation ensued. He could hear a flight attendant giving orders at the door.

Between two rows of seats, he found an elderly woman lying on the floor, sobbing. He carefully moved her to a sitting position and could see that her arm was badly broken. Suddenly the suffering, panic, and chaos became a personal burden. He felt a tightness in his chest and his breathing became labored. He was totally responsible for everything that had happened. He had failed to keep his passengers and crew safe. He began to think about where he had gone wrong. How could he have let this happen? The little old lady brought him back to reality.

"Thank you, captain. No one would help me, and I thought I would die in the floor between the seats."

Charlie became task-oriented once again and moved into action. The lady was not heavy, and he picked her up easily.

"Step aside, I have an injured person. Make way for an injury."

Two middle-aged men who looked healthy enough stepped aside to let him through, and Charlie ordered them to stay in the back of the line and look in each row to make sure everyone got out. He made his way through the crowd and reached the three-left door. Candace Whitten was herding people through the door and out onto the wing. Charlie shouted his way through the crowd and stepped out onto the wing with the lady in his arms. The escape slide at the over wing exits formed a rubber ramp that led out to the slide raft deployed outboard of the engine. Charlie could see huge pieces of jagged metal sticking up at the back of the wing and realized that the flaps had torn away. If one of the rafts encountered those shards, it would rip apart. He found Tony helping passengers off the leading edge of the wing and into the raft. The raft was already near its capacity of fifty people, and the two pilots handed the old lady down to a burly man in the raft as she thanked them over and over.

Charlie ran back to the door and directed the dwindling line of people to the wing exit on the opposite side. He sent Candace out to board the raft and take charge while he and Tony helped Mary Dobson herd the remainder of the passengers onto the right wing. The two men he had assigned to check the seat rows brought up the rear and assured him the cabin was clear. He ordered both Mary and Tony into the raft and told Tony to move it away from the airplane and try to join the other rafts if possible. There were only two doors remaining to evacuate: four-left and four-right at the very back of the airplane.

Charlie grabbed one of the emergency flashlights off the wall next to the door and began checking seat rows once again. He had not gone far when he found a man slumped forward in his aisle seat. The man's head lay against the yellow life vest at an impossible angle. The overhead compartment above was open and a heavy bag lay on the floor in front of the man. It was obvious that it had fallen on his neck like a guillotine while he was in the brace position. He checked for a pulse, although he knew there would be none.

He continued on, shining the flashlight between seats in the growing dimness and finding nothing but debris. The emergency lights were fading as the batteries grew weaker, and he knew they would not last much longer. He could hear shouts and commands from further back, and he hurried to reach the exits. The airplane had begun to list to the left and, with horror, he remembered the mangled flap tracks at the rear of the left wing. He realized that when they ripped away it probably left holes and the wing tanks must be taking on water. Ironically, the empty tanks had put them in the water and now the tanks were filling to sink them.

Briefly, he thought about the fact that when he reached the rear doors, the rafts might be gone, leaving him alone with his sinking ship. It was almost a relief to hear people screaming as he entered the last cabin. The aisles were clogged and panicked passengers were not moving. He could hear Alice Elon and Shelia Graham shouting orders. He pushed his way through the crowd, reassuring people as he went, and trying to calm them.

When he reached the aft galley area, the doors were open and the rafts deployed, but the flight attendants were trying to physically drag handicapped passengers to the rafts one at a time. Both flight attendants were grandmothers and taking gasping breaths like a heart attack was imminent. The process was extremely time-consuming, and the airplane was listing more and more by the minute. Charlie quickly set priorities.

He loudly commanded, "Don't block the aisle with those people, leave them in their seats for now."

He moved the man they were dragging to the door and passed him to Molly Jackson, who was helping people into the raft. He ordered Molly back into the airplane and Alice into the raft. With Shelia at one door and Molly at the other, he began to herd the other passengers into the rafts. Now the handicapped were screaming, threatening discrimination lawsuits, and calling him unspeakable names. He ignored them, and within two minutes all the mobile people were in the rafts.

The right side of the airplane was now several feet higher, and it was becoming difficult to drop into the raft on that side. Charlie ordered Shelia out the door and released the line attaching the raft. As they drifted away, Charlie told her to try to rendezvous with the others, but he did not have time for a survival lecture. He and Molly began releasing seat belts, dragging or carrying helpless people to the last raft, and handing them out to Alice. He told Molly to evacuate the smallest passengers first, and she was able to move several of them by herself. Water was lapping over the threshold of the door now, and he knew time was short. He could feel the cold water seeping into his shoes and wondered if anyone could survive in the water without the raft.

The few people left trapped in their seats were now screaming in terror as they saw the water in the aisles and knew the airplane was sinking. One of the remaining passengers was a huge man, and Charlie made a decision. He had Molly help him and it took all their combined strength to move the man to the exit. When he rolled into the raft, Charlie ordered Molly out the exit also. He would not allow her to perish in a sinking airplane after all she had done. He rationalized that she would be needed to help the survivors stay alive.

There were only three people left to evacuate, and Charlie could hear them screaming ten rows forward of the door. He sloshed through the aisle and unbuckled the first one he came to. The man's eyes were bulging, and he desperately grabbed Charlie's arms in a death grip. Charlie instinctively pulled away to free his arms, losing his balance and falling backwards. His foot caught under the seat, and a searing pain shot up his leg as all his weight forced the ankle to turn. His brain could not process the pain, and it began to shut down.

Dark shadows encroached at the edge of his vision, and he knew he was going to black out. He felt the airplane lurch and desperately wanted the screaming to stop. When he realized the screams were coming from his own throat, he closed his mouth. Before his vision narrowed to a pinpoint and went black, he heard a different faraway scream—a terrified female voice calling his name.

CHAPTER THIRTEEN

Ray was declared sober and released at three a.m., but it took him another hour to retrieve his truck from impound. He found the stolen cell phones still in the truck and tossed them into a dumpster in the parking lot of a strip mall. He was furious that the police had cost him a million dollars. If he could find a way to cause them misery, he would certainly do it. For now he had other things to think about.

By the time he got home it was too late to go to bed. At least he wouldn't be late to work. He reset the alarm clock before it went off and began his normal morning routine. He placed a bagel in the toaster and turned on the small television that he kept in the kitchen. The fuel dump system schematic was laying on the table, and he cursed as he ripped it into pieces. The local weatherman was spouting statistics that meant absolutely nothing to Ray. It was August, and it was hot. He could figure that out for himself. Then the screen filled with a breaking news icon, and the morning anchorwoman began the hype about the day's top story.

"We have just learned that an international flight is missing over the Atlantic Ocean. Our source at the FAA is confirming that the flight last reported to Gander in Canada and was bound for Europe. The airplane is now overdue by several hours and has not been heard from. Our source tells us that search and rescue efforts are underway. US Air Force assets have been dispatched from Goose Bay in Newfoundland, and US Navy aircraft from Rota, Spain, are involved in the search. The air carrier and type of aircraft have not been released, but we have learned that there were one hundred and ninety-seven passengers and a crew of eleven onboard. Our unofficial source cannot confirm or deny that terrorism was involved. We will obviously stay on top of this story and bring you more information as we get it."

Ray said to no one, "Well, at least part of the plan worked."

His bagel popped up in the toaster, and he removed it to spread butter and jelly on it. He knew that the jelly would become a part of his beard, and he would have to wash it out, but he had his routine and would not change it. He did not think of himself as obsessive; he was just comfortable with the way he did things. He noticed that he was thirty seconds ahead of his morning schedule and consciously slowed his chewing to compensate. By the time he finished his coffee he was back on schedule and headed for the shower.

Colt Adams stepped out of the shower in Madrid and turned on the English language news channel. He hoped to get some idea of the weather before leaving the hotel for the airport and the flight back to Atlanta. He continued to dress while waiting for the weather report. The British newsman began talking while the screen displayed the picture of a generic airliner. Colt had experienced an uncharacteristic feeling of tension since waking, and now an unexplained chill ran down his spine. His feeling of dread increased, and he sat on the bed to watch.

"Continuing our coverage of the tragedy over the Atlantic last night, we have learned that the airliner involved was an American carrier with as many as three hundred passengers on board. The airplane mysteriously disappeared in mid-flight, and search and rescue teams are combing the waters west of the Azores for clues as to what happened. The authorities have not officially released the details; however, our correspondent in Madrid is reporting that Tri Continent Airlines Flight Eleven is overdue, and family members awaiting that flight are being escorted to a secluded area. Officials tell us that terrorism cannot be ruled out at this point. We will continue to bring you details as we get them."

Colt sat staring at the television. This could not be happening. He had planned to be in the lobby when Charlie and his crew arrived at the hotel so he could give him a hard time about whatever he could think of. Charlie was one of his closest friends and one of the best pilots he had ever known. Charlie would not make a mistake.

Colt picked up the phone and dialed Tri Con operations in Madrid. The agent answered the phone in Spanish but quickly changed to English when Colt spoke.

"This is Captain Adams. I'm taking Flight Fourteen out in a couple of hours. I want to know everything you have on Eleven. What happened?"

"Captain Adams, can you verify your employee number?"

Colt gave him the number to prove that he wasn't a reporter.

"Thank you captain, we know that Eleven was operating on schedule and last reported forty west. Santa Maria didn't receive a scheduled position report at thirty west, and declared the flight overdue. After that, a Navy ship reported receiving a brief mayday

132

and copied the position at around thirty-four west. The ship received one more broken transmission and then lost contact. I wish I could tell you more."

"Thank you, I'll see you shortly. I'm leaving the hotel now."

Lieutenant Todd Gray arrived over the last reported position just before sunrise and set up a grid to systematically begin the search. Several air force and navy fighter jets had been on station for some time, but the weather prevented them from doing anything except orbit above the clouds and monitor the guard frequency for a signal from the emergency locator beacon. One air force jet had descended to one hundred feet and reported the visibility to be a half mile. The fighter jet's slowest speed covered the half mile in less than fifteen seconds so searching was impossible. Not to be outdone, a navy jet descended to fifty feet and reported the visibility as six-tenths of a mile. The machismo on the radio was palpable.

The fighters were basically useless in this situation, but Todd knew they would hang around as long as possible and log stick time. If they could organize a competition between the two services, so much the better. He just hoped they would play their games at high altitude and stay out of his way. He did not want to have to look for a fighter in addition to the airliner. He ordered the other airplanes to stay clear of the area and began a descent to one hundred feet above the water. This was a normal operating altitude for a sub hunter. His airplane was not glamorous but this is what his crew was good at. The Orion could operate much slower than the jets, but still, searching from a hundred feet with limited visibility was next to impossible. More assets were on the way, but the air search would be extremely difficult given the current weather. Helicopters did not have the range to reach the search area and the closest surface vessel was still the *Karuk*. Their only hope for quick success would be a signal from the emergency locator beacon. The beacon emitted a homing signal on the guard frequency which could be received by any of the airplanes in the area, and also by satellite. No signal had been received.

Todd knew that the sea surface temperature in the area was estimated to be sixty-five degrees, and survival time in the water could be as little as two hours even for a healthy person. Hopefully if there were survivors they were in a raft and not in the water. He and his crew scanned the ocean through the windshield and prayed that they would be successful.

Ray Slackman finished his shower, dried and fluffed his beard, then went back to the kitchen for a second cup of coffee. The weatherman was pointing to a map and prognosticating. He wasted several minutes stating the obvious. It was going to be hot today. The anchor woman appeared once again with more breaking news.

"We have just received new information on our top story. This is devastating local news. The FAA has released new details on the missing airplane over the Atlantic, and we now know that the flight departed Atlanta last evening bound for Madrid, Spain. Tri Con Flight Eleven carried one hundred and ninety-seven passengers and a crew of eleven. We cannot confirm how many of the passengers are from the Atlanta area, but an unofficial source tells us that the flight crew is based locally. The crew consists of three pilots and eight flight attendants. The names will not be released until families are notified; however, the FAA will hold a press conference at noon today. So far we know that the flight operated normally until something went horribly wrong over the ocean.

News networks in Europe are reporting that they have interviewed numerous passengers arriving at approximately the same time that Flight Eleven was scheduled, and several of them say that they witnessed the airplane going down with an engine on fire.

There has been no further word from search and rescue aircraft as to wreckage or survivors. We will obviously stay on top of this story and bring you details as we get them."

Ray sat down with his coffee and tried to get everything straight in his mind. He didn't get rich, but at least there was nothing to implicate that he had done anything wrong. The airplane was at the bottom of the ocean, and no one would ever know why. He felt sorry for the people on board, but they just happened to be in the wrong place at the wrong time. *Man, if I had been released earlier last night and called to warn Tri Con, that would have been a colossal mistake. They would have the airplane to inspect and find my handiwork. I must have been stupid drunk.*

He considered calling in sick and going to bed for a good sleep, but decided it might call attention to him. He carefully thought through the situation again and found no reason to be concerned. He was out the door right on schedule and ready to fight the day's battles.

✈

Phil James learned of the accident on the radio during his drive to work. He arrived at the training center and hurried to his office, where he was met by his supervisor.

"Have you heard the news, Phil?"

"I'm afraid so. What do we know so far?"

"I have a list of the crew members. You had Charlie Wells in class last week."

"Charlie was the captain?"

"Yeah, he was. I'm sure the FAA is going to want to talk to you about his training. Was anything unusual about the class?"

"No, not at all. Charlie is always prepared. He did very well, as usual."

They were interrupted by the telephone, and the supervisor spoke briefly with the caller, repeating "Yes, sir," several times.

"Phil, that was the vice president of technical operations. They're putting together the accident response team, and he wants you to be a part of it. They're meeting in the flight control conference room across the street. Keep me informed, and let me know what you need."

Phil gathered his briefcase and aircraft manuals and made his way across the street. He was met by a secretary who gave him a nametag and explained that the general briefing was about to begin. Afterwards, the group would split into smaller teams to use their particular expertise in gathering information and discerning facts. The general briefing had been moved to a larger room down the hall, and when Phil entered, there were probably fifty people milling about and looking for seats.

The vice president of flight operations opened the briefing. "Let's get started, people. We've got a lot to cover, and I don't want to waste time. Here's what we know from a flight ops perspective: Flight Eleven departed on time and operated normally through Gander Oceanic airspace. Gander handed them off to Santa Maria at the normal transition point, but they never reported in. Shortly after they became overdue with Santa Maria, a mayday was received by a US Navy ship in the area. Eleven reported a fuel emergency and gave their position. I'm not going to stand up here and read numbers to you; it's all on the briefing sheet that is being passed out. Search and rescue is under way; however, there is a low overcast in the area with very little visibility, and we are not hopeful of quick results. Our initial hypothesis is that they experienced fuel contamination or fuel exhaustion and were forced to ditch the airplane. That's strictly speculation; you are here to prove or disprove, and either way, we want to know why. Are there any questions before I turn it over to Tech Ops?"

Someone asked, "I heard on the news that eyewitness accounts say there was an engine fire. Is that true?"

The VP sighed.

"Every witness in the history of aviation has always said that they saw the airplane on fire as it went down. Number one, if our airplane ran out of fuel, there would be nothing to feed an engine fire. Number two, the spacing required between aircraft on the North Atlantic tracks would make it very unlikely that a passenger on another aircraft could be a witness to anything. When people see a news camera they become instant experts and say what they've heard other people say all their lives. That is, the airplane was on fire when it went down."

Next the vice president of technical operations spoke.

"Ship 826 was up-to-date on all inspections and airworthiness directives. The engines were low time and had no write-ups recently. The airplane underwent a routine service check yesterday, and no problems were found. The inbound flight had no squawks, and the logbook was clean. Line maintenance reported that the outbound crew gave a verbal request to check an access compartment door in the belly, the door was cycled closed, and no

137

logbook entry was made or required. Our group will obviously be focusing on the fuel system. Any questions?"

Someone asked, "Did the flight leave with the proper fuel load?"

"I'll let the dispatcher answer that."

The dispatcher gave a rundown on the fuel boarded and the fact that Charlie had called to discuss the fuel load before departure. They had both agreed that it was adequate, and left it as planned.

Next the meteorologist gave his report and stated that there were no storms or turbulence reported or forecasted for the route of flight. He added the current weather in the search area was forecast to persist with low clouds and restricted visibility due to a warm front that was practically stationary.

The FAA representative concluded the briefing.

"My name is Gene Clark. The Atlanta regional office has been given the responsibility to investigate the accident, and I am Tri Con's principal safety inspector. Later today the FBI and the National Transportation and Safety Board will also join the investigation. So far we have focused on the air traffic control aspects of the flight, and to this point, everything seems to be completely normal and routine. We will be looking into all facets of the operation and soliciting cooperation from each of your groups as we go forward."

Tom Hanes, the flight ops vice president, assigned meeting rooms for each of the various teams, and Phil went in search of the Tech Ops group. As he walked down the hall, he passed a large room with a group of civilian-looking people gathered in it. There was a handwritten sign on the door with the words, "Flight Eleven Crew Family Room."

CHAPTER FOURTEEN

When Jenny Kramer suggested that they join the other families at Tri Con headquarters, Pattie had resisted. She did not want to see anyone. Jenny gently persisted by telling her that they should at least visit to see if more information was available. She pointed out that there would be food available also, and Pattie needed to keep her strength up. Secretly, Jenny thought it would be good for Pattie to be with other family members faced with the same uncertainty she was feeling. Pattie finally agreed to go, but only for a short visit.

When they arrived, a representative escorted them to President Harold Collins' office. Collins was the exception to the rule in Tri Con management. He had started with the airline as a young man and remained throughout his career, whereas almost all the others in the management team were imported from other companies or other industries. Collins was a tall, gray-haired gentleman in his mid-fifties who was generally considered credible by the Tri Con employees because he had worked his way up in the management chain. He assured Pattie that everything possible was being done and that Tri Con was available for all her needs. He walked with them to the room reserved for the families and then left she and Jenny in the hands of a hostess assigned to the group. The hostess was a flight attendant who had been called in from the reserve crew list and was doing the best she could in a situation she was totally unprepared for. She gave Pattie a stick-on name badge and invited she and Jenny to help themselves to the brunch that had been catered for them. Leather recliners were lined along the outside walls of the room, and a large screen TV was installed at one end. Pattie felt lost and out of place as she stood there. A pretty young woman approached with tears in her eyes and looked at Pattie's name tag. "Mrs. Wells, I'm Robby Jenner's wife. My husband is the first officer."

The dam finally broke, and Pattie began to sob. They fell into each other's arms, and Jenny knew she had made the right decision to bring Pattie to be with the others. Eventually she was introduced to Britt Fowler's parents and the husbands, brothers, sisters, or children of other flight attendants. Tony Johnson was not married, but his parents were there.

Two chaplains were available and being kept very busy praying privately and publicly with various individuals and groups. The hostess made an announcement that a member of management would be updating them every hour or as warranted. Pattie wondered what it must be like on the other side of the field, where the families of two hundred passengers were gathered. She knew if Charlie were here he would take charge and provide leadership and guidance. She just didn't feel strong enough to do that, but she did somehow feel a sense of responsibility because her husband had been charged with the safety of all these people's loved ones. She must stay and do whatever she could to comfort them. She sat in a recliner, placed her head in her hands, and prayed.

The airplane lurched to the left, causing the raft to strain against the line attached to the door. Molly knew if the airplane sank it would drag them under with it. She screamed for Charlie and was answered by a chorus of screaming passengers from inside the fuselage. The airplane stabilized once again, and without thinking, she stood to enter the door. Alice grabbed the back of Molly's shirt and calmly said, "No, Molly, we can't jeopardize these people's lives."

Alice reached for the tether line to release the raft from the airplane. Tears streamed down Molly's face. "Wait! We have to give them a chance."

At the edge of consciousness, Charlie was aware of nothing but darkness. *Vertigo...floating...can't see.* His disoriented mind reverted to long ingrained habit pattern. His hand reached to turn on the landing lights but felt only emptiness.

The burning pain in his ankle, and the cold water that he lay in, brought him back to reality. A sense of urgency and a rush of adrenalin helped him to refocus as he forced himself to sit up. *Forget the pain...move.*

The three passengers were no longer screaming, having watched their last hope pass out in the floor. Now the man sitting in the seat beside Charlie looked at him with pleading eyes, "Help me," he whispered.

Charlie stood on one foot, "Grab the back of my belt and hold on."

Pulling himself from one seat to the next, he made his way slowly toward the door with the man sloshing behind him. *Please God...let that raft be there.*

Molly saw the white shirt appear in the door, "Charlie!"

"Help this man into the raft, I'll be back."

"I'm going with you to help."

"No! If the airplane moves, release the raft."

He hobbled faster without the burden on his belt. The floor was tilted more now, but he maintained his balance by holding the seat backs. He reached the next passenger and began to release his seat belt. The old man appeared to be paralyzed physically and resigned emotionally. He nodded to the seat in front of him, "Take him, and save yourself."

There was a much younger man sitting in the next seat quietly praying. The old man stared into Charlie's eyes and nodded once again, communicating more than words could ever convey.

Charlie moved forward and had the passenger latch onto his belt. He mentally suppressed the pain in his ankle and moved aft. Pillows and blankets were floating in the aisle now, and he ignored them. When they reached the door, the raft was actually higher than the floor. Molly and Alice had to pull the man up to get him aboard. Without speaking, Charlie disappeared back inside. He realized the airplane was slowly tilting more to the left, and he fought to maintain his balance without putting weight on his busted ankle.

He was only two seats away from the old man when the emergency lights dimmed and then cast total darkness in the cabin. *Oh God...please no!*

He held onto a seat back and fought panic. He opened his eyes as wide as they would go and was suddenly blinded by a bright light. "Over here captain. I never leave home without a flashlight."

Just as Charlie reached the seat, the airplane trembled and lurched again. "You shouldn't have come back, captain, I don't have the strength in my hands to hold on to your belt."

"Can you maintain your grip on the flashlight?"

"I think so."

Charlie removed his belt and looped it around the old man's belt at the back of his waist. "Just relax, and don't lose that light."

He had only dragged the man a few feet when the airplane began to roll slowly to the left. The wing tanks were filling and so was the cabin. Charlie gripped the belt and struggled on. The cold water, halfway to his knees, helped numb the pain, but slowed his progress. He only had one thought other than reaching the door, *Patti.*

Behind him, the old man said, "Take the light, captain, you can make it alone."

Charlie ignored him and grabbed the next seat to pull them closer to freedom. With the flashlight focused behind him, he reached forward again but found no seat to grip. He was standing in the door, but the raft was gone.

When the airplane began its steady roll, Alice had taken the initiative and released the tether line. Molly could not fault her decision and sat staring at the door as they drifted into the dark. From forty feet away, she saw the light in the door. She watched as Charlie reached down and inflated the passenger's life vest and then his own. When they were in the water, she saw that he had also pulled the tab to illuminate the little white lights on the vest.

Alice looked up to see Molly grab the tether line and dive into the water. She heard the pop of the vest inflating as she swam away. Charlie gripped the belt in one hand and swam with the other. He ignored the pain and kicked with both feet. He knew that the airplane still weighed almost 400,000 pounds and would create a tremendous undertow when it sank. Molly swam to the end of the tether and waited for Charlie to kick the last ten feet to meet her.

"Swap places with me, Molly." She held on to the passenger with one hand and Charlie with the other as he used the tether line to pull them to the inflated boarding station at the side of the raft. Alice and the passengers pulled them aboard, and they lay on the floor shivering.

Once Charlie got his breath, he found the survival pack and retrieved the paddle. They had to get away from the airplane. He began paddling and encouraged everyone seated at the sides to use their hands to help. They slowly moved away and watched as the airplane continued to list. With all the doors open, the fuselage filled quickly and moments later it rolled up on its side and began slipping away. The right wing was the last thing visible, and Charlie could see the section that housed the dump valves. Then it was gone.

"Listen to me. Everyone is safe. You're going to be all right. I want each of you to inflate one tube of your vest if you haven't done so already. Do not inflate both tubes. If you do you will be very uncomfortable, and we're only inflating one for insurance in case you get clumsy and fall overboard."

He could hear the little CO2 cartridges popping in the dark as vests inflated. A few people pulled the wrong tab and illuminated the little battery-powered white light on the vest. Eventually everyone sorted things out and the vests were properly inflated. "Now I want to balance our raft. We have too much weight on one side. If you are handicapped do not move. We will move other people first."

He began to choose people and move them until the raft evened out.

"Now, I want to know how many of you people are doctors, and don't all try to speak at once."

Someone actually laughed, which was a sign of courage or ignorance, but no one spoke up right away. A few seconds later a female voice said, "I'm an emergency room nurse, I'll do what I can."

"Very good, start a triage, and we'll go from there."

Charlie felt like he had succeeded in getting everyone focused on the proper priorities and a common purpose, which was the best he could hope for in the short term. He looked around and began to evaluate the situation. He thought he saw the lights of another raft for a moment, but he wasn't sure. The little battery-operated lights on his raft were growing very dim. Molly and Alice were using the flashlights to help the nurse look at injuries. He tried to remember what time the sun came up on his last trip, but knew it would be much later at sea level than at thirty five thousand feet and later yet under the thick cloud cover.

The nurse reported that she had not discovered serious injuries among the raft's occupants, only bruises and minor lacerations. Charlie used one of the flashlights and dug the first aid kit out of the survival pack, and she went to work. When everyone else was cared for, she wrapped Charlie's ankle and offered him Tylenol. The pain had subsided somewhat, and he refused the pills, thinking someone else might need them more. He had Molly do a head count and discovered that there were forty-two people in the raft, and twelve of them were handicapped. He and Molly discussed the situation with Alice, and decided that there was little they could do until daylight other than to encourage the people to talk and stay alert. They agreed that as crewmembers, they should exhibit as much confidence as possible.

Colt sat impatiently through the preflight and boarding process. When the agent closed the door, he taxied out to the runway as quickly as possible and then sat impatiently waiting in line for takeoff. It was driving him crazy to do nothing. He was determined to find a way to help. They finally received takeoff clearance and departed to the north. When departure control gave them a left turn, he rolled the airplane up into a tight turn to the west, asked for high speed approval, and lowered the nose to put the airspeed on the red line. He ignored climb performance and kept the speed up as they crossed Spain and headed for Portugal and the Atlantic.

He had plotted Charlie's last position on their chart and requested a westbound track that would over fly that position. When they were in range of Santa Maria, he got on the radio and asked for the latest information. There was none, so he asked who was leading the search. They told him Navy Rota was coordinating the operation. He asked who the on-scene commander was, and they gave him the call sign, "Navy Search Eight."

Colt kept the speed up, and approaching thirty west, he closely monitored the guard frequency and heard no activity at all. He decided to create some.

"Navy Eight, Tri Con Fourteen, on guard."

"Tri Con Fourteen, Navy Eight go ahead."

"Navy Eight, can you come up on air-to-air."

"Okay, we'll switch over."

"Tri Con Fourteen, Navy Eight on air-to-air. Go ahead, sir."

"Navy, we wanted to tell you guys how much we appreciate your help. Any luck yet?"

"No sir, the visibility is really bad, it's gonna be a slow go. We've got four Orions in grid but no joy so far."

"Who took the mayday?"

"That was *USS Karuk*, an oceangoing tug. He's down to the southwest steaming at flank speed to get here."

"Is he on guard?"

"Always, sir."

"Thanks guys, we're going to try to raise them if you want to listen in."

Colt switched back to the emergency frequency. Brian Davis had grabbed a nap after his mid-watch and was back on duty for the regular workday.

"*Karuk*, Tri Con Fourteen on guard, over."

"Tri Con Fourteen, this is *Karuk*, go ahead."

"*Karuk*, do you have 123.45 capability?"

146

"Yes sir, standby one."

"Tri Con Fourteen, *Karuk* on air-to-air."

"Thanks *Karuk*, I didn't want to tie up the emergency frequency. Thanks for helping out with the search. Do you have a word for word copy of the mayday?"

"Yes sir, I copied it myself. Standby one."

"Fourteen, are you ready to copy."

"Go ahead."

"Okay, we played the tape back several times, and this is it: '*Karuk*, Tri Con One-One, we have a fuel exhaustion emergency, present position, North 4443.7, West 03429.8, one zero thousand feet, two hundred and eight souls on board, over.' He came back again after the read back, and he was weak and broken. '*Karuk*, Tri—on—One, headi—ro, four—seven miles,—ect—' that's it word for word sir."

"Thanks *Karuk*. Navy Eight, are you still with us?"

"Affirmative."

"Listen, it sounds like he gave the mayday descending through ten thousand feet. Even with no engines, he would have a glide ratio of three to one, which means his splash would be thirty miles downrange. It sounds like the second transmission was trying to give a heading and distance to somewhere. I'm betting he was trying to make Lajes and splash would be about thirty miles on a direct line between the position he gave and Lajes. Does that make sense?"

"It sounds logical. We might need to rethink our premise. I'll run it by Rota and get them to plot it out to expand the grid."

"Thanks again guys, we're gonna lose you shortly. Good job *Karuk*. You too, Eight."

Colt knew that the investigation in Atlanta was underway, and he intended to be a part of it. He adjusted the cruise speed to maximum and ignored all fuel conservation measures. He stared at the clouds below and envisioned the waves beneath. At least the temperature on the surface was in the seventies and survivable.

Britt leaned against the side of the raft and wondered what the temperature must be. It wasn't cold, but the moisture in the air was thick, and everyone's clothes were damp and uncomfortable. The day was dawning gray and dark, but she was glad to have any light at all. The raft lights had long since gone out, and she was trying to conserve the flashlight batteries. Nancy had regained consciousness, and her ankle was swollen and discolored. The pain was bearable, but her source of distress, when she came to, was the sight of Allen Smallwood lying in the floor of the raft, soaked and shivering.

When she realized that he was looking at her, she said, "Hello, Mr. Smallman."

He shivered, stuttered, and blustered. "Smallwood."

After all that had happened, Britt was amazed that the skinny little grandmother's first priority was to antagonize Allen.

Nancy asked, "What happened, Britt?"

"We're safe. When we ditched, the galley collapsed on you. You took a blow on the forehead, but I think you'll be fine. Don't try to move around. Your ankle is sprained or broken also. Charlie and Robby put you into the raft."

"Where is everyone else?"

"I don't know how many others got out. The airplane sank after we drifted away from it. We have forty people in the raft, and you have the most serious injuries. Allen Smallwood is suffering from exposure, but he'll be all right. We fished him out of the water about ten minutes after we launched."

"Did you throw him in the water?"

"No, he panicked and jumped on the slide before I could disconnect it. He bounced and disappeared until we found him later."

Nancy glared at him lying on the floor, pouting.

"Britt, did you see Pam?"

"No, but I'm sure she's fine. You two are a tough old pair of grannies."

"What happens now?"

"I've been waiting for daylight to see what we can do. Surely the rescue teams are on the way. We just have to survive until they find us."

"Help me sit up."

Once Nancy was upright, she reached into her pants pocket and came out with several sheets of folded paper.

"I ripped these out of the *In-Flight Manual*, in case we made it this far."

Britt looked at the sheets and realized that they were the ditching section of the manual.

"Nancy, you are a genius."

They quickly found the pages describing the raft operation. They read about the survival pack and found it after a few minutes. The first aid kit contained the items they needed to bind Nancy's ankle, and then they set about making people busy. Two men were assigned the task of putting the canopy up. Another group was given the responsibility of figuring out how to use the desalination kit to make fresh water. They read about the sea anchor and deployed it to slow their rate of drift. More than anything else, their efforts gave people something to do and a sense of purpose. Once they had accomplished all that could be done, Britt sat down and looked through the remaining items in the pack. She could see no immediate use for the flare gun or signal mirror, and the referee's whistle didn't make much sense. She and Nancy decided not to mention the energy bars to anyone else so that they could be rationed later. The last thing they wanted to do was make people thirsty or feed them fiber. There were a few more items to be sorted out and read about in the survival book they found in the pack.

Everyone had quieted down, and they waited for full daylight to improve the foggy view. Britt and Nancy leaned against the side of the raft and read the survival book and the pages from the *In-Flight Manual*.

Nancy said, "I hear birds. Are we close to land?"

"I'm not surprised you're hearing little birdies. That was quite a blow to your head."

"I'm serious, Britt. I hear something."

They quietly listened and didn't hear anything at first. Then, very faintly, Britt heard it too.

"I think I do hear something, Nancy. What is that?"

Suddenly it occurred to her. She dug in the survival pack and came out with the whistle. She blew it, and it was so loud it scared everyone on the raft, including herself. She explained what she was doing, and everyone listened. When they agreed which direction the noise came from, they began taking turns with the paddle. After ten minutes, it seemed that they had barely moved, but it was hard to judge with no reference except open water. An elderly lady, who had not said much at all, tapped Britt on the shoulder. "Dear, shouldn't you bring up that sea anchor thing?"

The sea anchor was nothing more than a plastic bag on a rope, but after they retrieved it the raft began to make visible progress. They continued to blow the whistle and listen for the answer. The progress was maddeningly slow, but they were getting closer. The men in the raft took turns with the paddle, and after almost an hour Britt saw a brief glimpse of bright yellow. Soon everyone could see the other raft and began yelling to them. Britt could see two red vests in the raft, and as they came closer, she saw that Tony and Mary Dobson had survived.

After a frenzy of paddling from both rafts, they were finally close enough for Tony to throw a heaving line over, and they pulled the yellow tubs close and tied them together. Tony asked, "Are you okay, Britt?"

"I'm fine, but Nancy has an injured ankle. That's our only casualty, though. Are you all right?"

"Yeah, we've got a few bumps and bruises but nothing serious. I only have eighteen people, including Mary and myself."

"Did anybody else get out?"

"Yeah, Charlie and I loaded the other over wing raft and launched it with Candace. It was pretty full."

"Great. I know Robby launched at the one right door, but I don't know how many people he had. I think everyone in business got out, though."

"We just have to keep our faith. I transmitted our position to a Navy ship, so they'll be looking for us soon."

The *Karuk* was rocking and rolling. The big propeller on the little ship was making maximum turns and leaving a large wake. Unfortunately, the tug was built for power, not speed. It could tow an aircraft carrier, but not very fast. Captain William Maxwell convened a meeting of the ship's officers in the wardroom on the second deck.

"Gentlemen, Rota now has eight aircraft in the search area; however, none of them have rescue capability. Other surface ships are steaming to the area also, but I intend to not only be there first, but to complete the rescue before anyone else has a chance. Each of you will have the remainder of the day to prepare your respective departments. I expect all hands on deck with full capability and no excuses."

He turned to the engineering officer.

"Mr. Crouch, you will have your snipes check everything that can be checked. There will be no inoperative equipment. I want the electricians to test the carbon arc searchlights for night operations and I want them to test the small boat davits for launch. I want your best man on the propulsion switch board when we begin the search grid."

All the enlisted men who worked below decks on the ship were known as snipes. The engineering officer did not take offense. "Max, we can't test the small boat davits at flank speed."

"Well, that's the only speed you're going to see today, and if those boats don't lower when I say put them in the water, you can explain to a review board why you can't follow orders."

"Aye-aye, sir."

"Mr. Strickland, your deck apes will have all rescue equipment checked and in place by eighteen hundred hours. Be prepared to transfer whatever is needed to the small boats when we launch. I want sickbay prepared to take casualties, and you make sure Doc has what he needs.

Lieutenant Strickland was likewise not offended that his enlisted men working above decks were called deck apes, but he thought, *Doc is an enlisted petty officer medical corpsman, and sickbay is not much bigger than a closet with a box of Band-Aids in it. Give me a break.*

The captain continued. "Have the mess cooks clear some space in the ship's freezer, in case we need to store bodies for a few days. Next, I want a dive platform ready to be lowered, and I want the divers in wet suits prepared to go in the water if necessary. The small boats will launch and recover survivors to the platform, where they will be taken aboard. We have to expect two hundred survivors, and if necessary, they will be accommodated in the crew berthing compartments. The crew will sleep on deck. Are there any questions?"

Lieutenant Strickland said, "For those of you that haven't heard, the primary search grid has been relocated thirty miles to the east. It shouldn't affect our ETA very much, but initial operations will begin in the dark."

Captain Maxwell said, "That will be all gentlemen, carry on."

CHAPTER FIFTEEN

The room that the technical operations accident team had been assigned was on the south side of the building with windows that afforded the members a view of the airport. There were five people in the room poring over technical data for the fuel system. Each member had been assigned space at a conference table and provided a laptop computer in order to access the online maintenance manuals.

At mid-morning, the vice president of Tech Ops, Jake Smith, called for a roundtable discussion to sort out what had been learned so far. He asked Phil to begin the session.

"I have been trying to sort through the facts in order to establish what can be validated as credible premise. I believe we can eliminate fuel contamination, simply because the airplane had been in flight for several hours with no reported problems, and all tanks were loaded from the same source. In addition to that, the engines would have been feeding from separate tanks with a normal burn schedule. There could have conceivably been a problem with one engine but not all three. Therefore I think we should focus on fuel exhaustion."

Jake said, "That's good thinking, Phil. I should have told you that I just received a transcript of the mayday. It specifically states fuel exhaustion as the reason for the emergency."

"In that case, we only have to determine how and why. The position report at forty west mentioned no problems, and less than an hour later, they were out of fuel. That indicates a massive leak. Someone can double check my calculations, but it seems to me that with a normal fuel management schedule, the center aux tanks would be dry, leaving fuel in the mains and tip tanks only. The problem I'm having is understanding how both main tanks could develop such a huge leak. We've never experienced a difficulty with the integrity of the tanks, and the odds of two tanks having a problem are too great to consider. The only thing common to both tanks is the dump manifold."

Jake said, "You're right, but there are two failsafes to prevent dumping all the fuel, even if the valves opened inadvertently. The pilots normally program the flight management computer to automatically close the dump valves at max landing weight, and even if that failed, there is a standpipe level at twenty thousand pounds."

"I agree, but the only other possibilities I can come up with are fuel freezing or bird strikes rupturing the leading edge of the wing. The flight plan actually indicated a plus two for temperature at cruise levels. For thirty five thousand feet, that would be minus fifty-three degrees centigrade, which should not create a problem, even if they were there much longer than they were. We all know that there are no birds at thirty-five thousand feet, so that brings me back to the dump valves."

"Okay, Phil. I'll have someone double check with meteorology and see if the actual temperatures matched the forecast. Meanwhile, you can dig out all the dump system design information and start going through it. Check with engineering and see if there have been any modifications to the system recently.

Please don't find any evidence that we screwed something up to cause this. Who's working on the aircraft maintenance history?"

Another of the team members spoke up.

"I've got all the logbooks, Jake, and everything looks pretty routine."

"Have there been any squawks or routine maintenance on the fuel dump system?"

"There is no mention of the fuel system at all in the last couple of months."

"Maybe there should have been. Here's some information you'll love. Gene Clark and the feds want to meet with us after lunch. I'm not sure who will be with him, but let's share what we have and try to learn what they know."

Ray Slackman was having a bad morning. He had arrived at work with a headache and was finding it very difficult to focus on his duties. Even the routine maintenance chores were a challenge, and he made several glaring errors that required correcting before anyone noticed. He seriously considered feigning illness and going home, but he knew that it would only draw attention to himself. Of course, the topic of conversation among all the mechanics was Flight Eleven, and everyone had a theory. Ray avoided the discussion and tried to keep a low profile. He had not been approached by anyone with questions, and by mid-morning, he was beginning to relax. He told himself time and again that there was no evidence that he had tampered with the dump valves.

He decided to take his morning break as usual and stood before the vending machines perusing the choices. He almost bolted and ran when the foreman stepped out of his office and said, "Ray, I've been looking for you. I need to see you in the office."

Thoughts raced through his mind as he slowly walked across the room and into the foreman's lair. He had prepared a speech for this eventuality, but now his mouth was dry, and his tongue was thick.

"Come in and have a seat Ray. I suppose you know that ship 826 is the bird that went down last night. Did you see anything unusual at all when you did the service check yesterday?"

Ray tried not to sound defensive.

"No, nothing at all. Everything checked out normal."

The foreman said, "I don't know the details of what happened, but they seem to be focusing on the fuel system. I know there are no items on the service check concerning the fuel system other than the exterior walk around inspection. Did you see any evidence of a fuel leak around any of the tanks?"

Ray almost choked.

"No, of course not. I would have written it up if I had."

"Did you work on anything that's not in the logbook?"

"The lead flight attendant asked me to check out a coffeemaker, and I did, but it seemed to be working okay so I didn't put it in the book."

"Well, that sounds routine enough. If you think of anything else, let me know. It sounds like you did everything right, though. Thanks for coming in, Ray."

He walked out of the office and sat down at one of the tables. His knees were shaking, and he didn't trust himself to walk farther. Why were they looking at the fuel system? Lots of horrible scenarios went through his mind, but he concluded that there was still no evidence of wrongdoing, and now that he had been interviewed, that would be the end of it. The more he thought about it, the more confident he became. Tri Con had learned, like so many others, not to mess with Ray Slackman. The money would have made his satisfaction complete. His plan had been almost

157

flawless, and it occurred to him that there was no reason it wouldn't work again.

Charlie looked at the other forty-one people in the raft and felt the tremendous weight of overwhelming guilt. Twelve of his companions were handicapped, and he second-guessed his earlier decision in the airplane to leave them as a last priority to evacuate. He felt like each of them were staring at him and condemning his humanity. He could not get the image of the man slumped in his seat with a broken neck out of his mind. People who loved the man would suffer tremendous pain because of his death, and they would want answers. What would Charlie tell them? He was responsible and would have to be accountable.

Molly had been watching Charlie and could see what he was thinking. She crawled across the raft and sat beside him.

"Charlie, you saved a lot of lives tonight, including mine. I will always be grateful. I don't think there are many pilots who could have landed that airplane without killing everyone onboard. I know all you pilots are task-oriented and committed to completing the mission, but you accomplished an almost impossible task with great results. You are a hero."

"I don't feel like a hero, Molly. People died tonight, and more will probably die before this is over. Innocent people depended on me, and I failed."

"Charlie, you will not get sympathy from me. This is not your fault. You reacted to a terrible set of circumstances in a manner that most would have given up on. We don't have time to feel sorry for ourselves. We still have people we are responsible for."

"You're right, Molly. Thank you. We have to make these people as comfortable as possible, and see that they all survive. Our biggest problem is going to be water. We can survive a long time without food, but water is essential. Let's get someone working on the desalination kit. Then we'll ration what we have and make it last. I need to explain what happened to everyone first, and then see if we can get some teamwork established and make everyone feel involved and committed."

"Now you're talking, captain. Let's do it."

Charlie stood up. "Everyone, listen up. I'm Captain Charlie Wells. I want to explain our situation to you. First, I'm sure you want to know how we got here. I can tell you that we lost all our fuel and had no choice but to ditch the airplane in the water. I can't tell you why we lost the fuel, other than saying that it was a malfunction in the system that we could not fix. There will be plenty of time to assess blame, but that time is not now. Right now our only focus is going to be on survival until we are rescued. It will take a team effort to do that, and I intend to call on each and every one of you to contribute to the cause. Whatever particular talent or expertise you have, we will need it. We already have our nurse attending medical needs, and I appreciate that very much. Before we ditched, a message was transmitted to a Navy vessel giving our position. Resources are on the way to find us. The problem is, we don't know how long that will take. The weather is another problem, and until visibility improves the search will be difficult, but it will happen. Here are our priorities. If you have a medical problem, we need to know about it. The next thing we need is drinking water. I need three volunteers to operate the desalination process to make fresh water from seawater. Once we have that underway, we will have to ration the water to make it last. If it rains, we will catch as much of that as possible. Next, but not nearly as important, is food. We have a limited amount of energy bars in the survival kit, and we will ration those also, but

159

we can survive a long time without food. We also have a fishing kit. If you are a fisherman, we will need your skill."

A man spoke up. "Captain, I'm a commercial fisherman. Let me have the fishing gear."

Several other people talked at once and volunteered to make fresh water. Charlie passed out the equipment and thanked them.

One of the handicapped men said, "What can I do to help, Captain Wells?"

"Call me Charlie, and I have an important job for you. We need lookouts to spot the other rafts that were launched and to look for rescue aircraft or ships."

Charlie helped the man to the front of the raft and positioned him to look forward. Another handicapped person said, "Heck, I can do that. There's nothing wrong with my eyes."

Soon they had a person on all four sides of the raft and also a person to relieve them every thirty minutes. Molly assigned a woman to blow the referee whistle every five minutes or so, and another group worked on putting the canopy up. The sun was burning off some of the morning fog, and visibility was improving. Charlie thought, *Where there is hope there is…hope.*

Pattie paced the family room at Tri Con headquarters and refused to give up hope. She had faith in God, and she had faith in Charlie. She resolved to be brave and show courage in order to encourage the other family members. She had spent some time with one of the chaplains and gained strength from his words and the scripture he quoted. Robby Jenner's wife seemed to understand Pattie's feeling of responsibility, because her husband was the first officer and second in command. They had discussed the situation and concluded that they should make themselves visible and available to the other family members gathered in the room to provide whatever comfort they could.

There had been two hourly briefings since Pattie arrived, but very little information was available. The only good news was that they knew the aircraft's last position and rescue personnel were on the way. The company officials assured them that everything that could be done was in fact being done.

At noon, folding tables were brought in and set up, followed by a catered lunch. Pattie and Melissa Jenner were seated with the parents of both Britt Fowler and Tony Johnson. The conversation inevitably turned to family.

Mrs. Fowler asked, "Pattie, how long have you and Charlie been married?"

"We've always been together. We met in high school, went to college together, and were married after graduation. We learned several years later that I could not have children, so it's always just been the two of us."

Mrs. Fowler said, "Our Brittany was married for a few years, but it just didn't work out. We keep hoping that she will meet someone else, but I guess it's not that easy these days. She's our only child, and now that she's twenty-nine we worry that we will never experience grandchildren."

Mrs. Johnson said, "I know how you feel. Tony is thirty-one now and never married. He has always been so involved with other things. It seems that he never has time for a social life. First it was college and ROTC, then the Navy, and now Tri Con. We sometimes wonder if we will ever have a daughter-in-law, let alone grandchildren."

Mrs. Fowler said, "You must be very proud of his accomplishments. Do you have a picture of him?"

The next ten minutes were filled with exchanging photos of the four crewmembers and appropriate complements being expressed. A few tears were shed but not commented upon. They picked at the bountiful meal that Tri Con had provided, but no one really had an appetite. Still, it was nice to be doing something to occupy their minds and hands. Someone had tuned the big screen TV to the noon news, and as they finished their lunch, the anchor announced that they were going to the on-scene reporter at the airport.

"We're here in the airport terminal where relatives and loved ones of the passengers on the ill-fated Tri Con flight are gathering and demanding answers. Joining us now are Mr. and Mrs. Charles Chamberlin, who have been desperately seeking information about their ten-year-old daughter, Amanda. Mrs. Chamberlin, what is Tri Con telling you?"

The camera focused on the mother in tears.

"They have basically told us nothing. Amanda was traveling to Spain to see her grandparents. My father is in the Air Force and stationed at the base in Madrid. They told us that they would take good care of Mandy and that she would have someone with her at all times. Now we don't know what...wha—" She became too emotional to continue.

The camera focused on the reporter once again.

"As you can see, emotions are strained, and the grief-stricken loved ones who are gathered here are devastated. We expect the airline to release a list of the passengers later today, and we will learn how many local citizens were on the flight. We will bring that to you as soon as possible, but I can tell you from the number of people gathered here, it is going to be significant. We have learned that a local group of about twenty members, who are part of a social club, were traveling to Madrid for a convention of some sort."

The anchor asked, "Do we know the nature of the social club?"

"We know that they were all handicapped, but we have not learned what drew them together as an organization."

"Do we know if the airline violated any rules by placing that many physically challenged passengers on a single flight? For instance, I know we reported that there were only eight flight attendants onboard. I'm wondering what the rules and procedures are for emergency evacuations in this case."

"We just don't know the answer at this point, but our researchers are seeking that information. The NTSB will be on the scene this afternoon, and that will be a question we will ask. We are also trying to find out if there were other unaccompanied children on the flight, in addition to Amanda Chamberlin."

"Thanks for the report. We will come back to you later in the newscast."

The Fowlers and the Johnsons pushed their food away and felt guilty for complaining about not having grandchildren. Mr. Johnson said, "Can you imagine the devastation that little girl's grandparents must be going through? I feel so sorry for them. I wish there were something we could do."

Pattie said, "We all do. It's such a helpless feeling to sit here doing nothing, but I'm sure the crew did everything possible to help each passenger."

Two men dressed in business suits came in and spoke to the hostess at the door. She turned the TV volume down and said, "If I could have everyone's attention please, these gentlemen have some information for us."

The room became silent as everyone looked hopefully to the two strangers. The taller of the two stepped to the front of the room and spoke.

"My name is Gene Clark, and I am with the FAA. I'm afraid we still have more questions than answers, but I wanted to introduce myself and assure you that the full resources of the federal government are being utilized to investigate this incident. So far we have concentrated our efforts on gathering facts and putting together a profile of the flight. At this time we have not uncovered anomalies of any sort that would point us in a specific direction; however, it's very early in the process. As you know, the navy and air force are participating in the search effort, and the NTSB is sending a team of investigators to the Azores. They will be joined by officials from Portugal and Canada, since they both provided air traffic services for Flight Eleven. I want to introduce Special Agent Ed White of the FBI. Ed will explain his role, and then we will answer questions."

"Folks, I am here to provide liaison with the FBI and make available our resources and assistance to local and state law enforcement. We certainly want to leave no stone unturned in finding answers for you. I promise you that we want to know what happened as much as you do, and at some point, we hope to get to know each of you and provide an ongoing dialogue and information stream."

Pattie thought, *That means you will be doing background checks on all the crewmembers and seeking information rather than providing it.*

Mr. Fowler asked, "Does your presence indicate that the FBI suspects sabotage or terrorism?"

"No, sir, it's routine for us to offer our help in all air carrier accidents. I don't know where the investigation will take us, but at this time there is no evidence to indicate sabotage or terrorism."

Melissa Jenner asked, "Have you heard anything about the search?"

Gene Clark answered, "No, ma'am. There are eight Navy aircraft on scene, but the visibility is still poor, and they're limited as to capability right now."

Todd Gray made the turn at the end of the grid and started the run in the opposite direction. The ceiling had improved to three hundred feet, and the visibility was now one and a half miles. Even so, it was unrealistic to expect to see anything under these conditions. Normally they would have an aircraft at five thousand feet and another at fifteen hundred to cover a grid properly, and it would still be hard work. Even if there were survivors with flares and sea dye marker, they would be useless with the low clouds and fog. With each passing minute the odds of survival decreased, but that just motivated the navy crew more. They would not give up and continued to stare at the sea flashing by in a hypnotizing montage. Todd's radioman was in touch with the other seven aircraft, but there was no news.

The morning was gone, and as the day wore on, they discussed ocean currents and drift rates, but without a known starting point, it was like throwing darts. Within the hour they would complete the grid and be relieved by another aircraft from Rota. Todd thought his copilot was in a daze, but suddenly he shouted, "Two o'clock and a half mile! Mark the GPS."

The flight engineer pushed the button to freeze the digital readout on one of the GPS display units, thus recording their exact latitude and longitude.

"Got it."

Todd rolled the Orion up on its right wing and turned back.

"What did you see?"

"I don't know. It was small and white. It certainly was not an airplane or a raft; it was too little."

"Okay, everybody scan. Don't stare at one place. Use your peripheral vision to find it. Make sure the cameras are rolling."

Todd flew over the area three more times before they spotted the floating object again. He made two more passes to try to identify what they were looking at, but the speed of the Orion and the low altitude only gave them a few seconds to see it. The object was a light color in contrast to the dark water and appeared to be white or gray. Once Todd was sure they had obtained good video, he began the long climb to altitude and the rendezvous with their relief flight. He was dismayed by the fact that the cloud cover was still thick and showed no signs of breaking up.

After briefing their relief crew on the radio, he turned the Orion to the east and increased speed to max cruise. He had the technician upload the film to Rota, and then he called the *Karuk*.

"*Karuk*, Navy Eight, over."

"Navy Eight, *Karuk*, go ahead."

"What's your ETA for the search grid?"

"We're on schedule and estimating arrival at just after midnight."

"Okay, we're going home but we'll be back tonight. Good luck."

"Roger, Navy Eight. Have a good nap."

Flight Attendant Shelia Graham had thirty-six people in her raft, nine of whom were handicapped. After Charlie launched them from the rear door, they had floated aimlessly until the sun came up. Shelia had checked for injuries and found none that required more than minor care. She had opened the survival pack, used the first aid kit, and stored the flashlight away to preserve the batteries. Most of the other items made no sense to her, but she planned to read the survival book and make use of what she could. Hours had gone by, and she was still taking grief from the handicapped passengers for leaving them in their seats until everyone else had been evacuated. When her patience wore thin, she realized that she had to transition her persona from a genial hostess to a raft commander. That was when she explained to a rather verbose paraplegic that even though he could not walk the plank, she would happily help him over the side if he didn't shut up. Several other survivors, including some of the handicapped, applauded and offered assistance. Things settled down after that, and they contemplated their plight. Shelia quickly decided which of the men and women could be counted on for physical chores if needed and who could keep their head in a crisis. She had already imagined shark attacks, a hole in the raft, being capsized by a storm, and starvation.

Her morbid thoughts were interrupted by a lady in the front of the raft shouting, "There are people in the water! I can see people in the water!"

Shelia stood up and could indeed see several objects floating on the surface of the ocean in the distance. She remembered the paddle in the survival kit and quickly retrieved it. One of the men she had recruited volunteered, sat on the side of the raft, and began paddling. After a few minutes of making little, if any, progress, one of the handicapped men said, "Somebody help me up there."

The man's legs were paralyzed and atrophied, but his shoulders and arms were huge and well developed.

"I'm a state champion wheelchair racer, and I can paddle twice as fast as you. Let me up there."

Two men helped him into position, and water began churning. He turned to one of his buddies who was similarly built and said, "Randall, get up there on the other side so we can get this thing going straight." They began paddling and throwing the oar back and forth. The raft's momentum began building.

It soon became apparent that what they saw were not people in the water, but the flotsam from the remains of Flight Eleven. The first item they recovered was someone's carry-on bag containing personal toiletries and a few snack foods.

Shelia quickly declared, "Any food items that are recovered will be stored and rationed on an equal basis."

Everyone became excited and enthusiastic as the treasure hunt continued. People were shouting and giving directions to the oarsmen as they spotted more and more floating debris. Someone discovered the heaving line at the front of the raft and fashioned it into a lasso to retrieve items from a distance. Shelia decided that some of the people were excited to find items that might enhance their chances for survival, and others were enjoying the voyeurism of searching someone else's luggage. They stashed the occasional food items they recovered and a few soft drinks that were found in the bags, but the real treasure was three cases of bottled water from the airplane's galley. Their efforts were filling the raft, and they soon had to decide what to keep and what to jettison. Most of the clothing items, toiletries, and bags were tossed back into the sea, but Shelia could not bring herself to dispose of the cute little teddy bear that she had plucked from the water beside the raft.

Everyone groaned when the same woman that had first spotted the flotsam began pointing and shouting again.

"There's people! I can see people in the water!"

Shelia looked where the woman was pointing and saw nothing, but when she stood up, she saw something big and yellow on the horizon and heard a whistle blowing. Other people saw it too and began shouting and waving.

The oarsmen had been relieved by two other wheelchair racers, who were doing just as well at propelling them through the water. Among the items recovered from the sea were two skateboards, which were now being employed as paddles, along with a piece of metal from some part of the airplane. With four oarsmen at work, the distance closed rather quickly. Shelia saw three red vests in the other raft. She never thought she would be happy to see Mama Molly, but there she was with Charlie and Alice.

CHAPTER SIXTEEN

Gene Clark and Ed White arrived at the Tech Ops team room and were introduced by Jake Smith. Gene spoke first.

"Gentlemen, I can't overestimate the importance of what you are doing here. There has been a catastrophic mechanical failure of some sort to cause this accident. We can never know why that happened if we don't first know what happened. The crew reported fuel exhaustion in their mayday, and we have to determine how they lost the fuel and why. Jake tells me that you are looking at several possibilities, with primary focus on the dump system. I agree with your assessment. I know it's early in the process, but the rate of loss seems to correspond with the dump rate of six thousand pounds per minute. I'd like to hear your thoughts on how that could happen."

Jake said, "Phil, why don't you summarize what you've determined so far."

"Well, we know that the dump valves are electrically operated and can be controlled several ways. They normally have to be opened by physically pushing the dump switch in the cockpit; however, they can be closed three ways. The flight management computer can close them at a predetermined, programmed level;

the crew can push the switch to close them at any time; and there is a failsafe level at twenty thousand pounds to prevent inadvertently dumping to empty. The design is such that the valves are powered open but fail closed. In other words, it takes electrical power to hold the valve open. I've been looking through the electrical schematics, but so far I can't find a single power source that would maintain juice to the open side of the valves long enough to empty the tanks. Even if the crew held the switch in the cockpit, the computer or standpipe would close them at the proper time."

Gene said, "Have there been any modifications to the system recently?"

"None at all."

"Okay, gentlemen, let me introduce Ed White. Ed is with the FBI and will be assisting with the investigation."

Ed began.

"It's nice to meet all of you. I know very little about airplanes, so I admire what you guys do. I'll get right to the point, gentlemen. Gene said we have to know what happened before we can know why. My main purpose in being here is to focus on one possibility of the why. If the investigation leads us to believe that someone purposely caused the accident, we call that sabotage or terrorism. I ask that you do not discuss that possibility with anyone but me. Rumors run rampant sometimes and can hinder the good work that you are doing, so let's avoid that. Phil, that was a very good explanation of the dump system; even I understood it. I notice you used the word *normally* in your description. Could the valves be somehow rewired to bypass the failsafes?"

"Sure. Anything is possible, but I don't see that happening accidentally."

"That's my point. If you were going to do that, how would you do it?"

"Well, first of all, the power source could not be continuous, because the fuel would dump right at the gate. You would have to find a power source that would not activate the valves until the proper time; in this case, several hours after takeoff."

"Where would the most likely place to perform that modification be? Could it be done inside the computer?"

"Not likely. The programming is done in the hangar, and then the box is installed on the line. The location that would have the most common elements to the system would be the center accessory compartment in the belly of the airplane."

Ed said, "Okay, there is no evidence at all that anyone tampered with the system. I'm just trying to justify my job here, so please don't start rumors. Thank you for your time, gentlemen."

Something about the conversation was bothering Phil. He was missing something, but could not put his finger on it. It was like when you wake up and know you had a dream, but can't remember what it was about. He had been processing information all morning, and somewhere in that jumble of facts and figures, there was a tidbit that he could not quite pull into focus.

The two feds gave each team member a business card and asked him to call if anything came to light. After leaving the room, they walked down the corridor, and Gene asked, "What are you thinking, Ed?"

"I'm thinking something doesn't add up here. I'm putting all my marbles on the dump valves being the problem, but I can't see a scenario that would accidentally bypass all the failsafes. I'm thinking we should start looking at people, Gene. That's what I'm good at."

"I tend to agree with you, but we still have to know what and how."

"Didn't you tell me that Tri Con was making some personnel changes?"

"I knew you would get back to that eventually."

172

"Like I said, people are what I'm good at. Shall we visit the personnel department and examine some files? We already have agents doing background checks on all the passengers."

"I'll get the list of personnel we need to look at."

Todd Gray and his crew had lunch at the officer's mess in Rota. Before going to his quarters to get some sleep, he decided to drop by the intelligence section and see if the film had revealed anything of value. He didn't bother with official channels, but instead went straight to the petty officer who had analyzed the video. Entering the video shop was like walking onto a Star Trek movie set, and he was always amazed at what the Trekkies could do with a photo or video. He found the man he was looking for and said, "Rodriguez, you look like you haven't seen the sun in years. Did anybody tell you that there is actually a real world out there? It doesn't just exist on video."

"We have a documentary film that claims the same thing, Lieutenant, but it hasn't been authenticated."

"Is it the one with the Loch Ness Monster in it?"

"Yes, sir."

"What have you got from Navy Eight?"

"Was that you, Lieutenant?"

"Yeah, what have you got?"

"Let me put it up for you."

He ran the video in real time, and then slowed it down and stopped it.

"This is the best frame I could find to enhance."

The frame enlarged and refocused several times.

"You can see that it is definitely clothing, but the color is difficult to nail down because it's wet. My guess is light grey or tan. I can't be sure, but what you see just to the right appears to be an arm. I'd give it sixty/forty odds. Chances are better than even that you have filmed a human body, Lieutenant."

"Thanks for ruining my afternoon nap, Rodriguez."

Todd had to detour all the way around the room to avoid the Spanish-speaking civilian cleaning crew waxing the floor. He walked out into the fresh air and thought he should have dragged Rodriguez with him.

Pattie and the families had listened to the afternoon briefings by company officials with great anticipation, but heard nothing of real significance. The worry and tension weighed heavily on everybody, and the question most discussed was why there had been no signal from the emergency locator beacon, which brought disastrous thoughts and more worry. During the last briefing, the company meteorologist had explained the characteristics of a warm front and a stationary front to them and described low ceilings and visibility. He anticipated at least another day before improvement would begin. It was reassuring, however, to know that the temperature in the area was moderate. With the weather conditions hampering the search, and no signal from the beacon, it was like looking for a needle in a haystack. Pattie had talked to her sister several times on her cell phone, and by late afternoon, was considering going home to rest. Jenny Kramer assured her that she was available to take care of anything that she needed. As she considered what she should do, the TV in the room announced a breaking news bulletin.

Our coverage of the Tri Con disaster continues with late breaking and dramatic developments. News networks in Europe are now reporting, from unofficial sources, that bodies have been spotted floating in the waters of the search area. We know that US Navy aircraft are heading up the search and rescue efforts, and we are trying to get confirmation of these reports. We also are hearing that the search efforts may be suspended soon due to darkness.

In other developments, we can report that the FBI is now involved in the investigation. The Atlanta field office has confirmed that they are taking part, but describes their role as a routine support function for local and state law enforcement. However, coupled with earlier eyewitness reports of the airplane exploding in mid-air, the possibility of terrorism cannot be discounted. The FBI would neither confirm nor deny that as a factor in their involvement.

We of course will stay on top of this story. Stay tuned for more information as we get it.

There was an eerie silence. It was as if all the air had been sucked from the room. Pattie sat down and stared at the floor, as did everyone else. It seemed that every time they were offered a bit of encouragement or optimism, it was immediately ripped away from them. This was the low point of the day. She could not bear to look into the grief-stricken faces of the others. Her pain and fear was compounded by theirs. She closed her eyes and prayed for Charlie, herself, and the other families of crewmembers and passengers. She prayed for a sign that all was not lost and for the strength to go on while being faced with such horrible circumstances.

Someone touched her on the shoulder and spoke her name. Pattie opened her eyes and looked up at Colt Adams standing there, dressed in his captain's uniform.

"Pattie, I'm so sorry that Charlie was on that flight. It should have been me."

He sat down and put his arm around her. Pattie cried for a moment and then said, "Charlie was on that airplane for a reason. It has nothing to do with you."

"Thank you for saying that, Pattie. What are they telling you?"

Pattie related what they had been told in the briefings and what they had heard on the news.

"That's all speculation and mostly crap. Let me tell you what the facts are, Pattie."

"No, I want you to tell everyone in this room what the facts are, and you can be honest because they've already been devastated."

"That's exactly what I'll do."

Colt walked to the door, closed it, and then strolled to the front of the room.

"Ladies and gentlemen, please give me your attention. My name is Colt Adams, and, as you can see, I am a Tri Con Captain. I just returned from Madrid on the same flight your crew would normally be on tomorrow, and I came straight here to support my dear friend, Pattie Wells. Charlie is one of my closest friends and the finest pilot I know. I would trust him with my life. Is everyone here a family member of the crew?"

No one spoke. Colt turned to the hostess and said, "Who are you?"

The girl appeared to be in her thirties and had curly auburn hair and dark eyes. She was probably thought of as cute rather than pretty, due to a pattern of freckles scattered across her cheeks and nose.

She replied, "My name is Heather Navaro, and I'm the company hostess in charge of the room."

"Well, now you're the sergeant at arms. Go outside and don't let anybody in that door until I say so."

"I don't know if I should do that."

"Honey, get out of here so I don't have to use language normally reserved for imbeciles and idiots."

She went out the door, and Colt locked it.

"Sorry about that folks. I have little tolerance for pettiness today. As I was saying, I would like to tell you what I know and hopefully dispel some of the rumors and misrepresentation that you have heard. Pattie just told me what the news is reporting so let's start with that. Someone please turn off the idiot box back there."

Mr. Fowler walked over and turned off the TV.

"The news media is in the business of making money. Let there be no doubt what their motivation is. They dramatize, misrepresent, and justify it by saying things like, 'from unofficial sources.' That means they heard it from some homeless guy begging on the street. They end every bulletin with 'stay tuned for more information.' That's because they want you to watch the next five minutes of commercials that makes the money for them. I assign no credibility to the news media, and less than none when aviation is involved. Now, I talked to the Navy officer in charge of the search, and he told me the ceiling and visibility was so bad they could see almost nothing. There have been no dead bodies found floating in the water. I repeat, there have been no dead bodies found floating in the water.

"Next, the airplane did not explode and go down in flames. I repeat, the airplane did not explode and go down in flames. I talked personally with the Navy radioman who took the mayday call, and he read it to me verbatim. Is there someone here representing Tony Johnson?"

Mr. and Mrs. Johnson raised their hands, and Mr. Johnson said, "We're Tony's parents."

"Pleasure to meet you both. Tony was the relief pilot on the flight, and would have been operating the radios. The navy told me he was calm and totally in control. He reported fuel exhaustion as the problem and gave them a clear position report. I repeat again, the airplane did not explode and go down in flames.

"Now, I don't want to paint a rosy picture for you here. I can't say exactly what happened, but I believe Charlie made a somewhat controlled landing despite the fuel problem and the weather. If anybody could do it, he could. I'm not going to stand up here and tell you everything is going to be fine. I don't know what the survivability of the ditching was, but I'm betting a lot of people got out, and if they did, it was because of your crewmembers saving them. Now, I'm going to answer questions as long as you ask them. I know most of this crew, and I'm here as a friend. I'm not representing Tri Con or anybody else. I'm not worried about getting sued or fired. I'll tell you what I do and do not know, and we can speculate about the rest."

Britt Fowler's father said, "Thank you for coming, Captain Adams. One of the things that we are all concerned about is the fact that there has been no emergency signal to help locate them. Does that mean there was a catastrophic crash?"

"Absolutely not, and call me Colt. The ELT is designed to withstand a crash, but it's not indestructible. The transmitter is battery-operated and tested periodically. There has been more than one taken off the airplane for having a bad battery. There are several reasons why it might not send a signal."

Bertie Martin's husband asked, "Are there enough life rafts on the airplane for all those people?"

"Yes, sir. There are eight rafts, and they have a capacity of fifty people each. This flight only had a little over two hundred onboard. There are also life vests for everyone and plenty of extras if needed."

Someone else asked, "How long could they survive without food or water?"

"I don't know exactly, but it would be at least several days. Not only that, each raft contains a small amount of food and a kit to convert salt water to fresh water, so I don't think that's a concern at all right now."

The questions kept coming, and almost an hour passed before Colt opened the door and let the hostess back in. He apologized and asked if he might buy her dinner at a later date in order to make up for his rude behavior. She gave him her number.

Colt explained that sunset came much earlier in the search area, and that operations would not be suspended, but it might be a good time to get some rest and hope for better weather tomorrow. He promised to be in the family room early in order to be with them and explain whatever else might come up. Pattie could tell that he had provided a measure of hope for everyone, and his honesty had been refreshing and appreciated.

She decided to take Colt's advice and go home for the night. If anything happened, they would call her. She had been up most of the night and all day. Jenny Kramer offered to drive her home and stay with her as long as she wanted. Pattie was very concerned about Melissa Jenner, because she had no relatives close by to stay with.

"Melissa, I could use some company tonight, if you would like to come to my place. I have a spare room, and I really don't want to be alone."

"Are you sure? I don't want to be a bother, but I don't want to stay here all night, either."

"Of course I'm sure. You'd be doing me a big favor. Jenny will drive us, and we can have dinner together."

They said goodbye to everyone and agreed to meet back at Tri Con headquarters the next morning to resume the vigil. The ride home was slow in the afternoon rush, and Jenny turned the radio off to avoid the news. Colt's speech had been on target about the news media, and no one cared to hear more of their sensationalism.

When Jenny turned onto the street where Pattie and Charlie lived she said, "Oh no! Look at that."

There were three news vans parked in front of the house. Jenny drove on past and parked down the block. She said, "The company warned me about this, but I didn't believe it would be a problem. Pattie, you can't stay here but we need to get some things for you. Do you have your car keys handy?"

Pattie was petrified of the news people and did not want to confront them. Jenny took the car keys and told her and Melissa not to worry. She walked down the street and, by the time the media saw her and got out of their trucks, she had what she needed and was walking away. Two minutes later they pulled into the driveway as the garage door automatically opened. They entered and closed it. When they entered the house from the garage, the phone was ringing. Pattie rushed to answer it, but stopped when Jenny grabbed her arm. "That's going to be the vultures outside. If anyone important needs us, they'll call the cell phone."

Pattie noticed the answering machine had twelve messages blinking. She pushed the button and the recorder played message after message from news organizations requesting interviews.

"What's wrong with those people? Don't they know we've got problems enough without having to sneak into our own house and avoid our telephone?"

"I'm sorry, Pattie. Get what you need, and I'll take you and Melissa to a hotel on Tri Con's tab. I need to make some phone calls and warn the other families."

Pattie grabbed a bag and began packing what she needed. The doorbell rang, and she could hear someone saying, "Mrs. Wells, we would just like to ask you a few questions, please."

Pattie didn't know if she wanted to scream or cry. She had never been so angry in her life. Melissa calmed her down, and they loaded her bag in the car as Jenny finished her phone calls. When the garage door opened, the media was waiting with cameras and microphones. Jenny backed out without slowing, and Pattie pushed the button to close the door as they drove down the street.

Jenny said, "Melissa, I've arranged for a police escort to take you to get your things. They'll meet us at the hotel and take care of you. I'm sure you'll encounter the same situation at your house."

"Thank you. Did you notice that one of the news vans is following us?"

"Are you kidding me? These people are really sick."

Jenny sped around the next corner, quickly pulled into a strip mall, and stopped behind a delivery truck. The news van raced by and she pulled out and went the opposite direction.

At the hotel, Jenny went to the front desk and arranged the rooms while the two pilot's wives waited in the lobby. When she gave them the keys, she said, "Tri Con has taken the entire eighth floor for crew families. There will be a security guy at the elevator all night. That should solve the problem for us. Melissa, we'll wait for you to get your things and then have dinner together."

Jenny escorted Pattie to her room, where they would wait for Melissa to return. The window overlooked the airport, and they could see airplanes taking off and landing. Pattie looked down at the street to see if the news truck had followed them. The only trucks she saw were parked at the Cavu lounge.

CHAPTER SEVENTEEN

Pam drifted between nightmare and reality all day and couldn't decide which she preferred. Reality was the excruciating headache emanating from the lump on the back of her head and the fever her body was now suffering from due to whatever illness she had been coming down with before the crash. The nightmares were muddled dreams of sitting in her folding seat by the two-left door and hearing the screaming passengers as the airplane careened through the landing. She remembered assuming the crash position, the ceiling panels crashing down around her, and then nothing until she became conscious, lying on the floor of the raft. When she came to, not having any idea where she was, a small girl was applying damp cloths to her forehead. Pam's first thought was that she was being attended to by a little angel, but then the girl shouted, "Mommy, she's awake."

The girl's mother applied more damp cloths, and Pam realized she had somehow escaped the crash. She looked around the raft, saw only a few people, and wondered if this was all that remained of the passengers and crew. She asked questions that she wasn't sure she wanted to know the answer to and discovered that she had been saved by the family taking care of her. There was a middle-aged man and wife, two teenage sons, a younger son of about twelve, and the little girl. There was also an elderly Spanish couple who only spoke broken English: nine survivors from the two hundred and eight on board.

They explained that when the airplane stopped, they moved forward to the exits only to find the one on the right side completely blocked by debris that they couldn't move. When they cleared away the ceiling panels obscuring the other door, they found Pam underneath and unconscious. When the other panicked passengers saw the blocked exits, they all turned and ran to the rear. By the time the debris was cleared, they were the only people left in the area. The father and teenage sons had read the emergency escape cards in the seat backs and familiarized themselves with the door and slide raft. When they deployed the raft and loaded Pam, they checked once again for other passengers and discovered only the Spanish couple, then launched themselves. They watched the airplane sink and hadn't seen or heard anything since.

During moments of lucidness during the day, Pam had been given Tylenol with the worst tasting water she had ever had. Evidently there was art as well as science in making fresh water. Now it was dark once again, and after rationing an energy bar apiece, everyone settled in for sleep. The sea was black, and so was the sky. With no moon or stars visible, the darkness was total. They saved the flashlight to be used only in an emergency or to signal rescue personnel.

Pam slept and dreamed the horrible nightmare once more. The airplane was crashing through the water again and seemed to turn sideways to the direction they were traveling, and people were screaming. She knew the dream well by now and wasn't as frightened as before, but this time it ended differently. There was a tremendous bump and a loud squeal. Pam awoke to the little girl squealing and a bright light in her eyes. Totally confused between nightmare and reality, she tried to scream, but nothing came out. Then she realized it must be a dream because the voice of her best friend Nancy was shouting, "It's Pam! It's Pam in the raft!" Ignoring her painful ankle, Nancy shouted, "Somebody help me get over there!" The raft rocked back and forth, and then Nancy had her arms around Pam and cried as she asked questions but gave no opportunity to answer.

Incredibly, the two rafts had collided in the darkness. They could just as easily have passed within a few feet of each other without anyone realizing they were there. Nancy eventually ran out of breath, and Pam was allowed to ask questions of her own.

"Nancy, how did you get here?"

"I was in the raft with Britt. We escaped from the forward doors."

"You only launched one raft?"

"No, Robby launched with passengers in the other one. Our raft has forty people and we hooked up with Tony and Mary. They have eighteen, including themselves, in their raft. Now we have three rafts and sixty seven survivors."

"What happened to Robby?"

"We haven't seen him, so I don't know. Tony launched from the wing and says Candace got out with the other raft, but they haven't been seen either."

There was an air of excitement and optimism for a short while, and then fatigue and reality returned. Now the little flotilla of tired, hungry, and thirsty survivors trained along in the middle of the Atlantic Ocean, with no more chance of being rescued than before.

Nancy said, "Pam, you have a huge lump on the back of your head. Does it hurt?"

"I'm used to it, and it's not nearly as swollen as my bladder."

"That I can help you with. We've been using one of the bailing buckets. Britt, pass the bucket over here."

Nancy arranged the canopy for privacy, and the ladies lounge was open for business. Pam, as well as the little girl and the other two ladies, took full advantage.

It was almost midnight when Captain William Maxwell walked onto the bridge of the *Karuk*. The overhead lights were covered with red lenses, and the soft glow preserved the crew's night vision, enabling them to scan the sea outside the windows. The only other illumination came from the compass light and the green sweep of the radar scope probing the fog and darkness ahead. The radar antenna, high on the ship's mast, had been rotating since leaving Norfolk, but had not painted a target in days. Captain Maxwell had elected to retire to his cabin after dinner and sleep until approaching the search area. Now he was rested and prepared for duty. The mid-watch was beginning once again and Lieutenant Strickland greeted the captain.

"Good evening, sir. Did you rest well?"

"As well as expected, lieutenant. What's the situation?"

"We will enter the grid in about ten minutes, sir."

"Where's the Portuguese Navy?"

"They're several hours out, and will begin their search at the extreme eastern portion of the grid. The Spaniards and British are coming out too, but they're not due until late in the day."

"Good, I want to wrap this up before any of those glory hogs get involved."

"Yes, sir."

"I have command of the bridge, lieutenant."

"Aye-aye, sir."

Lieutenant Strickland announced, loud enough for everyone on the bridge to hear, "The captain has the con."

Maxwell ordered, "Helmsman, come left to new course three-six-zero."

"New course steady three-six-zero. Aye, sir."

"All ahead slow."

"Make turns for all ahead slow. Aye, sir."

The big wooden spokes of the wheel spun to the left, and the ship began to turn as the engine order telegraph rang. The handle was moved to all ahead slow. The bells were answered immediately, and the steady throb and vibration throughout the little ship decreased to a low murmur as the relative wind created by the ship's speed became just a whisper of five miles per hour.

"Lieutenant, tell the bow watch to keep a sharp eye. I don't want to run over anybody. In fact, place a double watch on the bow and have them rotate every thirty minutes."

"Aye-aye, sir."

The ship's crew had been ordered to modified battle stations and all watches, including the engine room, were plugged into the ship's intercom system. The captain's orders were passed along via the headsets the bow watch was wearing.

"Let's have both search lights now and order a continuous sixty degree sweep."

"Aye-aye, sir."

Everyone's night vision was totally ruined as the bright lights on either side of the bridge reflected off the fog and water, but it was too dark to see anything without them.

"Radio, are those air dales still up there?"

Brian Davis answered, "Yes, sir. They left two Orions orbiting above the clouds, but they're not actively searching until first light."

"Tell them where we are and that our mast is almost a hundred feet high. I don't want to meet them the hard way."

"Aye, sir."

The *Karuk* entered the grid and slowly worked north and then south across the area in a methodical search pattern. There was little wind to contend with and only a small, predictable current flowing west to east. They began the search a few miles west of where Todd Gray had photographed the object in the water and worked their way to the east.

After an hour with absolutely no results, Captain Maxwell climbed into the high-mounted captain's command chair and ordered coffee. After another fruitless hour, he propped his feet up and issued a few superfluous orders that everyone recognized as, "The captain's on the bridge" nonsense. When his eyes closed and did not flutter for fifteen minutes, the crew relaxed. However, you never really knew with captains. In the present circumstance, if he was asleep, everyone was happy about it; if he was faking it, everyone was happy to allow him to continue.

The question was answered when the enlisted man wearing the bridge headset said, "Bow lookout reports object in the water at one o'clock and fifty yards."

The captain sat up and ordered, "All stop, steady as you go, helmsman."

He stood up, wide awake, and lifted the binoculars hanging around his neck. He searched the water as the ship slowed and said, "Standby the starboard small boats."

The enlisted man repeated the order through the intercom, and the captain walked out the open hatch onto the flying bridge. The searchlight operator was tracking the object, and, as it drifted by the starboard side, a deckhand snagged it with a boat hook and lifted it aboard. It appeared to be an aluminum container of some sort.

"Have that brought to the bridge," the captain growled.

The crewman on the headset passed the order, and they watched as the deckhand climbed the starboard stairs. He placed the container on the metal deck, and, in the floodlights, they read the words stamped on the aluminum: Tri Continent Airlines. The deckhand tripped the latch on the container and opened it up to find the interior divided into slots and a tray with breakfast food in each one.

The captain ordered, "I want a three hundred and sixty degree sweep with the searchlights. Alert all lookouts."

"Aye, sir."

After a thorough search, nothing else was spotted. The captain went back to his chair and ordered, "All ahead slow, steady on course one eight-zero."

"All ahead slow and steady one eight-zero. Aye, sir."

"Radio, get a message off to fleet. Flotsam recovered, identified as Tri Continent Airlines property. Give them the lat long coordinates."

"Aye, sir."

No one wondered if he was asleep when he closed his eyes again.

An hour later they repeated the drill and recovered a suitcase with a Tri Continent bag tag and a Madrid destination code. A bumper sticker on the bag announced, "The handicapped have rights too."

The handicapped man propped his elbows on the side of Charlie's raft and tried to keep his sleepy eyes open. He had another thirty minutes of lookout duty before he would be relieved, and he knew sleep would come easy when he would finally lie down. He slowly moved his head back and forth, scanning like Charlie had taught him. He had learned that the human eye has a blind spot directly in front of it when focusing in low light or at night. By scanning back and forth, the peripheral vision allows the eye to detect objects which would not be seen looking straight on. He didn't fully understand Charlie's technical explanation involving cones, rods, and retinas, but he was secretly pleased that at least it was a handicap that everyone suffered and not just him. The constant moving back and forth caused his neck to chafe on the rubber life jacket, and the combination of raw skin and salt water was more irritating than his physical therapist, who he would like to torture in a similar fashion.

He thought he saw a flash of some sort off to his right, and wondered if a thunderstorm would add to their misery. He focused in that direction and this time definitely saw a glow of some sort. Somehow it didn't look like lightning, but maybe it was, because it was far away. He listened but did not hear corresponding thunder. He turned to the lookout in the rear of the raft, "Hey Tommy, did you see a flash of lightning off to the right?"

"Yeah, it looks weird, doesn't it? It's like slow-motion lightning."

"That's a good way to describe it. Maybe we should wake Charlie and tell him about it. If it's going to rain he probably wants to prepare."

Charlie sat up and asked, "Tell Charlie about what?"

"Oh, we thought you were asleep, Charlie. We saw a few flashes of lightning and wondered what we should do if it rains."

"If it rains we want to catch as much fresh water as possible, but warm fronts generally cause clouds and drizzle, not thunderstorms. Where did you see lightning?"

They pointed to the east, and Charlie watched. After a moment he saw a faint glow that seemed to slowly flare and then fade to nothing. He continued to watch and saw it once again. The dim flash seemed to have a rhythm to it, and Charlie smiled.

"Gentlemen, that is not lightning. What you see is either a lighthouse or a ship sweeping with a searchlight, and I promise you that there are no lighthouses hundreds of miles west of the Azores."

"Thank God," the two men harmonized.

"Indeed," said Charlie.

Their euphoria was short-lived as they watched the light slowly retreat to the south and finally disappear. The ship was moving away from them. Charlie briefly considered using the flare from the survival pack, but with the cloud cover and restricted visibility, he knew it would be wasted. He was buoyed by the fact that someone was searching. He prayed that they would return.

Shortly before dawn, Todd Gray and his crew aboard Navy Eight arrived back on station along with seven other Orions. As on-scene commander, Todd had assigned grids to each aircraft and carefully separated them to prevent collision concerns. The British had insisted on sending five C-130s out to search, but Todd had successfully lobbied to keep them far to the east and out of the way. From twenty three thousand feet the crew of Navy Eight could see a faint glow on the eastern horizon and noticed no tinge of red associated with it. This bode well for improving weather conditions. With all the sophisticated meteorological prognostication processes available to them, they still relied on, "Red sky in morning, sailor take warning. Red sky at night, sailor's delight."

Todd keyed his mic and transmitted, "*Karuk*, Navy Eight."

"Navy Eight, *Karuk*, go ahead."

"What are your weather conditions?"

"It's dark."

Todd answered sarcastically, "Thank you for that editorial. I forecast sunrise soon."

He received a sardonic response, "Thank you, sir. We appreciate whatever influence you can bring to bear."

"What's your position, *Karuk*?"

The radioman read off the coordinates and Todd copied them.

"Okay *Karuk*, keep your ears on. We'll talk to you soon."

Todd turned to his copilot.

"I don't know if we can find anything else, but I bet we can find that little tug boat."

The copilot smiled and fine-tuned the radar. Todd began descending and entered the clouds. At fifteen hundred feet, the radar painted the *Karuk* ten miles ahead. Todd continued the descent, and, at five hundred feet, they popped out of the clouds. He leveled at one hundred and fifty feet and approached the target from the rear. He turned off all the exterior lights on the airplane. At five miles they had a visual on the target and could see the red and green running lights on each side, the white light on the fantail, and the red anti-collision light on top of the mast. Todd increased speed to three hundred knots, and at two hundred yards he hit the bright landing lights and lit the ship up like daylight.

Captain Maxwell was sitting in his captain's chair with his feet up and his eyes closed. When the Orion roared past, vibrating the windows and lighting up the bridge, he didn't move a muscle. When everyone else recovered from their shock, he uttered one word without opening his eyes: "Juveniles."

Todd said, "That ought to wake them up."

The copilot said, "Aye-aye, sir."

With the ceiling and visibility improving, Todd was optimistic about the day's search and reported the weather to Rota and his other airplanes. He ordered two of the Orion's four engines shut down to save fuel and extend their search time, then waited for sunrise before settling into the grid pattern.

CHAPTER EIGHTEEN

Phil James tossed and turned most of the night. He knew that he was missing a piece of the puzzle and that the missing piece was within reach. He just couldn't quite put his hands on it. Since he couldn't sleep anyway, he decided to go into work early. With no traffic to hinder him, he arrived in record time. He walked down the corridor of the headquarters building, carrying his briefcase and aircraft manuals. When he approached the room that Tri Con had set aside for the crew families, he was surprised to see it half full of people already. Evidently they couldn't sleep either. He was even more surprised to see Colt Adams perched on the hostess' desk, talking to her. When Colt saw the ground school instructor, he stepped into the hallway and greeted him.

"Hey Phil, are you working on this?"

"Yeah, I'm on the Tech Ops investigation. Are you involved too?"

"Not officially. I'm here to support Pattie Wells and the other families. Come on in and have some coffee. I want you to meet Pattie."

Phil set his books down on a table and poured a cup of coffee, then followed Colt over to a table where two ladies were seated.

Colt said, "Pattie, I want you to meet Phil James. Phil is one of our ground school instructors and is working on the investigation."

Phil said, "Good morning, Mrs. Wells, I'm glad to meet you. Charlie is a friend and a great pilot, as you know. I hope Tri Con is taking care of everything for you."

"Nice to meet you, Phil. Charlie has spoken of you. Thank you for the work you're doing."

"I wish I could do more, and if I can be of help to you, I hope you'll allow me."

"Thank you again. Do you know Melissa Jenner?"

Phil turned to Melissa.

"We haven't met, Mrs. Jenner, but I know Robby well, and my offer extends to you also."

"Thank you, sir. I appreciate that, and I'm sure Robby will too."

Colt walked Phil out and asked, "What have you found so far?"

"Not much, but if you have a few minutes I'd like to go over it with you. Maybe you'll see something that I'm missing."

"Let me make sure everything is taken care of here and let Pattie know where I'll be."

"Good. The Tech Ops room is at the end of the hall on the left. I'll wait for you there."

Phil laid out all his material and booted up the laptop while he waited for Colt. He sat there looking out the window, watching airplanes take off and tried to find the clue he needed. A few minutes later, he was taking notes as Colt told him about his conversations with the search crews the day before. Colt said, "I doubt if any of that will help you, but I'd be interested to hear what you have discovered."

Phil went through his findings and why he thought it had to be the dump valves.

193

"I agree with you. But how could that happen?"

"That's the big question; I feel like I'm missing something, but I don't know what."

"Who else is on the team?"

"Several mechanics and engineers from Tri Con, Gene Clark from the FAA, and a FBI guy named Ed White."

"What's the FBI doing here?"

"He says just a support role, but you and I know what the FBI's interest in aviation is."

"True. As long as he doesn't get in the way, I guess there's no harm. Look, Phil, I don't know this technical data like you do, but sometimes the simple things are what get overlooked. Are you sure there were no logbook write-ups or verbal squawks?"

"Absolutely. There have been no fuel system squawks in months. Jake even talked to the crews that flew the last ten flights, and they didn't recall anything unusual. There was only one verbal that we know of, and it had nothing to do with fuel."

"What was it about?"

"I don't remember. Something totally unrelated. I've got it here in my notes somewhere."

Phil looked through his notes in reverse chronological order and didn't see it until he got to the first notes he had taken at the general briefing. He read what he had written under maintenance history and almost choked.

"Oh no, Colt!"

"What's wrong?"

"Oh man, I am so dumb. I should have seen this right away. The verbal was on the center access compartment door. It wasn't closed properly, and was showing a light in the cockpit."

"That seems insignificant, Phil."

"No it's not. The FBI guy asked me where the dump valves could be sabotaged and I told him the center access compartment. Someone was in there, Colt, and didn't close the door properly.

How did I not put this together? I've got to call this guy right now."

Phil dug a card out of his briefcase, pulled out his cell phone, and dialed.

"Mr. White, this is Phil James in Tech Ops. We talked yesterday about the dump valves. I think I might have something interesting."

Phil listened and then answered, "Yes sir, I'm in the same room right now."

He punched the phone off and said, "He's downstairs. He'll be here in two minutes. You better stay for this, Colt."

Phil dialed Jake Smith, the vice president of Technical Operations, and told him what he had discovered.

"Jake is on his way too."

Ed White, Gene Clark, and Jake Smith arrived at the same time. Phil introduced Colt and then explained what they had found.

"When we talked yesterday about where the dump system could be compromised, I said the center access compartment would be the place. Colt and I were just going over notes and remembered that the crew made a verbal request to close the access door. Someone was in there between the time the previous flight arrived and the time Flight Eleven departed. There were no scheduled maintenance functions that would require entry to the compartment."

Ed White said, "Now we're getting somewhere. Jake, how can we find out who it was in there?"

"Well, there was only one mechanic that worked on the airplane, and he just did a routine service check. There would be no reason for him to go in there, but he might have seen someone else around the airplane while he was doing the check."

"Are there any surveillance cameras in that area?"

"The only ones are on top of the terminal. I don't think they would show anything, but we'll pull the tapes and see."

Ed said, "Okay, we may have to interview everyone that worked that concourse on Wednesday."

"Actually, the airplane came in on day shift and left on afternoon shift," Jake said, "It could have been anyone on either shift."

"Right. There might be a simple explanation, but we need to find out. I guess the easy place to start is with the mechanic who worked on the airplane."

"Well, day shift is working now. Do you want me to get him over here, or do you want to go there?"

"I think it would be best to do it here. I'd like to get him out of his comfort zone and see how he reacts. I'm going to need to talk to all the mechanics on day shift, so you might bring a group over together."

"How about five at a time so we can stay in business?"

"That's fine, but bring the guy who signed the logbook in the first group. I'll need personnel files on all of them."

"All right, I'll get you an interview room and the files you need. The first group should be here in half an hour."

Ed said, "Gentlemen, we cannot have one word of this leave this room. If I find out someone is running his mouth, you'll answer to interfering with a federal investigation."

Colt smiled. "Thanks for inviting me over, Phil."

The line maintenance foreman called five mechanics into the office, including Ray Slackman.

"Men, you have been invited over to headquarters to tell the powers that be what you know about ship 826. Don't feel special. Everybody on day shift and afternoon shift is going over, five at a time. When you're finished, get back over here. I don't want to have flight delays because you guys are lounging around headquarters. There's a security van outside waiting to give you a ride."

Ray became tense for a moment, then relaxed when he knew everyone was being interviewed. He had made it through yesterday and spent several hours in the Cavu last night thinking things through. There was absolutely no way they could tie him to anything. The airplane was at the bottom of the ocean, and so was all the evidence. All he had to do was stay cool and tell a consistent story.

The security van was cleared across the runway and went straight to the headquarters building without having to leave the property, making the ride a short one. The mechanics joked about spending as much time as possible doing the interviews because there was a nasty brake job scheduled this morning, and they wanted nothing to do with it. Ray thought to himself that he would gladly do the brake job if he could get this over with quickly.

Ed White and Jake Smith waited in the interview room and thought about how the interviews should be handled. Ed said, "I don't want you to think that I have a suspect, because I don't, but this Slackman guy has an interesting file. I don't want him in here first. Let's place him third in line and give him a chance to relax."

"You're the boss, Ed. Why do you think he has an interesting file?"

"Several things. He transferred here from Dallas, but not voluntarily. He is divorced, possibly because of the transfer. I did some checking and found that his ex-wife had to obtain a restraining order against him because of threats he made toward her. He has elected not to stay at Tri Con as an Aero Mech employee, which means that now he and Tri Con are divorcing too, possibly generating the same animosity he felt for his ex-wife. None of these facts implicate him at all, but I see interesting parallels that I want to probe."

"Ed, half the employees at Tri Con are divorced, some of them more than once. And a lot of mechanics are not going with Aero Mech. I can't really blame them."

"Yeah, I know. I just always like to look at people who have no investment to lose, and this guy fits that profile. Humor me."

"Okay, I'll get the first guy in here for you. Good luck."

Ray waited with the other mechanics while the first one was interviewed. They were all anxious to question him when he came out. He told them that the guy asking questions was an FBI agent, but the questions were just routine stuff.

"He seems nice enough. They just want to know if we saw anything or heard anything, that's all."

Ray didn't like the FBI connection, but he could easily say he didn't see or hear anything. This should be easy. When the second mechanic came out, he reported the same thing. Then Ray was called into the interview room.

"Good morning, Mr. Slackman. My name is Ed White. I'm a special agent with the FBI, and I won't take much of your time today. We're just doing a routine follow-up on the accident."

Ray shook his hand. "No problem. I'm glad to help."

Ed watched as Ray sat down and crossed his arms on his chest. His posture, along with the thick beard and long hair seemed to make the statement, "I'm not a big guy, but I can hang with anybody."

Ed decided to enhance that attitude for him.

"You know, talking to you guys this morning makes me realize just how technical and important your work is. I can't imagine most people having the knowledge and skill to meet the requirements, not to mention the responsibility."

Ray uncrossed his arms and visibly relaxed. He puffed his chest up a little bit and said, "I've been doing it a long time, and if you know what you're doing, the responsibility is not a big burden."

"Even so, I admire what you do. Have you been in Atlanta your entire career?"

"No, I'm originally from Dallas. I've been here almost two years."

"Man, it's a pain to move, isn't it? I've had to do it twice with the FBI. I wish they'd leave me alone and let me stay in one place. My old lady threatens to cut me loose every time they transfer me."

"I hear that. My wife stayed in Dallas when I transferred, and we eventually divorced."

"I'm sorry to hear that. I hope it worked out for you. I guess being a single guy in Atlanta is not the worst social circumstance to have to endure, especially with an important position like yours."

Ray smiled.

"I enjoy my time off."

"Most guys would envy you. Well, I guess I should earn my pay from your tax dollars, sir, and I know you need to get back to your duties. Were you working on Wednesday?"

"Sure. I did a full day shift."

"Did you see ship 826 at all?"

"Absolutely. I did a complete service check on it."

"No kidding? That's great. What's a service check?"

Ed had a copy of the service check in his briefcase, and it had Ray's initials all over it, but he let him ramble on and on about how important the service check was and why everything had to be perfect before Ray would sign his name in the logbook.

"Wow. That must take all day to check that many things on an airplane. Did you have any help?"

"Nah, I do service checks by myself all the time. The boss knows I'm good at it."

"Man, it must be tough crawling in and out of all those compartments and wheel wells, checking everything out, especially on a big airplane like that. How do you get up there to see all those things on the outside?"

"Oh, it's not that hard if you know what you're doing. Most of it is done in the cockpit, and if there are no problems, you just walk around the outside and do a visual inspection. If you do have to check something out, we have tall wooden stepladders that reach the belly of the plane and give access to the accessory compartments."

"What in the world is an accessory compartment?"

Ray laughed.

"You have to go in through a door in the belly and inside is where all the black boxes are installed. We do a lot of our troubleshooting in there if a system has problems."

"Well, I certainly hope you didn't have to do anything like that all by yourself on ship 826."

"Nah, I didn't find any problems at all on the service check. I did a thorough walk around inspection and everything looked perfectly normal. No need to open anything up."

"Sure sounds like they had the right guy on the job, Mr. Slackman. If there was a problem, I'm sure you would have found it. You know, I don't understand all this technical stuff about airplanes like you do. They just sent me over here to fill squares, but with experts like yourself taking care of the airplanes, it seems impossible for an accident like this to happen."

Ray said, "Well, safety is always my first priority, but you can only do so much. Then it's up to the pilots, if you know what I mean."

"Yeah, I guess everybody has to do their job for things to work out right. You know, I've never talked to a pilot. What's it like working with those guys?"

"Some are better than others. I've never really understood why they pay them so much. When the airplane has a problem, they have no clue how to fix it, but they always expect us to repair it in five minutes."

"I guess it puts you under a lot of pressure sometimes, since everybody wants to leave on schedule. One of the other guys told me that some of the management folks don't understand what mechanics go through either."

"That's for sure. Most of them just look at the bottom line and judge everything by that. They don't understand how much we affect profit or loss."

"Speaking of that, I guess I should let you get back to work. I wish we had more time to talk, because I enjoy learning new things from people who know their stuff."

Ed stood up and they shook hands. "Thank you for coming over, Mr. Slackman. You've been a big help."

"No problem, just part of my job."

"Oh, one other thing. Did you see anybody else around the airplane on Wednesday?"

"Sure, there were a lot of people around all day."

"Did you see anybody that shouldn't have been there, or anybody doing anything out of the ordinary?"

"No, everything seemed normal to me."

"Okay. Thanks again."

Ray joined the other mechanics outside the interview room and thought to himself how much fun it would be to explain to them how he had outsmarted the FBI as well as Tri Con. When they asked him how it went, he restrained himself, assumed a confident posture, and said, "No big deal."

Jake Smith walked back into the interview room and asked, "What do you think?"

Ed answered, "I think Mr. Slackman has some issues with feelings of inadequacy and resentment. I'm sure you've heard of the 'Little man complex.'" He had plenty of opportunity, he has the knowledge, and possibly the motivation to do the deed. I may want to revisit him later."

The interviews continued with the other two mechanics in the group. In addition to the routine discussion, Ed slipped a few subtle questions in about their co-workers in general and Ray in particular.

CHAPTER NINETEEN

Tom Hanes, the vice president of flight operations, walked into the family room and all conversation ceased. The normal briefing had occurred just fifteen minutes before, and everyone knew there must be new information if he was back so soon. Colt had returned to be with the relatives, as he promised, and was talking with them individually and answering questions. Tom stopped at the front of the room, and everyone listened expectantly. Some were afraid of what he might have to say.

"Folks, I have some news, and I hope for once I may report this before the news media. The *USS Karuk*, the navy ship we have been waiting so patiently for, has finally arrived on station. The ship began a search pattern and within hours discovered items in the water that have been positively identified as being from our Flight Eleven. In my estimation, this is good news, because we know now that the search is being concentrated in the proper location. I wish I had more to tell you, but I'm afraid that's all I know for now."

Colt spoke up.

"For God's sake, Tom, don't you think we'd like to know what they found?"

"Oh, of course, I'm sorry. They recovered a meal carrier that still had meals in it and a passenger's suitcase. The carrier had Tri Con's name on it, and the bag had a Tri Con tag attached. Hopefully they will find more soon, and I'll come straight back as soon as I hear more."

Tom's cell phone chirped, and he answered it and walked out of the room.

Mr. Fowler said, "That was cryptic, wasn't it? Tell us what it means, Captain Adams."

The room's attention focused on Colt. He had become their source of hope and inspiration.

"I personally think this is good news, and it gives us reason for optimism. The fact that the suitcase, and especially the meal carrier, was found intact leads me to believe that the airplane made a controlled landing. They made no mention of charring, which means there's no evidence of fire. The food carriers are normally stored in the galleys, and the fact that it was found floating intact tells me that there is a good chance someone opened a galley door. That hopefully means a raft was launched, and we will find survivors. I freely admit that everything I'm telling you is speculation, but I certainly don't see bad news in any of this."

Mr. Fowler said, "I agree with Captain Adams, and I for one am glad to at least see progress being made."

Someone turned the TV volume up as the breaking news icon was shown. The anchorwoman was just beginning to speak.

"We have just received new information from our sources at the Department of Defense. The US Navy has recovered wreckage from the Tri Con crash in the Atlantic. We can't confirm exactly what has been recovered, and our source will not confirm or deny that the floating bodies reported earlier have been picked up. The bodies were spotted by reconnaissance aircraft earlier, and the number of fatalities has not been released. Eyewitnesses saw the Tri Con jumbo jet burning as it crashed into the sea more than twenty-four hours ago. There has been no evidence of survivors among the two hundred and eight passengers and crew aboard the doomed jetliner. We talked to a Tri Con official earlier today, who wishes to remain anonymous, and his comment was quote, 'It doesn't look good.' Now let's go to our reporter at the Tri Con terminal."

"We're here with the families of the crash victims aboard Tri Con Flight Eleven. We're talking to Mr. and Mrs. Chamberlin, whose ten-year-old daughter, Amanda, was a passenger on the flight. Thank you for talking to us Mrs. Chamberlin. What news have you heard from Tri Con this morning?"

"Tri Con has been very nice to us, but we have not been provided any information about Amanda. We appreciate the airline providing rooms for us at the Hilton, but we want to know when our Mandy will come home. We ask that everyone pray for our daughter's safe return."

"Well, folks as you can see, there is a somber mood here among the victims' families. We send you back to the studio now."

The camera scene shifted back to the anchor desk, and the anchorwoman pointing to someone off-camera and shouting, "Yes, the Airport Hilton. Get a crew over there right now." She saw the red light on the camera and smiled sweetly. "In other developments, we have learned that the FBI is interviewing a number of people in connection with the crash. We will bring you more information on their investigation as we get it. Stay tuned for late breaking news on this and other stories as the day goes on."

Colt said, "Here's where they make money on tragedy: the higher the ratings, the higher the advertising dollars. You might be interested to know there will be no Tri Con ads for a couple of weeks. All airlines pull their ads for a while after a crash. I suppose it's counterproductive to tell people how great you are with all the networks making you look as negligent as possible. Now we can look forward to the news crews harassing the families at the Hilton tonight. I hope someone sues them, and I hope all of you now realize the vagueness of their official reports. I promise you the Tri Con official they interviewed was a bag smasher."

Colt pulled his cell phone out and dialed a number. After a brief conversation, he put the phone away and said, "I just talked to Tri Con meteorology, and they have good news. The weather is finally improving, and the search effort should become more productive as the day goes on."

Captain William Maxwell returned to his command chair on the bridge after breakfast. The gray dawn had revealed increasing visibility, and the clouds were higher and not as thick and dark as the day before. He ordered the carbon arc searchlights secured. The electrician's mates waited for them to cool so they could replace the carbon rods and be prepared to operate them again if needed. When he was comfortable once again in his chair, he nodded at the officer of the deck and heard him command, "The captain has the con."

He looked out the forward bridge window and judged the visibility.

"All ahead two-thirds."

"All ahead two-thirds. Aye, sir."

He felt the vibration of the ship increase and watched as the bow wave grew larger. He intended to take advantage of the daylight hours and cover as much of the grid as possible. He turned to the officer of the deck.

"Let's double the flying bridge lookouts now that we can see. Pull one of the bow lookouts if you need to."

"Aye-aye, sir."

A few minutes later, they had four enlisted men with binoculars on the exterior bridge wings searching the sea. Everyone settled into the routine for a long day, but there was a sense of anticipation. Thirty minutes later, as they approached the center of the grid, the port lookout outside the hatch on the captain's left sang out, "Object in the water, ten o'clock, one thousand yards."

"Come left five degrees helmsman, all ahead one third."

The bow slowly swung to the left and settled a little deeper in the water as the ship slowed. Word went out on the interphone headsets and the deck apes prepared to recover the item from the sea. The deck apes were the young enlisted seaman who performed their duties on the exterior decks. All were in their late teens and early twenties. One of them had started a rumor that the bag previously recovered was full of hundred-dollar bills. He had been a journalism major before joining the Navy to see the world, and planned a career in the news business upon his discharge.

The ship approached the floating object a little faster than anticipated, and Captain Maxwell issued commands. "All stop."

"All stop aye."

The ship's momentum carried it on and the captain ordered, "Back one third."

The petty officer on duty at the propulsion switchboard in the aft engine room answered the bell by first moving the lever on his engine order telegraph to match the one on the bridge and then turning the electrical rheostat to reverse the propeller shaft. Captain

Maxwell was a little perturbed that his approach had not been perfect, but the deck apes retrieved the object nonetheless and brought it, dripping, to the bridge. The deck apes had already established that there were no hundred-dollar bills in the pockets of the baseball-style jacket they had fished from the sea. The gray wool jacket had leather sleeves that stood stiffly out to the side. It looked suspiciously like the body Navy Eight had reported photographing the day before.

Captain Maxwell conferred with his executive officer, and they marked a chart with the position of all the items they had recovered. They now had established a pattern. The executive officer said, "Max, the three things we have picked up are all relatively small. The drift rate of a raft or even a person in a life jacket would not be as great. Is it possible that we are downstream of the larger wreckage?"

Max replied, "I'm glad I thought of that. I'm going to change our search pattern and work from our present position to the western limit of the grid. I also think we should maneuver east and west rather than north and south."

The executive officer, who had been given his own command and would be leaving the *Karuk* in a matter of weeks, said, "It's a privilege to serve under a commander of such limitless intellect and flawless judgment. I'm overwhelmed by your capacity to lead."

Maxwell said, "I hope your exec turns out to be an insubordinate little weasel like mine."

They laughed as they turned the ship to the west and increased speed. The radioman on duty reported the jacket they had retrieved and informed Navy Eight that they were changing course and modifying the grid. Now that the *Karuk* was facing away from the morning sun, the glare off the water was much less, and the effective range of the binoculars was increased. The weather continued to improve, and as the horizon expanded, they increased the speed to fifteen knots. In twenty minutes, they had covered almost five nautical miles when the starboard bridge lookout reported, "Possible target, dead ahead, approximately three miles."

Captain Maxwell focused his binoculars, and in the next minute they covered over a quarter mile. He began to distinguish shades of yellow as the target grew larger and said, "All ahead flank speed, steady as you go."

A minute later there was no doubt he was looking at a raft. A minute after that he could make out people standing and waving.

"Sound the ship's horn."

As the loud blast traveled across the water, he could see people hugging each other as they waved.

"Standby the small boats. Make ready to lower the dive platform. Divers, prepare to go in the water. Radio, report survivors in raft, proceeding to rescue."

He slowed the ship and stopped several hundred feet away from the raft. He maneuvered the ship so that the raft was off the starboard side and ordered the lifeboats into the water. The people in the raft were still waving and screaming; they could clearly be heard over the noise of the lifeboat motors. The coxswain in the first boat stopped far enough away to tell the people to stay in the raft and not try to board the boat. He maneuvered closer, and a diver in a wetsuit swam to the raft and boarded. He was immediately embraced and kissed by a woman wearing a red life vest. The diver gathered himself and attached a line to the raft so it could be towed. Meanwhile, the dive platform had been lowered and stabilized beside the ship. The platform was twenty square feet. When the raft was secured beside it, the deck apes began transferring survivors to the platform and having them sit so the rig could be safely brought to the main deck level. The platform only had to be lowered once more to safely bring all forty-one survivors onboard. The ship's so-called doctor found only one injury as they boarded the *Karuk*. An elderly lady had a nasty break of the right arm, but other than that, dehydration seemed to be the most serious problem. After everyone was safely on board, the deck apes began the task of lifting the raft and placing it on the fantail, then recovering the small boats.

The crew directed the survivors to the mess deck, where they were given water and promised a meal as soon as the ship's cook could prepare it. Captain Maxwell entered and introduced himself, whereupon he was embraced and kissed by the woman still wearing the red vest.

"Captain, this is the most beautiful ship in the world. My name is Candace Whitton. I'm a flight attendant and the only crewmember on the raft. Have the other rafts been rescued?"

"I'm afraid not, Ms. Whitton. Perhaps you can give us information that will help."

Captain Maxwell assigned the ship's yeoman the task of listing everyone's name and other personal information while he tried to gather clues that might be helpful in the search.

Pattie didn't know how much more she could take. She had not slept, she couldn't eat, and she had cried till tears just wouldn't come anymore. Every muscle in her body seemed to ache from the tension and fatigue. She not only carried her own burden but that of everyone in the room. Over time each of them had shared their story, and the collective sadness and uncertainty was overwhelming. It was becoming more and more difficult to generate hope from tidbits of positive information. For every upbeat moment there seemed to be three of despair. It was difficult to absorb the devastation that pervaded the group, and yet she was terrified of being alone. It was as if she teetered at the edge of the abyss and would grab at any thread of news to keep from falling.

Tri Con President Harold Collins walked into the crew family room, and it was like someone had pushed the mute button. The group looked on in silence and anticipation.

"Ladies and gentlemen, I have some news to share with you. It's very preliminary and rather sketchy, so I know you will have questions that I will not be able to answer, but it's good news. Just a short time ago, the *USS Karuk* rescued forty-one survivors from Flight Eleven. They were recovered from a life raft several hundred miles northwest of the Azores. I can tell you that there were no fatalities among this group and only one injury. The injury is not life threatening. There is one crewmember in the group of survivors; however, I do not have a name. I know we would all like to have more details, but I'm afraid that's all we know so far."

Applause broke out, and hugs were shared around the room. The group had become close over the two days, and at least one family was going to be happy, even though they didn't know which one. The word survivor repeated itself like a mantra in their minds, and visions of their loved ones safe and sound took the place of the horrible scenarios that had haunted each of them until now.

Bertie Martin's husband asked, "Do you know if the crew member is a flight attendant or a pilot?" He immediately felt selfish for asking, but everyone looked on in anticipation.

Collins answered, "That was my first question too, but we just don't know yet."

Candace Whitton's daughter asked, "Won't the other rafts be nearby?"

"We certainly hope so, and the search is being intensified in that area, but I understand there are some variables. Captain Adams, maybe you can answer that for us."

Colt knew that the tendency would be to think that there were other rafts, which may or may not be true.

"There are some variables involved as to how fast and how far a particular raft might drift. The more people in the raft, the slower it would drift due to its weight. There is a canopy that may or may not be erected. If the canopy is in place, it would act like a sail. That would determine the wind's effect on the raft. In addition to that, the raft is equipped with a sea anchor to slow its drift rate. If the anchor is not deployed, the raft would obviously drift more than a raft using the anchor. Even so, this will definitely narrow the search and make the job much easier."

Mr. Collins said, "Thank you, Captain. I've been in the airline business thirty years, and I still learn something every day. Folks, I'm going to see what more I can find out, but I wanted to share this with you right away. I'll make sure you are kept up to date."

Ed White continued interviewing the day shift mechanics in groups of five. He had taken several pages of notes but discovered very little useful information. The cross-section of Tri Con employees was broad and varied. He tried to analyze the background of each one in order, to add context to the answers they gave. He was mildly intrigued by the subtle Cajun accent of Billy Ledieux, a mechanic who grew up in Delhi, Louisiana, and had received his training in the Air Force. The conversation had been routine, and Billy seemed relaxed and forthcoming with his answers. Ed was pretty much going through the motions and not expecting answers different than he had heard all morning.

"Did you perform any maintenance at all on ship 826, Mr. Ledieux?"

"No, sir, I was assigned to the aircraft at the next gate. We did a tire change and we replaced a cowling latch on one of the engines."

"Do you know if anyone worked on ship 826?"

"Oh sure, Ray Slackman performed the service check on it."

Ed flipped a page back in his notes and pretended to look for something.

"Oh yeah, I already knew that. You guys must help each other out sometimes when you're working on airplanes next to each other."

"Sometimes we do, but it's pretty much the luck of the draw as to who gets the easy jobs and who gets the tough ones. I think the boss tries to spread it around, but everybody takes their time when they get an easy job like a service check. You try to milk those as long as possible."

Ed laughed.

"I guess that's just human nature."

"Like I said, everybody does it to some extent, but Ray is really good at it."

Ed smiled.

"Sounds like a competition. Why is Ray good at it?"

"Oh, he can find all kinds of obscure things to look at on a service check to stretch it out. For instance, that day, me and another guy were jacking up a jumbo jet and changing a tire while old Ray was sitting on his rear end checking equipment cooling fans."

"That sounds important. What's an equipment cooling fan?"

"It's a fan that draws outside air in and blows it through the equipment racks to cool all the black boxes."

Ed felt like the hair stood up on the back of his neck.

"Well that sounds like something that should be checked."

"Not really. It's not an item on the service check, and it has all kinds of warning lights in the cockpit if it fails."

Ed tried his best to keep a straight face.

"Man, I'm learning all kinds of things about airplanes today. Where are the cooling fans located?"

"They're in the center access compartment in the belly of the airplane."

Ed had to be careful not to show his surprise and interest. He took a moment to frame a casual question and make it sound like he just wanted to learn about airplanes.

"How do you get in there to check them?"

"We have tall wooden stepladders that you have to drag out there to get into the compartment. I was joking around with Ray when I saw him coming out of there and accused him of hiding to take a nap. I even shamed him into buying me a beer after work at the Cavu."

"Now you've really lost me. What is a Cavu?"

Billy laughed.

"The Cavu has nothing to do with airplanes. It's a bar over by the Hilton."

"Mr. Ledieux, I really appreciate your time. Thank you for coming over to talk to us. I hope you don't have to change tires again today."

"We all want to help, Mr. White. I wish I could tell you something more useful."

Billy and the other four mechanics went out to the waiting security van, and Ed hurried down the hall to the Tech Ops team room.

"Jake, I need to talk to you and Gene Clark in the interview room."

When the three men were alone, Ed said, "This Slackman guy is looking better and better for this. One of the other mechanics told me that he saw him coming out of the center access compartment on Wednesday. Slackman told me he didn't open any belly compartments. Jake, is there any reason at all that he would need to go in there on a service check?"

"Not unless he discovered a problem, and he obviously didn't find anything wrong, because there were no logbook entries."

"Okay, we know now that he's lying to us. I can only think of one reason why he would. Unfortunately, lying is not against the law in most cases. We need more than this to make a move, but I'm going to take a much closer look at his background. We also don't want to do anything until we know if other people are involved."

"Ed, you don't think he would do something like this for money, do you?"

"It's possible. I promise you there are a lot of organizations that would love to take down an American air carrier jet over the Atlantic, and they wouldn't hesitate to pay big bucks to do it. But if he's our man, I would bet on good old fashioned revenge for being terminated."

Jake said, "I can't imagine anything that would create enough animosity to intentionally do something as heinous as this."

"You don't want to imagine some of the things I've seen, Jake. Let's keep this between the three of us for now. I don't want to spook him."

Billy Lediuex thought Ray looked like he had just seen a ghost. Ray was in the break area when Billy returned from headquarters, and Billy decided to have some fun with him. "Hey Ray, I think the FBI might arrest you for taking a nap in the center access compartment the other day. I told him you were in there, and I heard loud snoring when I walked by."

The color drained from Ray's face, but he didn't say anything as he walked to his locker and strapped on his tool pouch. When he passed back through the break room, Billy said, "Man, you don't look so good. Are you okay?"

Ray composed himself enough to answer, "Yeah, I think the hot weather is getting to me. I need some fresh air."

He walked out onto the ramp and away from the maintenance shack. He needed to be alone and think.

CHAPTER TWENTY

"*Karuk*, Navy Eight over."

Brian Davis was back on duty in the radio room.

"Navy Eight, go ahead."

"*Karuk*, give me your position. We're going to concentrate the search in your grid. We've got good ceiling and visibility right now, and we don't want to waste it while we still have daylight."

Brian gave him the latitude and longitude of their position.

"We copy, *Karuk*. Are you still working east to west?"

"Affirmative, we're steering a two-seven-zero course. The captain thinks we're on the eastern portion of the debris field based on the flotsam we've picked up."

"Tell him we agree. Did you guys get the word on the number of rafts?"

"Yes sir, a total of eight possible. The flight attendant we picked up said she's sure others were launched, but she doesn't know how many."

"Roger, we'll see you guys in a few minutes."

Brian removed his headset and turned the volume up on the speakers so that he could walk out to the bridge to refill his coffee cup. Lieutenant Strickland agreed to listen up for radio calls, and Brian walked out onto the bridge wing for a breath of fresh air. The temperature was in the seventies, and now that the sun was peeking through the clouds, it was becoming a very pleasant day at sea. Brian looked aft and saw that a number of the survivors had moved out onto the fantail of the ship, three decks below, and were being entertained by the deck apes. The ship was underway once again and leaving a churning wake behind.

He heard one of the lookouts call, "Aircraft approaching, six o'clock low."

Brian looked and saw the gray P3 Orion low on the horizon. He watched the airplane get bigger and realized it was no higher than the ship's mast. Unlike the earlier high-speed pass, this time the flaps were down and they were moving slow. The people on the fantail were pointing in horror because they could see that the propellers on the two outboard engines were not turning. It looked like the airplane was in trouble. As they flew slowly past the starboard side of the ship, the wings dipped and rocked a friendly wave. The smell of jet exhaust from the two turboprop engines permeated the air.

Brian walked back onto the bridge just as the radio crackled.

"Hey *Karuk*, we like your little boat. Do you still have the box it came in?"

Brian answered, "Nah, they didn't have boxes in 1943. Did anybody tell you two of your engines aren't running?"

"Yeah, we know. I think the rubber bands broke or something. We'll send a guy out there to rewind them before we go home. We're going to blanket the northwest corner of your grid. We'll be in touch."

"Okay Navy Eight, we won't go far."

"Somehow I don't doubt that."

Brian watched out the front bridge windows as the Orion climbed to search altitude. He prayed that they would be successful. He went back to his chair in the radio room and wished he could be outside enjoying the fresh air.

Tony thought that if he never experienced fresh ocean air again for the rest of his life, it would be too soon. The people in the three rafts were hungry, and they had not had a lot of success with making drinking water. The rubber rafts were hard and uncomfortable, and after thirty-six hours everyone was miserable and incredibly tired. Tony knew that the priority was survival and not comfort, but nonetheless he felt frustrated in his efforts to care for the survivors, who were becoming increasingly despondent. He was concerned for Nancy and Pam. The fact that there was little he could do for their injuries was frustrating. It was almost certain that they had both suffered at least mild concussions, and he worried every time they slept. Nancy's ankle was terribly swollen and possibly broken. He knew it must be very painful. He admired their courage and mental toughness in the face of such adversity. In fact, it had caused him to have less sympathy for the few whiners in the group than he should have. Britt had quietly explained who Allen Smallwood was and why Pam and Nancy continued to antagonize him. Tony himself had quickly grown tired of Allen's silly questions and self-serving attitude and was happy to let him sulk and pout alone.

The polar opposite was Britt, who refused to complain and continued to exhibit the optimistic attitude that seemed to inspire the others. Even he had drawn strength from her refusal to give in to the terrible circumstances that they found themselves in. With all that had happened, it seemed like a long time ago that he had first seen Britt in the briefing room and noticed how attractive she was. He had been so preoccupied, however, with learning his new duties as an international pilot that he had not allowed himself time to think of a social agenda. But now, time was all he had. They had talked late into the night, and Tony had quickly discovered that she was not only attractive but also intelligent. After evaluating their chances for survival and planning their strategy, the conversation had turned to their personal lives, and Tony now felt that he had known her for years. He was reminded once again how a crisis could strip away all pretension and reveal one's true character and core values. After thirty-six hours adrift in a wet life raft, Britt was filthy, with no hint of makeup remaining and damp, stringy hair plastered to her head. Yet Tony still found her attractive.

With the weather improving as the day wore on, Tony had rewarded the people's patience with a small ration of the energy bars they had discovered in the survival pack and also a mouthful of the foul-tasting water they had distilled. His own lips were parched and felt like they would soon crack. He knew that dehydration would soon become their biggest enemy. He laid his head back against the side of the raft and closed his eyes in order to concentrate on what else he could do to improve their conditions and odds of survival.

During the morning, the raft had settled into periods of dead silence as everyone tried to conserve whatever energy that remained. Now it was so quiet that Tony thought, *This must be what outer space is like*. Tony became conscious of a faint noise that sounded like a portable fan running. He opened his eyes and scanned the horizon, but saw nothing at all. The sound seemed to increase in volume and had a slight irritation to it. Then it became downright annoying as he recognized the one thing that all pilots could not stand. It was not one fan running, but two, and they were out of sync. Somewhere nearby there were two propellers out of sync, and, for once in Tony's life, it was a beautiful sound. The low throb and thrum was clearly audible now, even though he still could not see anything. He scrambled across the floor of the raft and opened the survival pack. He removed the flare gun and the sea dye marker. He moved to the downwind side of the raft. No one else had heard the airplane, and they all watched, wondering if their leader had lost his mind.

Tony pointed the flare gun high and slightly away from the raft, then pulled the trigger. A red fireball streaked into the sky and arched across the sea. Next he popped the sea dye and put it in the water, turning it bright green as it spread in an increasing fluorescent circle around them. He jumped into the other rafts and retrieved their flare guns, but did not fire them. He hoped he would not have to. The droning noise was getting louder, and now everyone could hear it. Suddenly the most beautiful P3 Orion Tony had ever seen popped up over the southeast horizon and went into low orbit over the three rafts. People were screaming, waving, crying, and celebrating all at once. It was an amazing feeling, but not as amazing as how he felt when Britt hugged him.

"*Karuk*, Navy Eight."

"Go ahead, Navy Eight."

"You guys have more work to do. We've got three rafts at your one o'clock and eleven miles. We'll orbit until you get us in sight. Suggest a two-nine-zero initial heading."

"Outstanding, Navy Eight. Copy two-nine-zero and eleven miles. We're on the way."

Captain Maxwell heard the report over the speakers and immediately ordered, "Come right, new course steady two-nine-zero, make turns for flank speed."

"Steady, two-nine-zero and flank speed. Aye, sir."

"Radio, find out how many people are in those rafts and give them an ETA of forty minutes."

Brian had been on the ship over a year and Maxwell still called him Radio. He always gave the same response: "Radio, aye, sir."

"Navy Eight, *Karuk* estimates forty minutes en route. How many people in the rafts?"

"Looks like sixty or so total. The rafts are lashed together, and it's hard to get a count."

"Thanks, Eight."

That was close enough for Captain Maxwell.

"Lieutenant Strickland, I want you to go below and organize a field day for the crew berthing compartment and head. Notify the crew that those spaces are off-limits to them until further notice. As soon as it's clean, you can move the civilians in and set a schedule for the showers to be used by the ladies and then the men. Make sure they understand what a navy shower is, or we'll be out of fresh water before dark. The crew can sack out wherever they can find a place on deck. The snipes sleep in the engine room half the time anyway. Talk to the chief and make it happen."

"Aye-aye, sir."

Twenty minutes later, the Orion had modified its slow orbit to a racetrack pattern and climbed to twenty-five hundred feet so the *Karuk* could spot them sooner. As Todd made the turn at the northwest corner of the pattern, one of the crewmembers in the back keyed his interphone and reported, "Skipper, we got another flare at three o'clock in the turn."

Todd rolled right to a sixty-degree bank, and as he muscled the airplane around, he spotted the flare dying out but leaving a clear smoke trail hanging in the air. The copilot said, "This is like looking for the pot of gold at the end of the rainbow."

Todd said, "Remind me to tell you my leprechaun joke later."

The Orion increased speed and flew away to the north, causing Allen Smallwood to jump up and down, screaming at them to come back or face litigation. It wasn't until Tony pointed out the smoke from the *Karuk*'s single stack approaching from the east that he calmed down. Britt commented that the twelve-year-old in Pam's raft was more mature and probably more intelligent.

"*Karuk*, Navy Eight."

"Go ahead, sir."

"We've got more business for you. We're orbiting a single raft four miles north of the first group. Looks like about twenty customers aboard."

"Roger, Navy Eight. Copy four miles north and twenty souls."

"You guys have enough chow for all these people?"

"Yes sir, it's mystery meat tonight. There are always plenty of leftovers."

Robby Jenner and his eighteen raft mates did not know they would be served mystery meat, but they would enjoy every morsel.

Melissa Jenner pushed the food around on the plate, but had little appetite for the lunch that Tri Con had provided. The group was considerably more encouraged since the report of survivors, but Melissa somehow innately knew that the rescued crewmember was not Robby. She and Pattie had discussed the emotional peaks and valleys of the last two days, and when someone turned the TV volume up, she braced herself for more pessimistic sensationalism.

"This just in from the Department of Defense. The US Navy has recovered survivors from the Tri Con crash in the Atlantic. A public information officer is confirming that forty-one people were found floating in a life raft earlier today and are now aboard the *USS Karuk*. There were no names released, but we are pursuing that information now. There were over two hundred passengers and crew aboard the doomed airliner, and the spokesman could not offer encouragement that more survivors might be found. The tragic loss of that many lives has generated a public outcry against the airline and its operations. We're hearing that Tri Con's bookings have fallen off drastically and many people are canceling reservations. As we reported earlier, the federal government is investigating the airline and its safety practices. A spokesman for the National Transportation Safety Board confirmed that investigators are onsite at Tri Con headquarters, and others are on their way to the Azores. In addition to the NTSB, the FBI is also investigating the possibility of terrorism.

Summing up what we have learned, forty-one survivors have been rescued with little hope of finding more. At six o'clock we will be interviewing more of the victims' families and also the federal officials conducting the investigation. Stay tuned for more late-breaking details that we expect to report soon."

The anchorwoman's image faded and was replaced by a commercial for a trial lawyer specializing in accident litigation. By now Colt had educated everyone as to how phony the news media could be, but they looked to him for his analysis anyway. He pointed out the fallacy of the report and explained that the trial lawyer would have paid a premium for the commercial spot immediately following the sensational report that the federal government was investigating, which of course was entirely routine in any accident. The lawyer had probably helped write the news bulletin.

The family hostess quietly approached Candace Whitton's husband and daughter. "Mr. Whitton, could I have a word with you and your daughter please?"

They followed her into the hallway without anyone noticing. Bob Whitton was in his late sixties, and his daughter was in her early forties. They both automatically assumed the worst.

When they were alone, the hostess said, "Mr. Collins would like for you to join him in his office for a few minutes if you don't mind. If you'll follow me, I'll take you up there now."

"Do you know why he wants to see us?"

"I'm afraid I don't, sir. The message just said he would like to speak to you in private right away."

They followed her, forcing themselves to put one foot in front of the other and bracing themselves for what they might be about to hear. Harold Collins was waiting for them in the corridor outside his suite of offices. They were encouraged by the smile on his face.

"I have great news for you. Candace is aboard the navy ship, and she is just fine. I thought you might like to hear this in private before I share it with everyone else." Tears came to both of their eyes, and they embraced each other and then Harold Collins, who also had tears on his cheeks.

"Would you like to accompany me to tell the others?"

"Yes, we would. I think we should stay and support everyone else until we get more news."

"I'm sure they will appreciate that. I can't yet tell you where or when we can reunite you with Candace, but we'll make whatever arrangements we have to."

Candace Whitton stood on the deck of the *Karuk* and watched as the ship approached the little flotilla of three rafts. She watched the small boats being lowered in the davits. She was familiar with the routine from her own rescue. She strained to see who was in the rafts, but the ship had stopped too far away to recognize individuals. She could, however, pick out several red life vests, and she knew they were crewmembers. When the first boat approached the rafts, she knew they would be told to stay put so that the boat could tow them safely to the ship. Knowing that, she watched in amazement as an individual wearing a yellow vest jumped up on the side of the raft, waving his arms and gesturing wildly. His weight on the inflated rubber sidewall caused the raft to become unbalanced, and his arms began wind milling as he fell over the side, making a huge splash of saltwater. He continued to flail with his arms until one of the divers reached him and helped him into the lifeboat. Even from a distance, it was apparent that the occupants of the rafts had been burdened with some sort of mental midget who had succumbed to the forces of fear and paranoia. Thankfully she had not had to deal with that in her raft.

The divers separated the rafts, and the boats towed them alongside the dive platform. The first people brought aboard were Pam and Nancy with their injuries. Candace gave them both big hugs before they were taken to the little sick bay below decks. She waved to Britt, Mary Dobson, and Tony in the rafts alongside. She also now recognized the imbecile in the lifeboat as Allen Smallwood. The next group to be brought aboard was women and children, although Britt and Mary refused to leave until all the passengers were transferred. Candace noticed that the young boy and girl, who had helped their family save Pam, were not traumatized, but were in fact treating the whole affair as a great adventure. It never ceased to amaze her how different individuals responded in terms of courage, confidence, and faith.

Once everyone was aboard and the boats recovered, the ship moved off to the north in the direction of the circling Orion. An announcement was made alerting everyone that another rescue was already underway and the Tri Con crewmembers waited in anticipation to see who else would be picked up. They calculated the total survivors to this point and came up with one hundred and eight aboard the *Karuk*, including the six crewmembers.

It only took a few minutes to cover the four miles, using the circling Orion as guidance. They could soon see the single yellow raft and its waving occupants. Tony borrowed a set of binoculars from one of the lookouts and informed the others that Robby Jenner would be joining them shortly. The *Karuk* deck apes had become proficient at the rescue procedures, and they pulled this one off without anyone falling in the sea. Robby's first words to Tony and the flight attendants were, "Do we get paid extra for this?"

Captain Maxwell ordered the search to resume immediately and had the yeoman start collecting personal data from the new survivors. He had Brian Davis transmit a message conveying that the *Karuk* now had rescued one hundred and twenty-seven, including seven crewmembers. The mess deck and the fantail were now crowded with people, so the captain convened the surviving crew in the wardroom. He ordered Doc to bring Pam and Nancy, and they arrived with deck apes carrying them on stretchers. Allen Smallwood had been taken below deck to get out of his wet clothes and have them dried in the ship's laundry. The men working in the laundry had found clothes for him to wear temporarily. The bellbottom dungarees fit in the waist but were about eight inches too short and fell well above the ankle-high boondocker boots and black socks. The blue work shirt was several sizes too large and bloused out around the waist. He was not in danger of being featured on a recruiting poster.

The captain addressed the flight crew seated at the wardroom table. "First, let me congratulate you on your performance. Each of you are to be commended for saving lives and providing leadership in trying circumstances. I know you want to rest, but before you do we need to discuss what you might know that will help me find other survivors. I want to hear from each of you individually. I think it would be a good idea if you write notes as we talk, so you can record your thoughts while they are relatively fresh in your mind. I've provided notebooks for each of you, and you can keep them to continue keeping record of anything you think you will need later. We should probably start with the pilots."

Robby spoke first.

"Thank you, Captain. I have a request. When we finish here, I would like for Tony and myself to transmit what we know about the cause of the accident to Tri Con. There might be other airplanes in danger of the same problem, and they'll want to inspect them."

"That's not a problem. It will be our next priority."

Robby said, "As far as other survivors, I was on the flight deck during landing, and afterward myself and Captain Wells were trapped by a jammed door for a short time. Once we hacked our way out, we found Britt had begun the evacuation at the one left door. Nancy was unconscious at the other forward door. Charlie and I moved her to Britt's raft and then cleared the one right door. We launched the two rafts with all the business class passengers, and Charlie went aft to help the others."

Tony went next.

"I was at the over wing area for landing, and Candace, Mary, and myself deployed both rafts from there. Charlie showed up, helped us load and launch, and then went aft to the rear doors."

Maxwell said, "Okay, two rafts were launched at the front doors and two at the over wing area. Where was the fifth raft launched?"

Pam answered, "That would be my raft at the two-left door, but I won't be much help. I was knocked unconscious during the crash and came to in the raft later. I was saved by a family that was smart enough to open the door and deploy the raft."

"All right, I was led to believe that there were eight possible rafts. Is that correct?"

Robby answered, "That's right, we have not accounted for the two-right door or the four-left and right doors at the very rear."

Pam suddenly gasped.

"Oh no! Bertie was at the two-right door. She had that little girl with her. The family in my raft told me that the entire exit area was covered with heavy debris that they couldn't move. They told me that all the other passengers went aft when they saw the door blocked. It's all a blank to me, but I should have helped Bertie."

Britt said, "Pam, how could you help if you were unconscious? There was nothing you could do. We can only hope that Charlie helped her or she went aft with everyone else."

"If she went aft, Britt, she would be in the raft with Tony or Candace. Did either of you see Bertie or the unaccompanied minor?"

They both said no.

Maxwell said, "I'll speak to the family that opened your door and see what they can tell us, but for now can we assume that raft wasn't launched?"

Everyone agreed it probably wasn't.

"Now, that leaves the two rafts at the rear of the airplane. Is there any way to know if they were launched before the airplane sank?"

No one could say with any certainty one way or the other.

Britt said, "Captain, I should tell you that there were a large number of handicapped passengers in that section of the airplane. It would have been time-consuming to evacuate them. I only hope that at least some of them escaped. There were two flight attendants back there, and I also sent a flight attendant supervisor to assist them. She just happened to be traveling on the flight and offered to help."

Tony added, "Don't forget, Charlie went aft also, after he helped us launch."

Captain Maxwell said, "All right, based on what we know I think we have to continue to search for at least two more rafts, and that's what we're going to do. I'll leave you to enjoy the hospitality of the *USS Karuk*, but keep the notebooks handy and write down anything that might help now or later. I'll be available twenty-four hours a day if you think of anything. For planning purposes, I assume we will be relieved by other ships soon, and at that time I have been led to believe that we will be ordered to proceed to the Azores, where you will be provided transportation."

Everyone thanked the captain again. He turned to Robby and Tony, "If you gentlemen will come with me, I'll take you to the radio shack, where you can compose and transmit your information. I'll put you in the capable hands of my best radioman. His name is Brian Davis, but he likes to be called Radio."

Neither pilot noticed the smile on the captain's face as he turned away.

Pam and Nancy were returned to sickbay, which was located next to the ship's laundry. They quickly befriended the laundry workers, and Allen's Armani suit would mysteriously disappear and never be seen again.

CHAPTER TWENTY-ONE

At Tri Con headquarters, things were happening fast. Harold Collins had received two communications in the last few minutes from the *Karuk* via the Department of Defense. Both required immediate attention. He couldn't do two things at once, so he elected to delegate. He told his secretary to put out the word for Jake Smith to report to his office right away. Then he had her dial the crew family room and see if Colt Adams was there. A moment later his intercom buzzed, and she said, "Sir, Captain Adams is on line three."

He picked up the phone and said, "Colt, I'm glad you're still there. I need a favor."

"What can I do for you, Mr. Collins?"

"Look, I appreciate what you've done for our people down there, and I can tell they all look up to you. I want to share some information with you and then ask you to pass it on to the relatives. I can't come down there because I also received other information that I have to act on right away. In fact, when you're finished there I'd like for you to come to my office and discuss this other thing too."

He related what he had learned from the Department of Defense and Colt agreed to tell the families. When he hung up the phone, he walked over and closed the door. This time he told the hostess she could stay but she had to sit by the door and not let

231

anyone open it. She was now thinking about cooking dinner for Colt instead of going out with him.

He moved to the front of the room and asked for everyone's attention.

"Mr. Collins asked me to pass along some good news that he has received. He apologizes for not coming down himself, but he wanted you to get this without delay. More survivors have been rescued. The USS Karuk now has one hundred and twenty-seven survivors on board, including seven crewmembers. And, just to prove that I could never be a newsman, I'll add that there are no known fatalities."

The room erupted in applause.

"Now, since all the crew has not been rescued yet, there's no good way to handle this, but after all we've been through together, I'm simply going to read the names to you. Then we're going to deal with it as a group."

There was an audible gasp from some of the family members because they had not expected to receive actual names, based on what happened earlier.

Colt said, "The only reason we have names is because one of the crew was able to send an official message concerning the cause of the accident, and instead of signing it with one name he signed it with seven. That was Robby Jenner."

Melissa almost fainted. She sat down and buried her head in her hands.

"Tony Johnson was also rescued. I'm sorry Pattie; we haven't heard from Charlie, but we will. The lead flight attendant, Britt Fowler, is safely on board, as are Mary Dobson, Nancy Hammond, and Pam Arnold. We already know that Candace is okay, so that makes seven crew in all. This is just more proof that the landing was survivable, and I'm confident we will get more good news. Mr. Collins promised that he will let us know as soon as he gets more information."

The celebration in the room would have been much more ebullient, were it not for the fact that four families plus Molly Jackson's mother still suffered in limbo. Allen Smallwood's wife had been invited to join them, but elected not to. Colt offered encouragement to them and was happy to see that everyone remained to give their support.

Colt explained to Pattie where he was going and quietly left the room. When he arrived at Collin's office, the secretary escorted him into a conference room where he found Collins, Jake Smith, Phil James, and the two federal representatives, Gene Clark and Ed White. Harold Collins filled Colt in on what Robby had reported. The dump valves had mysteriously opened and could not be closed. Phil had not been able to find any plausible scenario that would allow that to accidentally happen to one dump valve, much less two. Now that they knew what happened, it was all about how and why. Ed White was reluctant to name Ray Slackman an actual suspect, based on what they knew so far.

"Gentlemen, we simply don't have any real proof. No matter what we think we know, the justice system requires certain benchmarks that must be met in order to accuse someone. We have to keep looking if this is going to stick."

As Ed was talking, his cell phone was vibrating. He looked at the caller ID. "Excuse me guys, I have to take this."

He walked to the end of the room and took the call. Jake and Phil continued to explain that what happened couldn't happen. Colt went through the scenario in his mind and could not think of anything that Charlie could have done to prevent the accident.

Ed ended his call and walked back to the group.

"We may have a break. The local office received a call from a woman who claims she may have information for us. She's agreed to come here to talk, and I've arranged transportation for her."

Colt asked, "Who is she?"

"An employee at a local bar, The Cavu Lounge. Her name is Annie Jordan, and she should be here shortly."

Twenty minutes later, Ed walked into the interview room.

"Ms. Jordan, my name is Ed White. I'm a special agent with the FBI. Thank you for coming by to talk to us."

Annie shook hands and said, "I don't know if I can help or not, Mr. White. I don't want to get anyone in trouble, but I couldn't sleep last night thinking about this."

"Well, this is quite a tragedy, ma'am. If you can shed any light at all on it, you'd certainly be doing the right thing. Our policy is to keep information as confidential as possible. Why don't you just tell me what's on your mind?"

"Well, I've heard a lot of employees talking about the crash, and last night some of the mechanics were talking about the fuel system and saying the airplane ran out of gas."

"That's one of the theories we're looking at. Do you have reason to believe that's what happened?"

"Mr. White, I don't know anything about airplanes at all, but since everybody is talking about the fuel system, I remembered seeing something a few days ago that had to do with airplane fuel."

"Can you tell me what that was about?"

"Well, one of the Tri Con mechanics was in the bar this week, and he was pretty upset that he was going to be let go. He had quite a few beers and was looking at some papers he had with him. He told me it was a love letter to Tri Con's bottom line, or something like that. I didn't think much about it at the time, but when he went to the restroom, I wiped down the bar and picked the papers up so I didn't get them wet. There was a Tri Con logo at the top of the page and under that it said something about fuel. Like I said, it may not mean anything, but I keep thinking about all those people dying and thought I should say something."

"You absolutely did the right thing, Ms. Jordan. We depend on good citizens like you to come forward, even if the information turns out to be unrelated. Can you remember exactly what was on the paper?"

"I don't think so. I just remember it was about fuel."

"Was it all writing and words or did it have pictures or something like that?"

"Oh, wait a minute, I remember now. It was a diagram of some sort, and it had a funny word at the top that sounded technical. I think it started with an *s*."

"Did the diagram have thick lines or double lines like pipes, or were they thin lines like electrical wires?"

"Oh yeah, it said something about electrical too."

"Okay, was the technical word *schematic*?"

"That's it! I've been trying to remember that word."

"You're doing great, Ms. Jordan. Now, the fuel system involves a lot of different things, but the electricity usually opens and closes valves and operates pumps. Did the paper say anything about valves or pumps?"

"Oh wow! I do remember what it said. It was something like, Electrical Schematic Fuel Dump Valves."

"Great. Sometimes you remember much more than you think. By the way, do you remember this mechanic's name?"

"Oh sure, he comes in all the time. His name is Ray Slackman."

"Can you think of anything else that might be relevant, ma'am?"

"I don't think so. None of this may mean anything."

"You may be right, but can I get some information on how to reach you if I need to?"

Ed wrote down the information and escorted Annie out. He asked her not to discuss her visit with anyone, and she agreed.

A few minutes later, Ed rejoined the others in the conference room.

"Gentlemen, I think we have our why and how. We have a viable witness who can attest to the fact that Ray Slackman harbors a grudge against Tri Con and can also place in his possession documents that could be used to sabotage Tri Con Flight Eleven. I don't think we have enough to charge him with sabotage at this point, but we're close. It's time to bring him in. I plan to get a warrant for his arrest and charge him with lying to a federal officer and obstructing a federal investigation. I think he might fold under interrogation, but if not, at least he will be in custody while we gather more evidence."

Charlie had seen no evidence of rescue since the pre-dawn sweeping searchlight. The day was slipping away, and the shadow of the raft was growing longer. He shuddered to think of another night in the crowded raft. Most of the twenty-one handicapped people were taking prescription drugs of one sort or another and had watched them sink with the airplane. No one had considered taking time to recover personal belongings in the rush to evacuate. They had been very fortunate to get themselves out and had barely made it in time.

The distant searchlight had been so encouraging and yet had resulted in absolutely nothing. The weather had also been a plus today. Ceiling and visibility had improved steadily, and a search plane could have spotted them from miles away. Charlie and Molly struggled to find any little sign that would offer encouragement and hope to the survivors, but they were losing credibility as the hours passed with no sign of civilization. Even Molly's skill at finding positive solutions to difficult circumstances was being severely tested. The one advantage they had was that all of the handicapped passengers had faced extreme challenges before and had learned to deal with it.

Charlie still suffered periodic bouts of guilt and depression because he blamed himself for everything that had gone wrong. He now wished that he had fired the flare when they saw the searchlight earlier. He had not experienced many options during the entire ordeal, but he felt that he had consistently chosen the wrong one when given the opportunity. In addition to everything else, he had begun to worry about Pattie. He knew what she must be going through, and once again he blamed himself. Those thoughts were compounded by realizing that everyone in the rafts had loved ones grieving for them also. Charlie offered up many silent prayers as the day wore on.

Another thing that he and Molly had discussed several times was what happened to the other rafts. They had all begun at the exact same place and time, and yet even with the increased visibility, the others were nowhere in sight. Charlie knew for a fact that seven rafts had launched. Only the two-right door had been inaccessible. He had personally seen all other rafts away. He tried to think of all the factors that would affect how far and fast a raft would drift. He finally concluded that the other rafts probably drifted farther away than his raft. Both Shelia's raft and his were relatively heavy and had both deployed the sea anchor early on. This presented another rare option. Should he pull the sea anchors and drift to the east or leave them deployed and stay in the area? They would never catch the other rafts with a two-day head start anyway, and every survival manual said stay with the wreckage. They actually had no wreckage, but at least they could stay near the last reported position.

He took some satisfaction from the fact that he could still think logically and rationalize facts, but it wasn't going to make a difference in this case. His thought process was interrupted when someone made a loud whooping noise. Both rafts erupted in shouts and applause when the grinning fisherman held up a wriggling fish about ten inches long. Shouts of, "Sushi for dinner" and, "Start the fire" made everyone laugh. Molly encouraged the celebration to continue by making jokes and funny comments. Any break from the monotony was a good thing, and everybody wanted to enjoy the moment. The rafts were joyous, rowdy, and extremely noisy. Nobody saw or heard the P3 Orion until it roared overhead at one hundred feet.

Suddenly there was a stunned silence in the rafts. Seventy-eight people sat with their eyes wide and mouths open. Charlie felt a moment of panic when he thought the airplane had not seen them, but it only went a short distance before pulling up into a lazy chandelle to reverse direction. It went into orbit above the rafts. He closed his eyes and said another silent prayer of gratitude.

"*Karuk*, Navy Eight."

"Go ahead, Navy Eight."

"You better tell the cook to get out more mystery meat. We've got two more strays for you to round up. Looks like seventy to eighty hungry people."

"Roger that. The more the merrier. I've already been thrown out of the berthing compartment, and I have to make an appointment to use the restroom, so a few more won't matter."

Ed White made the call and obtained the federal warrant, then called the airport division of the local police. He faxed the warrant and asked them to pick up Ray Slackman. He planned to interview Ray at the airport holding cells and confront him with the new information that he had received. With a little luck, he could get a confession and be home for dinner. He was still talking with Harold Collins and Jake Smith when his cell phone vibrated.

The conversation was short, and when he ended the call, he said, "We've got problems. Slackman hasn't been seen all afternoon."

Collins asked, "Do you think he knows we're on to him?"

"Yeah, I think he figured it out somehow. I put out an all-points bulletin on him and his truck, and the local police are sitting on his house. I also asked for a search warrant for his locker at work and his home. We've got plenty of probable cause now."

Jake asked, "What can we do to help, Ed?"

"There is one thing. I'd like to borrow Phil James for a while. I'm going straight to Slackman's house, and I don't have a clue what I'm looking for. Phil might recognize something to do with airplanes that I would overlook."

"I'll get him for you."

Thirty minutes later, Ed and Phil stopped in front of Ray's house. It was an older, single level home on a quiet residential street near the airport. Ed identified himself to the police officers in the patrol car guarding the house, and a minute later, two more FBI agents arrived with the search warrant. They opened the trunk of one of the cars and removed an evidence kit. When they approached the front door, Ed had Phil wait to the side, and one of the agents walked to the rear of the house. Ed and the other agent went through the formality of knocking on the door and identifying themselves. Once they were sure nobody was there, the other agent asked, "You want me to kick it open?"

Ed faked a shocked expression, "How primitive. There's a policeman right out front. We could be arrested for vandalism."

The other agent laughed as Ed reached into his coat pocket and removed a small tool kit. Ten seconds later the cheap lock was open. Ed gave Phil a set of booties to put over his shoes and a pair of latex gloves to wear. He instructed Phil not to touch anything unless he asked him to.

The three agents were thorough and meticulous. They had obviously had a lot of practice, and went through the house one room at a time, not missing anything along the way. They looked in places Phil would never have thought of and found very little of interest, other than a twenty-two caliber pistol in a dresser drawer and some irate letters from his ex-wife concerning alimony payments. The patrolman outside came to the front door and called Ed without coming inside. He passed the message that Ray's truck had been found in the employee parking lot and apparently had not been moved since he arrived early for his day shift. Ed said, "There's a good chance he's still on the airport property somewhere. He'll show up eventually."

By the time they began searching the kitchen, the only things they had bagged for evidence were the gun and a laptop computer, which would be examined at the lab. One of the agents went to the small trashcan and started picking through the items one at a time. Phil noticed that he began carefully laying scraps of paper on the kitchen table. After a few minutes the agent called to Ed.

"We might have something here, boss."

Ed went to the table and started rearranging the scraps of paper.

"I hate jigsaw puzzles."

The agent drew another scrap from the trash and said, "This looks like part of a Tri Con logo."

"Phil, you better look at this."

Phil looked at the scraps and immediately recognized the layout of a Tri Con maintenance manual page. He said, "I've seen a million of these, let me put it together."

Ed made sure Phil had the gloves on and said, "Knock yourself out."

Two minutes later the entire page was reassembled on the table. Phil said, "I don't believe this."

"What is it?" Ed asked.

"It's the dump valve electrical schematic, but the interesting thing is the handwritten notes. He rigged the dump valves to open when the aft transfer pumps powered up. I would never have figured this out on my own. This is incredible. I need to analyze this against the flight profile of Flight Eleven, but I'm betting it's going to fit perfectly with the timeline of the accident."

"How long will that take?"

"I can set it up in the simulator, fly the profile, and see exactly how it would play out. Once we program it, I can fast forward to somewhere east of Gander and then watch in real time. We'll know in a couple of hours."

"Beautiful. All we need now is Mr. Slackman. I'm going to call for a new warrant charging him with sabotage, terrorism, and possibly murder. We need to get more men around the airport and comb till we find him."

One of the other agents said, "Ed, he's already inside the security perimeter. TSA won't be any help at all."

"Maybe they can help keep him inside, but he could be anywhere on the property."

Phil said, "This might not be easy, Ed. There are lots of places to hide on a huge airport, especially with an employee badge."

"We'll find him."

Ed made several digital photographs of the page on the table, and then they bagged the scraps for evidence.

"I'll print you a copy of this, Phil, for your analysis. Let's go for a simulator ride."

CHAPTER TWENTY-TWO

Charlie watched the Orion climb to a higher altitude. It began lazy circles above the raft. Now that they had been located, he wondered how the rescue would take place. He assumed a surface ship would eventually show up; he scanned the horizon, hoping it would come soon. Now that the crisis was over, the people in the two rafts cheered him as their hero and lifted his spirits. They waited for over an hour, then spotted the black smoke on the southeast horizon signifying the arrival of the *Karuk*. The little ship maneuvered to within a few hundred feet and then turned broadside to the rafts. Charlie was elated to see the deck railings lined with civilians and realized that many others had also survived.

Alice Elon had tears in her eyes.

"There's Britt and Mary Dobson."

Charlie spotted Robby and Tony, and they waved and saluted. Molly continued to banter with the people in the rafts, and she and Charlie declared that since the handicapped were the last off the airplane, they would be first to leave the rafts. The long ordeal was over, and the looks of relief on passengers' faces were a beautiful thing to see.

The rafts were towed alongside the dive platform, and the handicapped were taken aboard. The process was time-consuming, as they were assisted from the rafts and then physically carried onto the ship once the platform was raised to the main deck. Charlie insisted on being the last to leave the raft, and Molly insisted on waiting with him. When the two of them were finally lifted to the deck, a loud cheer went up from the passengers and crew. Charlie waved as he limped aboard on his sprained ankle, and Molly took a slow bow as her red hair cascaded across her face. Captain Maxwell greeted Charlie with a salute and a handshake.

The Tri Con crew, along with Molly Jackson, was once again assembled in the wardroom to debrief. Charlie refused medical attention until after the meeting. Captain Maxwell announced that the number of survivors on board now totaled two hundred and five. Charlie said, "I can confirm one fatality. I left one deceased male passenger in the mid cabin with a broken neck. I planned to go back and recover his body, but there just wasn't time. I had hoped he was the only fatality."

Britt said, "Charlie, the other two missing people are Bertie Martin and the unaccompanied minor. They were sitting at the two-right door, and one of the passengers reported that the exit was completely blocked with heavy debris that couldn't be moved. The same passenger saved Pam, who was unconscious, and launched her raft at two-left with his family and a couple of other people."

Charlie looked down and paused a moment, then raised his eyes once again.

"I saw the debris at two-right, and it did appear to be impassable, but when I noticed the raft at two-left was gone, I assumed everyone left in it. I should have taken time to check closer."

Captain Maxwell said, "It sounds to me like you did the right thing, Captain Wells. You have to base decisions on the greater good, and you obviously did that. You saved the greatest number of people in the shortest amount of time. Taking the delay of trying to move the wreckage at the door might have doomed all the people you evacuated after that. You barely got them out as it was."

Pam said, "You can talk to the passenger who tried to move it, Charlie. He had two teenage sons with him and they couldn't budge it. There is no way you could have done more by yourself."

Captain Maxwell said, "I think you all performed heroically. I'm sure you will be commended and your deeds celebrated. Let me fill you in on the situation as it stands now. There are numerous ships in the area, with more on the way. We have been relieved of our search duties. The mission will continue for quite some time, and of course, as much wreckage and flotsam as possible will be recovered. As for us, we will be underway shortly and proceed to the Azores. I expect to make port late tomorrow. We will dock at the island of Terceira. The port is located at Praia da Vitoria and is only a few miles from the air base at Lajes. Meanwhile, we will make you as comfortable as possible while you are with us. I'm afraid we don't have enough berths for everyone, but the accommodations will be better than another night in a life raft. Fortunately, we have plenty of food and beverages, and I've instructed the cook to have open mess from now until midnight. My officers and I are available at all times for any request or concerns that you may have."

Charlie said, "Captain, we would all like to let our families know that we are safe. Is that possible?"

"Already underway, sir. My yeoman is compiling the information as we speak, and it will be transmitted shortly. In fact, if you'd care to join me on the bridge, Captain Wells, we'll make sure that happens right away."

Charlie followed Maxwell, hobbling up the stairs to the bridge, and looked out over the vast ocean as they waited for the yeoman. Captain Maxwell was giving him the tour when the speakers came alive. "*Karuk*, Navy Eight is going home. Well done, gentlemen, it's been a pleasure working with you."

Maxwell said, "Standby, Radio."

He turned to Charlie, "Would you like to respond to that, Captain Wells?"

Charlie took the mike from Brian Davis.

"Navy Eight, my name is Charlie Wells. I'm the captain from Tri Con Eleven. On behalf of my crew and passengers, sir, thank you for saving our lives. There are two hundred and five men, women, and children here who would like to shake your hands. That Orion was a beautiful sight when we thought we might die."

Lieutenant Todd Gray replied, "You're very welcome, captain. Congratulations on a job well done yourself. There would have been no one to save if you had not made a great landing. Did you dead stick it?"

"No, we had one engine operating to help control the approach, and we got very lucky. We owe you our lives."

"Give the credit to *Karuk*, captain. All we do is sit on our butt and look out the window."

"Your modesty is wasted on me, sir. You and your crew are heroes, like it or not."

"I'll pass that on to them, captain, but I like to keep them humble as much as possible. Enjoy your cruise on *Karuk*, sir. So long."

"Roger that Navy Eight, so long."

He handed the mike back to Brian and turned to see the yeoman arrive with the latest list of survivors. Brian loaded the information and data linked it via satellite to fleet. Charlie looked out the bridge windows to the east and watched as dusk approached over the sea. Suddenly he was starving.

Pattie Wells heard her stomach growl and looked around to see if anyone else heard it. Fortunately, everyone was talking, and she did not have to be embarrassed. It was appalling that she could be hungry at a time like this. What would the others think if they saw her stuffing groceries down her throat when her husband's fate was unknown? She looked at the food on the table and fought back the urge, but there was no doubt that her appetite had returned with a vengeance. She thought the pressure must be getting to her, because it was as if Charlie was laughing at her in her confusion. She sat alone and tried to sort out her emotions, but was interrupted by her cell phone ringing. She opened it and said, "Hello."

"Pattie, it's Colt. I'm still in Harold Collins' office, and you've got to keep a secret for a few minutes."

"What are you talking about, Colt?"

"A new message just came in, and Harold is on his way down to announce it, but I wanted you to know right away. Don't say anything to the others, because I don't have all the details, but Charlie has been rescued, and he's in good shape."

Pattie couldn't speak.

"Pattie, are you there?"

"Yes, thank you Colt. Are you sure?"

"I'm positive. I'll be down in a few minutes."

Pattie closed the little phone, got up from her seat, and walked to the buffet table. She heaped food onto a plate and didn't care what anyone thought.

As she sat down to eat, Harold Collins called the room to attention.

"Folks, we have more good news. Seventy-eight more people have been rescued, and three of them are crewmembers. Charlie Wells, Shelia Graham, and Alice Elon have been picked up and are in good health. Mrs. Jackson, I'm happy to say that Molly is also aboard the ship and in good shape."

The room erupted once again and hugs were shared. When it quieted down he said, "We only have one more crew member to find, and that's Bertie Martin. I understand that Bertie's husband has left for a doctor's appointment, but I hope you will all continue to support him when he returns. I plan to speak with him personally and pledge that our efforts will continue unabated. In fact, we can now concentrate all our resources on this one task. Unfortunately, we have two other passengers unaccounted for, and I ask that each of you continue your prayers.

"I also have another announcement. We have been informed that all the survivors are en route to the Azores aboard the *USS Karuk*. They expect to arrive in port late tomorrow. I would like for all of you to be on the pier when they dock, and I have set up an airplane to make that possible. You and any family members you choose are welcome to make the trip. We will provide hotel rooms and whatever else is required. We have a tentative departure time of eight o'clock this evening, and Captain Colt Adams has graciously volunteered to be your chauffeur. I hope that will give you time to go home and pack. I suggest we meet back here at seven and go to the airplane together. If that's a problem for anyone, please let me know as soon as possible. I also suggest that you pack a change of clothes for the crew. I doubt if they saved their luggage."

Jenny Kramer was still babysitting Pattie and Melissa and offered to drive them home to pack. She had security check to make sure the media hounds were not still camped in front of their houses, and then they left with Pattie munching a roast beef sandwich and a pack of chips. Jenny informed them that she too had volunteered to fly the trip as lead flight attendant, and the family room hostess would be a part of the crew also.

When they arrived at Pattie's house, Jenny and Melissa watched TV as Pattie packed. The news bulletins had been coming fast and furious all afternoon, and the public had been served a steady diet of trial attorney advertisements following each one. The latest bulletin was introduced with a graphic of a Tri Con jet and the superimposed words "Tragic investigation." Of course, this was accompanied by dramatic music symbolizing a funeral procession.

"We continue to gather facts and information on the Tri Con tragedy. It now appears as though the death toll may be just three people. We have learned that one flight attendant and two passengers are still missing and presumed dead. The passenger list has not been released, but we can report that the crewmember listed as a fatality is sixty-two year old Bertha Martin. Ms. Martin is a local resident and is survived by her husband, two children, and four grandchildren, who all live in the Atlanta area.

"We reported earlier that all three pilots survived the crash and will be facing investigation as to why they failed to complete the flight safely. Captain Charles Wells was in command, and repeated attempts to interview his wife, Mrs. Patricia Wells, have resulted in 'No comment.' Stay tuned as we continue to monitor developments."

Now that the death toll had been drastically reduced, the bulletin was followed by an Amtrak commercial. The three women were incensed that the pilots were being defamed and that Pattie had been quoted as "No comment," although it was technically correct, since she had not spoken at all. They hoped that Mr. Martin had not seen the bulletin and learned of Bertha's demise in such a callous manner. How could you explain that news report to a grandchild? They should be required to precede the news with an adults-only disclaimer.

Ray Slackman was in a full-blown panic. He had watched from a distance when the airport police had converged on the maintenance shack, and he had no doubt who they were looking for. He hated Billy Lediuex, and he hated the FBI agent who had skillfully manipulated him. Billy would pay for this. His only choice now was to run. He thought of jumping on the employee bus and making his way to the parking lot, but he knew they would be watching his truck and guarding his house. He thought of going to the main terminal and catching the Marta train to downtown, but surely they would be watching that too. Besides that, he only had thirty dollars and a maxed-out Visa card in his wallet. Somehow he had to buy himself some time and think of a plan. He decided he couldn't stay in the ramp area without being seen and recognized. By remaining underneath the concourse and following the twists and turns of the conveyer belts and trains of baggage carts, he was able to eventually make his way to the north end of the complex. He found what he was looking for in a storage bin in the baggage service area. The airline kept RON kits available for passengers who missed a flight and had to unexpectedly *remain overnight*. Among the items in the amenity kit was a razor and shave cream. If he could get rid of the beard and mustache, maybe he would not be recognized as easily.

Now he had to get away from the concourse and move to a more remote part of the airport, away from the co-workers who knew him. Through the open end of the complex, he could see a row of baggage tugs that would not be used until the evening push of international flights. He walked out to the tugs as if he was supposed to be there and climbed on the first one in line. There were no keys for the tugs—they all had a simple start button—and it fired right up. Ray drove away from the concourse and joined a line of other tugs waiting for a jet to exit the ramp. When the airplane was clear, the line moved to the next concourse. Ray followed the traffic until he reached the service road that circled the airport perimeter. He went north on the road and drove past the fuel farm and a maintenance hangar, onto the remote pad where spare jets were parked until they were needed. Today there were five airplanes on the pad.

At one end of the ramp there were several pieces of ground support equipment parked, and Ray placed the tug between an air conditioning cart and a portable generator. He walked down the row of airplanes until he found one that had a set of portable stairs in place at the entrance door. He bounded up the stairs and glanced at the number on the nose wheel door. It was ship 827; the sister ship to the one at the bottom of the Atlantic. Ray had no time to consider trivia. He opened the big entrance door and entered the aircraft. Once inside, he closed the door and looked around to make sure he was alone. This would be the perfect hiding place for now, and he needed time to think of a better plan.

He went into the lavatory and filled the sink with water so he could shave the hair from his face. He had grown the beard several years before, and shaving was not a habit he was used to. When he finally finished, he was nicked and cut in several places, but satisfied that his appearance was sufficiently changed and wouldn't be recognized from a photograph that the authorities might have. He placed the remainder of the amenity kit into the trash bin and then walked to the back of the airplane. He decided to rest until dark, and then find a way to escape the airport property. He still wore his tool belt. He removed it and reclined a seat to nap in.

✈

After driving Pattie and Melissa to their homes to pack, Jenny stopped by her apartment near the airport and changed into her Tri Con flight attendant uniform. Since becoming one of Molly's assistants, she had not had occasion to wear it often, and she was pleased that it still fit. She threw some things into her rolling travel bag and found room for an extra pair of jeans and a shirt that she hoped would fit Molly. It distressed her that the outfit would probably look better on Molly than it did on her. She collected Pattie and Melissa from her living room, and they drove to the airport.

At six thirty, the three of them arrived back at the crew family room to find most of the group already waiting. Bertie's husband was there, surrounded by his daughter, son, and four grandchildren. The grandchildren ranged in age from about eight years old to fifteen. Pattie hugged him and told him not to give up.

"I appreciate your encouragement, Pattie. I have to go and do what I can, no matter what, and I want my family with me."

"I think it's exactly the right thing to do. Bertie would do the same if roles were reversed."

The Fowlers and the Johnsons arrived, having driven together to gather their belongings for the trip. They seemed to have become close friends in the short time they had been thrown together by the crisis and had found much in common. When they were introduced to the Martin grandchildren, they immediately focused their attention on caring for them. The room was filled with joy, elation, and relief now that the families knew that their loved ones were safe. The atmosphere was tempered only by the fact that Bertie was not among the survivors. Mr. Martin and his children made it clear that they too celebrated the rescue of the other crewmembers, and they graciously accepted the empathy of

251

everyone else. Even in their distress, they felt loved and supported by the other families.

Harold Collins came into the room to announce the departure plans.

"I regret that I will not be able to accompany you, but I have to remain here as the investigation continues. Our departure plans for the Azores are all set, and we'll get you on your way to reunite with your loved ones very shortly. We're waiting for a few more people who are staying at the hotel to check out and return here; when they do, we'll put you all on a bus and take you directly to the airplane. The crew is already on their way to do the preflight, and they'll be ready for a timely departure when you arrive. I want you all to know how much I admire the way you have come together to support each other, and I want you to know how proud I am of the heroic effort our crewmembers have made to save so many lives. There will be a total of forty-four family members on the flight tonight, and there are fifty business class seats, so I hope everyone can stretch out and get some rest. I know Captain Adams will give you a good ride, and most of you know Jenny Kramer, who will be your lead flight attendant. The other crewmembers are also volunteers who wanted to do this on their days off. In fact, we had over one hundred volunteers, and had to turn most of them away. You know, it's times like this, when people pull together, that make me proud to be a human being. We'll all be waiting to welcome you home in a couple of days."

The room gave him an enthusiastic round of applause, and many individuals personally thanked him. A few minutes later, a crew of bag smashers arrived to load the luggage on the bus, and an agent arrived to check IDs against the passenger manifest as they boarded the bus.

CHAPTER TWENTY-THREE

Ray couldn't actually sleep, but he had pulled the armrest up on a row of seats and stretched out with his eyes closed for over two hours. He was anxious to get away and had thought of several ways to escape the airport once darkness fell. The longer he waited, the more nervous he became. His eyes popped open when he heard a noise at the front of the airplane. The first thought that came to his mind was police, but then it occurred to him that if they knew he was here, they would have come for him sooner. The other possibilities were that maintenance was here to perform some sort of work, or the airplane was being prepared for a flight. Either way, he could not leave the airplane without being seen, since the only stairs were at the front door. He quickly came up with a lame cover story for being on the airplane if he was spotted, and then waited to see what would happen.

His first big clue came a few minutes later when he heard the APU start; shortly thereafter, the air conditioning system began blowing cold air through the outlets above the seats. The airplane was being prepared to fly, and he needed a plan if he was to escape. It wasn't dark yet, and he would have to not only find a way off the airplane, but also a new place to hide. Then it occurred to him that his thinking was far too simplistic. What better way to leave the airport than on the airplane? All he had to do was stay put and soon he would be in another city, free and clear. This new train of thought was intriguing, and he began thinking of how it could be accomplished. There were several places he would like to hide, but all of them required going to the front of the airplane, where he would surely be seen and questioned. He also knew that time was running short. Soon either a mechanic or one of the crew would be doing a walk around and inspecting the interior of the airplane.

He came to the conclusion that there was only one place that he might be able to remain aboard and not be discovered. He peered around the edge of the seat and didn't see anyone. He assumed that whoever started the APU must still be in the cockpit. He hurried around the partition at the last row of seats and was out of sight from anyone at the front of the airplane. From his position, he could access the rear galley without being seen, and he quickly went through the drawers until he found what he needed. He located a packet of Tri Con stationery and a magic marker. He wrote, "Out of order," on the paper and used a roll of masking tape to attach it to one of the lavatory doors. He added a big X pattern of masking tape to the exterior of the door and replaced the items he had taken from the galley. He had performed this task many times before, when the toilet malfunctioned and there was not time to repair it before departure. There were several other lavatories at the rear of the airplane, and it wasn't uncommon to be dispatched with one out of service. Now he moved into the lavatory and locked the door from inside. He sat down in the small space and hoped the flight would be a short one.

He thought his plan through and was satisfied that it would work. Like most mechanics who wore a tool belt all day, Ray had a habit of resting his hand on the flashlight in the loop at the front of the pouch. When he moved his hand down now, he panicked when

254

he realized the pouch was not there. He had left it in the row of seats he had been resting in. Just when he thought he was home free, he had made a stupid mistake. The tools in the seat would be a red flag that someone would investigate, and his name was on the pouch. He would have to retrieve them. When he cracked the door and peeked out, he could hear voices from the forward part of the cabin. He couldn't make out the words, but he watched through the thin opening. He saw a mechanic walk out the front door onto the stairs. He quickly opened the door while watching the front of the airplane and grabbed the tool pouch. He ducked back into the lavatory without being seen and locked the door once again. Ray settled down for the long wait and visualized himself walking off the airplane scot-free.

Colt had managed his time well during the afternoon. He went home, packed his bag, showered, shaved, and then got into his uniform. On the way to the airport, he stopped at the ATM for some cash and made it to flight operations by six o'clock. He stopped in crew scheduling to see who the copilots would be, then answered questions and dispelled rumors for the schedulers. He knew they gossiped more than a ladies' knitting club, and he didn't want them spreading wild stories or becoming an unofficial source for the news media.

He found the briefing room the flight had been assigned and began the flight planning. By the time the two copilots arrived at six thirty, he had completed most of the task. Glenn Rodgers and Rick Stanley were both senior first officers and made short work of the remaining paperwork.

After that the conversation turned to what had happened to Flight Eleven and Colt told them as much as he could without risking the wrath of the FBI. They went to the flight attendant briefing room and found Jenny with her crew. Heather, the family room hostess, smiled at Colt. He said, "Heather, I hope you have not been spreading unfounded rumors and untruths about me."

Jenny spoke up, "We've tried to dissuade her from encouraging you, Colt, but she's young and foolish."

Colt spoke to the other flight attendants.

"Ladies, don't listen to these surly, insubordinate women. My name is Colt Adams, but you can call me Your Majesty, Your Honor, or whatever other similar superlative you choose. Tri Con has had the good judgment to assign me as your leader tonight. I won't demean you by talking about the weather and other such trivia, but there are a couple of important things for you to know. One is that I take one cream and no sugar; the other is that I prefer the beef over the chicken. The two underlings accompanying me are scallywags of the first order, and I would not recommend allowing them to sully your good reputation."

He took a sheet of paper from his pocket and handed it to Jenny. The page contained a very thorough and professional briefing with all the pertinent details about the flight, so that she could include the information in her briefing.

Colt added, "I'll leave you to continue your discussion and remind you to discount any personal insults that Ms. Kramer might direct toward me. The airplane is on the remote pad, and I've ordered a van to transport us in about fifteen minutes. I look forward to flying with you, and I think, with a little effort, this could quite possibly be the finest flight of our entire collective careers."

Jenny said, "Thank you, Your Majesty. We'll try to demonstrate worthiness of your kindness and compassion."

Colt took a bow, and all the girls giggled as he and the copilots left the room.

Jenny spoke to the girls at the table.

"If you haven't flown with Captain Adams before, don't be deceived by the facade. He's one of the finest pilots you'll ever fly with, and even though he likes to keep everyone entertained, if you screw up, he will hold you accountable in a most unpleasant way."

One of the ladies drew a scornful look from Heather when she asked, "Does he have a wife?"

"Several. Don't go there," Jenny answered.

Jenny continued her briefing and included all the information Colt had written on the page he had given her. At the conclusion, she went over the passenger list and related what she knew about each family. She noticed two slips of paper clipped to the manifest and recognized the familiar forms. "Ladies, I'm not sure what this is about, but we have two gentlemen added to the manifest. As you can see from the little blue forms, they are authorized to carry weapons. The authorizing agency is FBI, so we have two gun-toting feds with us. I don't have to remind you that this means that no alcoholic beverages are to be served to them."

Jenny looked at the girl who had asked about Colt, "It doesn't say if they're married or not."

That drew a laugh from everyone else and a blush from the girl. Jenny went on to explain that even with the two feds, the total number of passengers was only forty-six. Therefore she planned to seat everyone in business class and use only the forward and mid galleys to serve.

"I want everyone to sit at your normal duty station for takeoff and landing so that we have all the doors covered, but other than that, we can all hang out up front. Plan on about a three-hour break so everyone will have a chance to sleep."

A few minutes later, the entire crew was gathered in the lounge, and the transportation arrived to deliver them to the airplane. Two vans were required to accommodate the eleven people with their bags, and they caravanned around the perimeter road to the remote ramp on the north side of the field. Colt was the first one to climb the stairs to the forward entrance door with his travel bag in one hand and his brain bag in the other. As he neared the top, a mechanic came out to greet him.

"Afternoon, Captain. I just started the APU and got the air conditioning going for you. The logbook is clean, and the fuel truck is on the way. I'm supposed to hang around until departure in case you need anything."

Colt said, "I appreciate that. Feel free to wait inside where it's cool if you want to."

"Okay, is this a charter flight or something?"

"Yeah, we're going to pick up the Flight Eleven crew, and we're taking their families to reunite with them. The other passengers are being accommodated on Air Portugal."

"I knew it must be something important. Operations is treating it like Air Force One."

Colt made his way to the cockpit and began making his nest in the left seat. He was joined shortly by Glenn, who had lost the coin toss for the return leg. They settled into the routine, and a few minutes later, the preliminary checklist was complete, except for checking the fuel load after the truck finished pumping. Colt looked out the windshield and saw a Tri Con employee bus entering the security gate, followed by a black Crown Victoria with antennas protruding in various places.

He left the flight deck and waited at the top of the stairs to greet the passengers. Rick returned from performing the exterior walk around and watched as each man shook Colt's hand, and each lady gave him either a hug or a kiss on the cheek. Not knowing the background, he concluded that the captain possessed a more magnetic personality than he had thought. Colt knew that most of his passengers had just lived vicariously through their loved one's terror filled experience. He sensed their apprehension about getting on the same type airplane to fly the same route, and he admired their courage and sense of loyalty to their family. Colt had mentally put himself in Charlie's place and wondered if he could have performed as well.

At the end of the parade, the last three men up the steps had short hair and wore dark suits with white shirts. They looked like they were cloned in the basement of a federal building somewhere.

Ed White said, "Good to see you again, Colt. I wanted to come over and introduce you to Special Agents John Lehman and Joe Rand." Handshakes were exchanged all around. Ed continued.

"John and Joe will be going with you and conducting the initial interviews of the crew. We want to get their thoughts while everything is still fresh in their minds."

Each agent handed Colt a copy of the in-flight gun-toting authorization.

He said, "Gentlemen, we're happy to have you with us. I know you're legal to carry your weapons on the flight, but I remind you that once we are underway you are not authorized to use them without the captain's permission. Since I know everyone on the airplane personally, I can't imagine it becoming an issue, but nonetheless, those are the rules."

Lehman answered, "We understand perfectly, Captain, and it will not be a problem under any circumstances."

"Welcome aboard. We have plenty of seats. You can enjoy a business class seat or an entire row of tourist if you want to stretch out horizontally and sleep. The flight attendants will know that you are carrying, but the passengers will not. You are also welcome in the cockpit anytime."

Ed said, "We appreciate your help, Colt. I wish I could come along myself, but you know the situation here."

"Any luck locating this guy, Ed?"

"Not yet, but it will happen, believe me."

"I do believe you. I'll keep these two fed and watered for you until we get back in a couple of days."

Colt escorted the two agents inside and introduced them to Jenny, who compared their IDs to the little blue slips she had with her paperwork.

The passengers had settled into their seats, and Pattie and Melissa had taken the two front seats on the left side. The Fowlers were in the middle two seats, with the Johnsons taking the two on the right. The ladies had taken aisle seats across from each other so they could converse. Colt took a few minutes to speak with Molly's mother and to encourage the Martins, who had taken seats in the rear of the cabin. Before leaving headquarters that afternoon, Colt had learned that the two missing passengers were a Spanish man traveling alone and the unaccompanied minor. He didn't have the heart to tell the Martins that a ten-year-old girl was missing with Bertie. He took some time with Bertie's granddaughter of about the same age and tried not to think of the possibilities or what the outcome might be. When he heard the fuel truck driving away from the right wing, he went to the cockpit to prepare for departure.

Jenny inventoried the forward and mid galleys and was satisfied that they were catered and supplied properly. There were an abundance of premium meals and desserts, and lots of goodies for the kids. She went to the video cabinet and loaded the movie racks with the latest releases, including several for the youngsters. She sent Heather and one of the other girls to the rear of the airplane to check the emergency equipment and to secure the galleys. There was nothing more embarrassing than having a galley drawer slide open and crash to the floor during takeoff. Each door and each drawer had a rotating bar that could be positioned to keep them securely closed.

The two girls went chattering through the empty rear portion of the plane checking fire extinguishers, oxygen bottles, megaphones, first aid kits, and flashlights. When they reached the rear galley, they began checking all the drawer locks while talking about the fact that neither had ever been to the Azores and what they must be like. When they were satisfied that everything was closed up tight, they went back to the front.

Jenny asked, "Is everything ready back there?"

Heather answered, "Yeah, it's all buttoned up. Did you know one of the johns is blocked off?"

"No, which one?"

"The one on the left in the very back."

"It's not in the cabin logbook. The last crew must have forgotten to write it up."

"I don't know, but the door is taped up and has an out of order sign on it."

"Okay, thanks. I'll see what Colt wants to do."

Jenny walked into the cockpit and said, "Colt, let me see if I've got this right. You like beef with one sugar and no milk with your chicken. Is that correct?"

"Ms. Kramer, need I remind you that I have two armed federal officers at my disposal, and you are flirting with charges of interfering with a flight crewmember in the performance of his duties. I suggest you take notes if your memory is failing you in your advanced years."

"My sincere apologies, Your Honor. We have a lavatory blocked off in the back cabin. Did anyone tell you that?"

"No, it's not in our book."

"It's not in mine either. Somebody screwed up. What should we do?"

"Well, we're going to be ready to close the door in about five minutes, and we've got seven other toilets. I'll get it fixed if you want, but with only forty-six people I'm not sure it's worth the delay."

"No, we don't need it. I just wanted you to know it's out of service. I'll put it in the cabin logbook, if that's okay."

"That would be great, Jenny. I'll get somebody to check it out when we land."

"Okay, can I get you guys anything?"

"Heather already beveraged us, but thanks. By the way, I'm going to leave the cockpit door open for the entire flight. If anyone wants to come up and visit, they're welcome anytime. I'll mention it on the PA."

As Jenny left, the agent walked in with the final paperwork.

"Forty six and zero. Gentlemen, any last words?"

Colt said, "Check with the flight attendants. You know women always have to get the last word."

"I hear you, captain. I understand all of you are volunteers. The rest of us want you to know we appreciate what you're doing."

Colt answered, "It was either this or a TV dinner at home by myself."

The agent laughed.

"We still appreciate you guys, have a good trip."

Glenn put the final numbers in the computer and checked the center of gravity and stabilizer setting. They watched the entrance door light blink out and they were ready to go. As they waited for the stairs to be moved away Glenn said, "Looks like the vultures came out to film our departure."

Colt looked up to see a satellite truck and a news crew parked on the road outside the security fence.

"How do they find out everything that goes on?"

Rick said, "They must have spies in every department of the airline and law enforcement."

"Well, since they took the time to come out, I guess we should try to look good for the cameras."

When the tug driver came on the interphone, Colt requested that they push him straight back and let him make the turn out under power. A few minutes later, he set the brakes, and Glenn started all three engines while the tug disconnected and drove away. He returned the agent's salute and then waited for him to clear the area. The flight number had been assigned appropriately as One Eleven, like a continuation of Flight Eleven. When they were ready to taxi, they could see the cameraman standing next to the fence with the camera on his shoulder and a reporter with a microphone standing next to him. Colt pointed the nose right at them, turned all the landing lights on high beam, and taxied straight at them as far as he dared. When he turned, he did a one-eighty, pointed the tail at them, lightly held the brakes, ran the two wing engines up to about half power, and created a horizontal tornado. As they taxied away he said, "Stay tuned for further developments."

At the ramp exit, Glenn called ground control.

"Ground, Tri Con Triple One on the north ramp with information Kilo."

"Tri Con Triple One roger. Are you the Flight Eleven recovery flight?"

"Yes, sir."

"Can you use Runway Eight Right for departure?"

Glenn looked at Colt, and he gave him a thumbs-up.

"Affirmative. That would save us a long taxi."

"Roger, Tri Con Triple One, turn right on Alpha, taxi to Runway Eight Right, hold short of Eight Left at the end."

"Triple One, right on Alpha hold short of Eight Left. Thank you, sir."

"No problem. Expect an immediate departure at the end."

Colt said, "I didn't see this coming. Rick, sit the girls down quick and then run the taxi checklist."

As they approached the end of the taxiway, Jenny reported that they were ready for departure. Just as Colt was slowing for the turn, ground control came back on the frequency.

"Tri Con Triple One, cross Runway Eight Left, contact the tower on one-nineteen-five."

"Triple One cleared to cross Eight Left and nineteen-five thanks again."

"Bring them home safe, guys."

"Will do."

Colt continued the taxi, and Glenn changed frequencies.

"Tower Tri Con Triple One with you."

"Triple One, are you ready?"

"Yes, sir."

"Tri Con Triple One, I have an amended clearance. Are you ready to copy?"

"Affirmative, go ahead."

"ATC clears Tri Con Triple One direct Boston, then as filed. Climb and maintain flight level two-three-zero, and you're cleared for immediate takeoff."

Glenn read back the clearance as Colt turned onto the runway and pushed the throttles up. When Glenn thanked the tower for the direct clearance, the controller replied, "That's the best we could do from here. Boston will work with the Canadians to get you something direct when you get there."

With so few passengers and no cargo, the airplane was much lighter than a normal flight. The takeoff run was short, and the climb was quick. Once they contacted Atlanta center, they were cleared to cruise altitude without delay. Colt realized how much work and coordination had gone into the unprecedented direct clearance, and it made him proud to be part of the aviation community. There were hundreds of airplanes in the air between Atlanta and Boston and four air traffic control centers, but they had somehow worked together to clear every conflict to make the clearance possible. Climbing through eighteen thousand feet, he flipped the seat belt sign off and picked up the PA. He announced the flying time of seven hours and explained the time zone difference and the weather they could expect. He elaborated on the clearance they had received and what it meant in terms of respect for their family. He added that it was the kind of thing that would never be reported on the news because it would not sell a product. Lastly he invited anyone who would like to visit the cockpit to come up any time as his honored guest. It was against the rules, of course, but it was his way of also paying respect. He would deal with the consequences, if it came to that.

Ray stood up in the tiny lavatory and tried to stretch his legs. His entire body was becoming stiff from inactivity, and even though he was short and thin, there was barely enough room to turn around in the small room. He had heard the flight attendants talking about the Azores before takeoff and wished he had paid more attention in geography class. No matter where the Azores Islands were located, it would be better than Atlanta and the police. Later he had listened as the captain made his PA announcement and was disheartened to learn that he would be trapped in the toilet for seven hours. He was confused by the talk of special clearance and open cockpit, but he assumed he had chosen some sort of unique charter flight to stowaway on.

Ray was careful to remain as silent as possible, but there had been very little activity in the galley area. That worried him. He had listened as the girls preflighted the galley, and he had heard them talking again when they sat in the seats by the door for takeoff, but then nothing at all. They were not cooking meals or serving drinks, and no one had used any of the other restrooms in the rear of the airplane. They had been airborne for almost an hour, and he had not heard any activity at all. The only explanation he could think of was that the passenger load must be very light, and everyone was seated up front. He hoped that was the case, and that it would lessen the chances of him being discovered. Once they landed, he would wait until everyone left, then leave the airplane and make his escape. With his Tri Con uniform and ID, he should be able to bluff his way off the airport and disappear into civilian life. For now he could relax. His only concerns were the hunger pains he felt. There was water to drink in the lavatory, but he had not had food since breakfast. He would just have to tough it out. He had removed his tool belt and placed it in the sink to keep it from making noise when he moved around.

He stretched as best he could and then sat down and leaned his head back to try to sleep.

Charlie could not sleep. The women and children had been given the crew's berths, and everyone else tried to stretch out on the deck, but every time he closed his eyes he saw the dark water in the landing lights or the man with a broken neck in the passenger seat. Most of the people who had chosen to rest on the exterior decks were on the open fantail at the back of the ship. Charlie decided to take a walk and try to clear his mind. He held on to the rail and moved forward along the main deck, keeping as much weight as possible off his tightly wrapped ankle. His white uniform shirt was smudged and hardly recognizable, but the warm salty wind on his face felt refreshing. The mess deck was located at mid-ship, and, when he passed the open hatch, he could see a few passengers and *Karuk* crew sitting at the tables drinking coffee. He considered joining them, but didn't feel up to answering the questions he knew they would ask. He continued forward in the dim light provided by the sparse deck lights and stopped to lean on the rail and watch the foaming water slide alongside. He thought of Pattie and wondered where she was and what she was thinking.

He sensed that he was not alone and glanced forward toward the bow. Near the front of the ship he saw Tony Johnson and Britt Fowler sitting on an equipment locker and holding hands while they quietly talked. It was hard to imagine anything good resulting from the tragedy they had all experienced, but maybe there was an exception. He felt like an intruder and moved back toward the mess deck. When he came to the starboard stairs, he decided to climb them and visit the bridge. Each step was a challenge, and his progress was slow and deliberate, giving him cause to consider his handicapped passengers and how much he had come to admire their perseverance and ability to deal with adversity. He was welcomed by Captain Maxwell and provided with hot coffee.

"Who is the enamored couple using my bow for a rendezvous?"

Charlie smiled, "I'm afraid that's my first officer and lead flight attendant. I hope they're not breaking Navy regulations."

Maxwell laughed, "I'm sure they're discussing official business."

Charlie looked around the bridge and saw the navigation equipment, radar, helmsman, and radios. He thought that he and Maxwell had a lot in common. They basically did the same things, but Maxwell did it at fifteen knots and Charlie did it at six hundred. In some ways, Charlie envied the leisurely pace, but he knew he could never adapt to it. Ten miles a minute was the pace that he liked to think at, and even that seemed slow and unchallenging sometimes. In the distance, Charlie could see the lights of another ship and asked about it.

Maxwell said, "The British finally made an appearance. That's one of their aircraft carriers, which will be plowing around the eastern portion of the grids in hopes of recovering more debris from the airplane. International diplomacy dictates that they do something to make us indebted to them in the future. It's an endless game played out by childish world politicians every day."

Maxwell excused himself to return to his cabin and do the reports generated by the day's activities, but he invited Charlie to relax in the command chair on the bridge as long as he cared to. The big leather chair was comfortable, and Charlie sat there watching the bow slowly rise and fall in the darkness until fatigue finally overtook him, and he fell asleep.

CHAPTER TWENTY-FOUR

Flight Triple One was streaking up the east coast of the United States at eighty five percent of the speed of sound. Point eight-five Mach at 39,000 feet equaled six hundred and forty-two miles per hour ground speed, when the prevailing westerly wind was added. With the clearance of a lifetime, Colt poured the speed on and gave not one thought to Tri Con's fuel conservation concerns. He intended to repay the air traffic controllers' courtesy by clearing the airways for other flights as quickly as possible. Each time the controllers handed them off to the next sector, they did so with the request that their best wishes be passed along to the Flight Eleven crew.

In addition to setting speed records, Colt was hosting the passengers who visited the cockpit. He entertained the kids by testing the various warning systems and causing horns, bells, and lights to activate. At the speed they were flying, the sun quickly faded behind them in the west. They watched as a dome of darkness steadily rose in the eastern sky as the curved shadow of the earth interceded with the sun. History recorded another day over the northeastern United States. The combination of the earth's rotation and the airplane's speed would result in a very short night.

Jenny had decided that eight flight attendants were far too many in the one cabin and sent four of them on break. She, Heather, and the two others served beverages, then the main dinner meal, and then dessert. Afterwards they dimmed the main cabin lights so that people could sleep or watch movies as they chose. Pattie and Melissa selected a chick flick to watch, but after two days of sporadic sleep at best, they both were in la-la land ten minutes after the opening credits.

By the time the flight crossed the coast of Newfoundland and headed out over the Atlantic, most of the passengers had reclined their seats and covered themselves with blankets to sleep. The notable exception was the two FBI agents in the last row of business class. They had their briefcases out and papers spread in order to prepare for the upcoming interviews.

The flight attendants picked up the food trays and put them away. They now had little to do until the breakfast service just before landing. The flight was scheduled to land at approximately eight a.m. local time on Terceira Island. Jenny and Heather sat on the flight attendant folding seat at the one left door and discussed the incredible events of the last few days. They tried to imagine how the Flight Eleven girls had handled the horrific emergency and looked forward to hearing their story firsthand. Their conversation was interrupted when Colt came out of the cockpit.

"Are you two still conspiring against me?"

"Your name came up once or twice."

Colt laughed. "I won't make further inquiries. Carry on, ladies. I'm going to get my beauty rest for an hour before I deliver you safely to the islands."

"Don't disturb my passengers. I just got them tucked in," Jenny said.

When they approached the midpoint of the flight, Jenny woke up the girls on break and then called the group together in the mid galley. She laid out her duty plan for the remainder of the flight. She told Heather and the other girls going on break that they would not be needed until preparation for landing, and therefore could plan on sleeping until thirty minutes before touchdown. That sounded like a great plan to Heather, but it was her custom to read in order to help her fall asleep. She informed Jenny, "I'm going to read my cheap novel for a while before I sleep. I'll go to the rear cabin so I can turn on the reading light at the seat without disturbing anyone, and then I'll stretch out in the middle row and snooze. Wake me up when you need me."

On her way to the back she stopped and spoke to the FBI agents, "Can I get you gentlemen anything before I go on break?"

John Lehman answered, "No, thanks. We know where the coffee pot and the cups are, and that will keep us going. We're almost done anyway, and hopefully we can get some sleep too."

When she moved into the dimly lit tourist cabin, she saw Colt stretched out in the first long row of middle seats, sleeping. She quietly walked all the way to the back of the airplane and sat down in the last row. The reading light above the seat was perfect, and she opened the paperback and removed her bookmark. It occurred to her how strange it was to be sitting in a cabin with over two hundred empty seats. She remembered the ghost stories she had heard as a kid and looked around to make sure she was alone. Those thoughts receded as she read the novel and tried to predict the direction the plot would take next. When she became aware of activity at the front of the cabin, she looked up to see one of the flight attendants giving the wake-up call to Colt. A glance at her watch told her she had invested an hour of her break in the novel. She calculated that she still had two hours to sleep and forced herself to close the book. Both Colt and the flight attendant had disappeared into the forward cabin, and Heather decided to ensure two hours of uninterrupted sleep by visiting the restroom before tucking herself in.

Over a period of several hours, Ray had tried ten different positions to get comfortable in the tiny space. His efforts were finally rewarded when he dozed off sitting sideways on the seat with his head against the forward wall and his feet in the sink. A bad dream involving his ex-wife woke him with a start, and it took him a terrorizing thirty seconds to figure out where he was. That was followed by a strong desire to return to the other nightmare. Once he decided this was the reality that he must deal with, he began taking inventory of his senses. He had a sore back, a stiff neck, and numbness in his legs. His mouth tasted like an army had marched through while he slept, and many of the soldiers had personal hygiene issues.

Once he generated enough circulation to actually stand up, he realized that all the water he had drank earlier, in lieu of lunch and dinner, had gathered in his bladder. There was little he could do for his other maladies, but he was in the right place to cure this one. He took a few seconds to make sure his legs would actually support him and then relieved himself. A glance at his watch indicated that if he had calculated correctly, the flight would land in a little over two hours. That was not a proposition he wanted to embrace, but he had little choice. The thing that amazed him the most was that he had not heard a single person outside the lavatory since takeoff. Maybe his fortunes were changing at last. With that happy thought in mind, he lowered the lid and pushed the flush button.

HMS Integrity plowed through the dawn waters, making thirty knots and providing a relative wind across the flight deck to aid the launch of her surveillance aircraft. Admiral Geoffrey Harrison sat in one of the two bridge command chairs alongside his air wing commander, Captain George Newman. Both officers were adamant soccer fans, and they listened to the radio traffic between the carrier, using the call sign Goalie, and the search aircraft, using the call sign Striker. Ten airplanes were launched, and they watched as they formed up and then disbursed into various areas of the search grid. Harrison and Newman were still chapped because the Americans had exiled the huge British carrier to the easternmost sector of the search area, while the tiny US salvage ship basked in the glory and headlines of rescuing over two hundred survivors.

They felt extremely demeaned to be relegated to the status of garbage scow as they picked up various and sundry bits of useless trash as it drifted east into their sector two days after the crash. The hangar deck held a small pile of clothing and bags, along with seat cushions and pillows.

Now that the aircraft were safely away, Wing Commander Newman ordered the Sea King helicopters onto the flight deck. They saw the elevator lift the first one from the hangar deck and watched it being towed into launch position. Admiral Harrison ordered the carrier to all ahead slow, and they loitered along at a speed of ten knots. The Sea King crew walked out of the ship's island superstructure wearing life vests over their flight suits and carrying their helmets in their hands. One of them wore a wet suit and also carried a pair of flippers to put on his feet, should he have to go into the water to rescue another suitcase.

Harrison and Newman were both in foul moods and heaped abuse on the bridge crew as they barked orders and dreamed of retribution. The sun was now above the horizon, and Harrison ordered the helmsman to turn the ship to the north because he didn't want to put his sunglasses on. Such was the privilege of command. The two officers munched scones with their coffee and discussed the soccer season to distract from the depression of their duty assignment. The ten search aircraft began making idle comments to each other over the radio to relieve the boredom. Newman picked up the mic and let loose a barrage of colorful verbiage, none of which would be condoned by his own policy of radio etiquette that he demanded of his pilots. This was followed by a series of double clicks from each airplane's mic button, but no words. The double click was universally accepted worldwide as an informal roger, but was not mentioned in manuals describing radio procedure or accepted technique. The response further irritated Newman. He now suffered the silent treatment from the bridge crew as well as the airplanes.

The silence only lasted a minute or so and then a very formal and technically perfect transmission was heard.

"Goalie, Striker Six, over."

"Striker Six, Goalie, go ahead."

"Goalie, I've got a large debris field in my location, over."

"Striker Six, radar shows you eight miles northwest. Is that correct?"

"Affirmative. The debris field begins here and runs to the west."

"Copy Striker Six."

Newman ordered, "Launch the first Sea King and give him a call sign of Striker Eleven. Vector him to the reported debris location."

A few minutes later, the helicopter's huge blades began to turn, and the jet engine wound up to a roar. The pilot turned it into the wind and then lifted off with the rescue jumper sitting in the open door, dangling his feet over the side. From the bridge, they watched it disappear to the northwest. Harrison commented that if the Americans didn't want their garbage back, they could have a yard sale and buy beer for the crew. They waited with little enthusiasm to hear what the Sea King discovered.

That, however, was not to be. The next voice on the frequency was not from the Sea King but from the search plane. "Goalie, Striker Six! Goalie I've got a raft in sight! Goalie do you read Striker Six!"

The radioman thought to himself, *I can hear you but I can't talk to you until you let the transmit button go.*

"Striker Six, Goalie, understand raft in sight, can you confirm survivors?"

Harrison and Newman were on their feet now.

"Negative, Goalie. There is a canopy in place and I can't see inside."

Newman took the mike.

"Make a low pass, man, and see if you get a response."

The pilot recognized the voice.

"Yes, sir. Proceeding with low pass."

Newman said, "Radar, vector that Sea King in right now."

"Yes sir, he's on frequency and listening."

"Goalie, Striker Eleven, give me a heading."

"Striker Eleven, fly heading three-three-five, approximately six miles."

The bridge was alive now that there was an opportunity to rectify an American oversight and revive their ship's importance and credibility.

"Goalie, Striker Six, there was no response from the raft when I made a low pass."

Newman responded, "Striker Six, did you make a low pass or just a flyby?"

"Sir, I was at raft level. I could see under the canopy and observed one occupant, but no response."

"Good, man. Wait for the Sea King."

"Goalie, Striker Eleven, I have the raft in sight, ETA two minutes."

The Sea King could not hover directly over the raft for fear of overturning it with their rotor wash. They dropped the rescue diver a short distance away and waited for him to swim to the raft.

"Goalie, Striker Eleven, diver in the water."

"Roger, Striker Eleven, standing by."

The men on the bridge knew that it was counterproductive to ask questions at this point. The diver could communicate with the helicopter but not directly with the ship. They would have to be patient and wait for information to be relayed.

"Goalie, the diver reports two occupants, one female and one child, both unresponsive."

They waited and prayed.

"Goalie, Striker Eleven, diver reports weak vital signs in both survivors. We're beginning recovery. ETA at Goalie in fifteen to twenty minutes."

Harrison ordered, "Notify sick bay, two victims inbound. Have them standby on the flight deck to receive them."

Unlike the *Karuk*, the *Integrity* possessed a full service hospital, complete with doctors and surgeons. Four hospital corpsman were dispatched to the flight deck with rolling gurneys. After a short wait, the Sea King could be seen approaching from the west.

"Goalie, Striker Eleven, three miles west for landing."

"Roger Striker Eleven, you're cleared straight in approach and cleared to land amidships. Wind is north at ten and altimeter is 1014 millibars." The British used millibars instead of inches of mercury for barometric pressure.

The Sea King pilot aimed for a point a half mile behind the carrier and then racked the chopper around to approach over the fantail and land alongside the huge island. Four minutes later, Bertha Martin and Amanda Chamberlin were in ICU with bags of fluid dripping into their arms. Royal British Navy doctors argued over the best course of treatment.

276

Heather left her book lying on the seat and stood up to stretch, then walked toward the restroom. The nearest lavatory was broken, so she would have to use the next one. She was just passing the taped-up door when she heard the familiar sound of the flush motor. Working in the aft galley and sitting on the flight attendant seat by the door, she had heard the flush motor a thousand times. The finicky motors were famous for screwing up in any number of ways, one of which was to activate on their own for no apparent reason. Sometimes if they did that often enough, it would cause an overflow and blue water would run out into the floor. Heather decided she should check it out to make sure that wasn't going to happen. However, it could wait until after she used the restroom. The door to the broken toilet was locked, but every crewmember knew how to unlock it from outside, in the event a passenger became incapacitated while using the restroom. She moved on to the next one and went inside.

After flushing the toilet, Ray was looking at his nicked and cut face in the mirror and thought that he would need practice shaving. He could see the reflection of the startled look on his own face when the other lavatory door opened and then closed. He could feel his pulse rate increase, and he could hear someone bumping around in the other john. *No need to panic, no one has bothered to check the broken toilet so far and there is no reason to do so now.* He remained quiet and waited. Eventually the toilet flushed, and he could hear water running in the sink. *Just be still and just be quiet,* he silently told himself.

The other door opened and then noisily closed, causing him to flinch, but his heart almost stopped when he realized someone was unlocking the door he was hiding behind. Instinctively, he reached into the sink and pulled an eight-inch screwdriver from his tool pouch. He was filled with rage and had come too far to give up now. There was no doubt in his mind that everyone was out to get him, and he would no longer submit to ridicule and mistreatment. He was ready when the door opened. The flight attendant froze when she saw him. Her mouth opened to scream, but before she made a sound, he grabbed her. He pulled her inside and covered her mouth with his hand while his other arm went around her neck. She tried to kick him, but there was no room in the tiny space.

He pulled her head back as far as it would go and put the screwdriver to her throat. "I haven't killed anybody all day, but I bet you would be fun. You're all mine now, and you can live or die. I don't care." He closed the door and twisted her arm behind her back. He looked for something to restrain her with and spotted the plastic tie wraps in his tool pouch. The plastic strips were used to tie wiring into bundles and were basically the same thing that police officers used as temporary handcuffs. He pulled her other hand behind her back and quickly placed a wrap around both wrists, placed the end into the self-locking receptacle, and pulled it tight. He listened at the door but didn't hear anyone outside.

He turned her around and put the screwdriver in front of her face.

"Is anyone else out there?"

"I don't know."

He pushed the screwdriver against her throat.

"I don't have time for games. Is anyone out there?"

"No, I don't think so."

"Why are you back here?"

"I'm on sleep break."

"Where are the other flight attendants?"

"They're all up front. We only have business class passengers."

"Why did you come back here?"

"I wanted to read, and the light would have disturbed other people."

"When does your break end?"

"Right before landing."

"Okay, you're going to do exactly what I tell you to, and for now that means sit tight and keep your mouth shut."

Ray looped several tie wraps together and circled Heather's head with the plastic running between her teeth, very effectively silencing her. "If you move or make a noise, you'll be wearing a screwdriver in your neck. Don't be stupid."

He cracked the door open, and when he was sure they were alone in the back of the airplane, he moved into the galley area and scavenged for food. He only found cookies and peanuts, but he ate them with gusto. He knew he had to make a plan now that things had changed. Tri Con was going to pay for ruining his life, and he would not let anyone stand in the way of achieving his goals. From what the flight attendant told him, he figured he had two hours to decide what to do.

The bright sun was peeking above the horizon now, and Colt slid the green sun screen around its track above the windshield and positioned it to block the glare. They had passed thirty degrees west longitude earlier and were talking to Santa Maria Control. Colt had formed a plan to make the last hour of the flight interesting and had asked for an early descent. The airplane was now two hundred miles from Lajes and cruising at flight level two-three-zero. The flight attendants had finished the breakfast service for those who wanted it, and since Jenny couldn't sleep anyway, she had helped them. Colt briefed her that there might be a short delay, but they should touch down in less than an hour.

"Santa Maria, Tri Con One-One-One, how soon can you hand us off to Lajes approach control?"

"Tri Con One-One-One, I'll hand you off to Santa Maria radar shortly. They own about one hundred and fifty miles of airspace, sir. They will send you to approach when you get closer."

"Thank you, sir."

Colt switched to the number two radio.

"*Karuk*, Tri Con Triple One on guard over."

There was a momentary delay.

"Tri Con Triple One, this is *Karuk*, go ahead."

"*Karuk*, can you meet me on 123.45."

"Yes sir, standby."

"Tri Con Triple One, do you read *Karuk* on twenty-three forty-five?"

"Affirmative, *Karuk*, understand you have a couple hundred stowaways on board."

"Yes sir, we look like the Staten Island Ferry."

"Like they advertise, it's an adventure. We're inbound to Lajes to take some of them off your hands. What's your present position?"

"We're ninety miles west, estimating docking at three p.m. local." He read off the latitude and longitude of their position.

"Thanks *Karuk*, you guys are our heroes. There will be a beer bust tonight at a time and place to be determined. We'll get the word to you later."

"Roger that, sir. We'll standby."

Colt patiently watched the mileage decrease until he heard, "Tri Con One One-One, contact Santa Maria Radar on 132.15, good day, sir."

Colt changed frequencies.

"Santa Maria, Tri Con Triple One at two-three-zero."

"Tri Con Triple One squawk 2364."

Colt changed the transponder code to 2364 so they could be identified on radar.

"Tri Con Triple One, radar contact, you're cleared direct Koker. Lajes is landing Runway Three-Three."

"Direct Koker, and we'd like to get lower and deviate south, traffic permitting."

"We heard you call *Karuk* on guard earlier and thought you might want to deviate. The only traffic we have is military activity in the search area one hundred miles west. Tri Con Triple One is cleared direct Koker descend at your discretion to maintain 2500 feet. Deviate as necessary."

"Direct Koker with deviations, we're out of two-three-zero to maintain 2500 feet, say your altimeter."

"Altimeter is 1015 millibars. Let us know when you're ready for approach."

"Tri Con Triple One, thank you very much, sir."

Colt plugged the *Karuk*'s position into the computer and tracked the magenta line while descending.

Charlie slowly opened his eyes to bright sunlight pouring in through the windows of the bridge. He couldn't believe he had actually fallen asleep in the captain's chair and that he had slept so long. The hatch to the bridge wings were open and fresh ocean air permeated the space. Captain Maxwell stood on the starboard side of the bridge with his hands folded at the small of his back like a grown-up Napoleon.

"Good morning, Captain Wells. Did you enjoy your nap?"

"I feel like the firehouse dog, laying around in everyone's way."

"Not at all, you needed the rest. Would you like coffee?"

"I would love some."

The two captains drank coffee and discussed the arrival in Lajes. Maxwell updated the ETA and explained the procedures to Charlie. They would be met by a harbor pilot, who would come aboard and assist them with docking at the unfamiliar pier. The harbor charts were laid out on the navigation table, and Maxwell was pointing out the landmarks they would use. They were both surprised when the bridge speakers came to life with radio traffic.

"*Karuk*, Tri Con Triple One."

Charlie couldn't believe he was hearing the familiar voice.

"Go ahead, Tri Con."

"Gentlemen, we decided to drop by and pay our respects on the way to Lajes. We're at six o'clock and five miles at 2500 feet. Didn't want to surprise you unannounced."

Charlie and Maxwell walked out onto the bridge wing and looked aft. Maxwell ordered an announcement be made on the ship's PA, and they could see people on the fantail looking up. The huge Tri Con jet drew closer and Charlie could see the gear and flaps were down to allow the slowest possible speed. Everyone cheered as they roared by on the starboard side of the ship and then rolled into a left turn to circle.

Charlie found a mic and said, "Colt, are you having fun?"

"Of course I am, Captain Wells."

"Then it must be illegal."

"Be that as it may, I have someone who would like to speak to you."

Charlie listened and then heard, "Charlie, can you hear me?"

"I hear you, dear."

"I love you, Charlie."

"I love you, too Pattie."

Colt came back on.

"We'll meet you in Lajes, and you can tell the other crew members that I have forty-four of their loved ones on board."

"I'll pass that along. We appreciate it, Colt."

"Does this mean you'll still swap trips with me in the future?"

"No. Over and out."

Maxwell watched the big jet disappear into the distance and realized that he and Charlie shared many things in common, but they lived in two very different worlds.

Heather had been locked in the lavatory for over an hour. Her hands were numb from the restraints, and her back hurt from sitting in the awkward position. She had racked her brain trying to determine what she should do. All the training she had received in dealing with hijacking didn't seem to help in this situation. No one had told her what to do if she was tied up and locked in the toilet. The only idea she came up with was to push the flight attendant call button in the lavatory, but she knew that the hijacker would hear the chime and see the light above the door. If someone did come to investigate, he might panic and hurt them. She thought about the two FBI agents, but had no way to warn them. Her only option was to wait and see what happened next. She could sense that the airplane had descended, and it felt like they had circled in a holding pattern for a short time. It would not be long before they landed, and she knew one of the other girls would come to wake her and sit by the emergency exit for landing.

She had not heard the man moving around outside the door in quite some time, and it occurred to her that he might have fallen asleep. If she could get to the interphone, the crew could be warned. For that matter, if she could somehow sneak past him, she would simply run to the front. Even though she had been threatened if she moved, she decided to take the chance. When she stood up, she had to wait for the circulation to return to her legs before she felt confident enough to maneuver. The slide latch that locked the door and illuminated the occupied sign was high on the door, and she could not reach it with her hands restrained behind her. She was able to move into position so that she could get her nose against it and move it a little bit. It took several tries and almost a full minute to unlock the door. Now her nose hurt almost as much as her wrists and hands, and the plastic strap in her mouth made her teeth and jaw extremely sore.

She leaned against the sink and slowly pivoted her feet until she had fully turned in the tiny space. She felt behind her for the door handle and realized that her fingers had very little feeling in them. At last she gripped the handle and pushed down on it. At that exact moment, the airplane rolled to the right and the door flew open. Heather lost her balance and rolled out into the galley floor. She screamed as loud as she could but it came out as a mousey squeak with the gag in place. When she gathered her senses, she was laying in the floor looking at a pair of nasty work boots a few inches in front of her sore nose.

She helplessly watched as one of the oil soaked boots moved against her hip and rolled her over. Ray reached down, grabbed a handful of her shirt collar, and jerked her up on her feet. He shoved the screwdriver in front of her face and said, "I should have shut you up for good. You must be as stupid as my ex-wife."

He pushed her back into the lavatory face first and grabbed her hands behind her back. In the tiny room, his body odor and fetid breath would have gagged her without the plastic tie wrap in her mouth. She desperately wanted to cover her nose and mouth with her hand. He closed the door and pressed against her in the cramped space. She felt nauseous and tried taking shallow breaths through her nose to keep from throwing up. Heather was beyond fear now and into full-blown fury. This ugly little sub-human smelled worse than a cow barn, and his face looked like somebody's cat had used it for a scratching post. The only thing that could make him look more ridiculous would be a beard.

She braced herself and shoved backwards, pushing him against the closed door. He grabbed her by the hair and pulled her head back, forcing her to look at him. He laughed at her, unleashing more bad breath, and shoved her back.

Nothing would please him more than to teach her not to mess with Ray Slackman, but for now at least, he needed her. He had formulated his plan and explained Heather's role through a fog of halitosis.

"I need money and transportation to a safe place. Tri Con is going to provide both, and you are my insurance policy. I'm going to take the gag out of your mouth and you are going to call the cockpit and talk to the captain. If you scream or do anything I don't like, I'll need a new hostage, and I'll get one easy enough. Do you understand me?"

Heather shook her head yes. Ray took a wire-cutting tool out of his pouch and cut the tie wrap. Heather worked her stiff jaw back and forth and found that it still worked.

"Why are you doing this?"

"Don't ask stupid questions. Just do what I tell you."

"How can I help you if I don't know what's going on?"

"You can help by keeping your mouth shut and doing what I tell you."

Before he could give her instructions, the seat belt sign came on and the tone sounded through the speaker in the lavatory.

Everyone on board was thrilled to actually see the little ship that had rescued the crew and passengers. Even the FBI agents were impressed. Colt had climbed back up to five thousand feet and was flying direct to the approach fix they were cleared to. He turned on the seat belt light and told Jenny she had thirty minutes to prepare for landing. He and Glenn Rogers briefed the approach plates for Runway Three-Three and set the landing minimums for the arrival, even though the weather was CAVU. Colt was glad the flight was almost over and that there was nothing left but a routine landing. The flight attendant call chime sounded, and Colt wondered why Jenny didn't just walk into the cockpit instead of calling.

Rick Stanley was sitting in the relief pilot seat and answered the phone.

"Yeah, right, Heather. You're a very funny girl."

He listened again and became serious.

"Colt, I'm talking to Heather in the aft cabin. She says we have a stowaway on board, and we're being hijacked."

Colt didn't know if this was a joke or not, but he didn't think it was funny. "Give me the phone, Rick."

"Heather, what are you talking about?"

"I'm serious, Colt. This guy is a Tri Con mechanic, and he hid out in the lavatory. He has a screwdriver to my throat and says he'll kill me if you don't do what he says."

The words, "Tri Con mechanic," struck home, and he knew who it must be. "Okay, do you know what his demands are?"

"He wants a million dollars first, and then he wants to go to Syria."

"Will he talk to me?"

He could hear her talking to someone, and then a new voice.

"Is this the captain?"

"Yes, sir, it is. I'll be glad to do what you want, but you can't hurt anybody. If we work together, everybody can go home happy."

Now Ray felt an enormous sense of power. He was in control, and nobody could stop him. He was the man.

"You know what I want, Captain, and I don't care who gets hurt. I planted a bomb on board in Atlanta, and Tri Con can pay me or lose their airplane and all the people in it."

"I understand, sir. We'll do what you want. You can call me Colt. What's your name?"

"Nice try, captain. You can call me sir."

"No problem. Can I come back and talk to you so we can work out the details?"

"You can come back here alone. If I see anyone else, the flight attendant will die."

"That would cause more problems than any of us need to deal with. Let's keep it simple, and you'll get what you want. Give me a few minutes to brief my crew and tell them to do what you say, then I'll come back there alone, and you can tell me how you want to do this."

Both copilots had heard the entire conversation. "Rick, get Jenny and the two FBI guys up here. Glenn, tell Santa Maria that we're going to hold at the next fix. Request twenty-mile legs, and tell them to standby. Explain the situation and declare an emergency if you have to. You fly the airplane until I tell you different."

A few minutes later, he had explained the situation to Jenny and the FBI agents. Jenny looked pale but seemed to be under control. Colt related who he thought the hijacker was, and the agents knew right away whom he was talking about. They were up to speed on the investigation and familiar with the prime suspect. Colt told them in no uncertain terms that they were not to interfere unless he asked them to.

When he walked into the aft cabin, he could see Heather standing in the galley with the screwdriver at her throat. The man holding her also had some sort of electronic device in his hand. Colt was more than a hundred feet away, but he could sense the anger and determination on Heather's face. He continued down the aisle, and when he was about ten rows away, Ray spoke up.

"That's close enough, Captain. I can hear you just fine from there."

Colt had to control a surge of anger when he saw the bright red streaks on Heather's cheeks where the plastic gag had cut into the skin. "Look, we're going to give you whatever you want. There's no reason to hold the flight attendant. Why don't you let her go, and we can talk about how to meet your demands."

"She's my insurance. Just do what I say, and she won't get hurt."

"The bomb you planted is plenty of insurance. You don't need her, too." Colt could now see that the electronic device the man held was a simple voltage checker that all the mechanics carried in their tool pouch. It was obvious that there was no bomb aboard.

"Don't tell me what I need, Captain. Just get my money and take me to Damascus. There are organizations there who will appreciate an aviation expert who understands airline operations."

"I intend to do just that, sir. My only concern is the safety of my crew and passengers. I don't care how much money Tri Con gives you or what you do in Syria."

"I'm glad to hear that. Make it happen."

Colt could sense that Ray was really enjoying his position of power. It must be frustrating to go through life and never have the opportunity to control or influence another person. He could see that Ray was living his dream, and it had nothing to do with money.

"I'm glad you understand airline operations, because you know we've been flying for seven hours and we're low on fuel. We need to land and refuel, and we can get your money for you."

"I've already thought about that. You're going to land and taxi to the most remote part of the airport. I want one fuel truck with one man on it to refuel us. If I see anybody else, I'll blow the airplane up on the spot. Next, I want the money delivered, and then we'll be on our way to Damascus."

"That sounds like a good plan. I don't see any problem doing that, but I want you to let the girl go."

Ray turned red in the face.

"I'll decide what happens here. I'm in charge. Don't try to tell me what to do. You land the airplane and get the fuel and the money. I'll let you know what happens next."

Colt turned around and walked away without speaking, but he was thinking about what he would do to this cretin at the first opportunity.

He convened the FBI agents and Jenny in the cockpit and filled them in on what was going to happen. He explained what he wanted them to do and how and when he wanted them to do it.

Next he coordinated with Santa Maria to get the clearance to land and taxi to the remote area. Glenn and Rick had filled the controllers in on the hijacking and declared the emergency. Colt gave the controllers the details on what he planned to do and ordered them not to interfere unless he asked them to. He did not want Ray to see any activity outside the airplane.

They ran the descent and approach checklist and prepared for landing. Colt flew along the southern coast of Terceira Island at thirty-five hundred feet, and near the eastern end, he turned left to intercept the Runway Three-Three localizer. They could see the runway ten miles ahead and tracked the glide slope down. There was a mountain to the left of the airport, and the town of Praia da

Vitoria passed beneath them. As they neared the runway, Colt ordered the gear down.

The runway was over two miles long, and Colt gently touched down in the first thousand feet. The runway had a pronounced slope, and they were coasting uphill. Minimum reverse thrust and little braking allowed them to decelerate to taxi speed as they approached the end. Colt stowed the ground spoilers and ordered the flaps up before leaving the runway. The airport chart indicated a concrete run-up pad on the taxiway at the northeast corner of the airport, and Colt spotted it as he made the right turn to exit the runway. He slowly taxied to the pad and turned the nose of the airplane to the northwest, pointing it out over the farmer's fields and pastures that gently sloped downhill between the airport and the ocean. The entire airport complex was now behind them, allowing any and all who cared to approach the airplane to do so unobserved from inside. The APU had been started before landing, and now Colt set the parking brake and shut down all three engines. He had ordered that there be no intervention without his approval, but he looked around the area to try to spot where the tactical snipers would be deployed in case he changed his mind. They must be doing a good job, because he didn't spot them.

He left the two copilots in the cockpit and walked to the back of the airplane. He found Heather and Ray where he had left them before and stopped twenty feet away when he saw that Ray was becoming nervous.

"Heather, are you all right?"

"My hands and shoulders hurt, but other than that I'm okay."

He turned his attention to Ray.

"Look, you're hurting her for no reason. The bomb threat is enough to make sure you get what you want, and it's no skin off my teeth that Tri Con is giving you a million dollars. I don't owe Tri Con anything. I just work here. But I do care about my crew. I don't want anyone to get hurt, including you. I'm sure you have your reasons for what you're doing, and it's none of my business, but there is no excuse for hurting her when there's no cause to."

Ray replied, "Do you have my money?"

"Of course not. We just landed, but they're working on it."

"When will it be here?"

"I don't know, but we can ask them on the radio. Why don't you come up front so we can talk to them?"

"No way. I'm not going to try to keep my eye on all those people at once. Me and Heather will stay back here."

"Well, I can't keep running back and forth with messages. What if they call with the money, and I'm back here? Why don't we send everyone else back here and the three of us will stay up front with the radio?"

"How could we do that?"

"Easy. You and Heather go up the right side aisle, and I'll send everyone else down the left side. You'll never be close to them. Not only that, but all the food and drinks are up front, and I haven't had breakfast. We can eat while we wait for the fuel and money."

The thought of food weighed heavy on Ray's decision. He was starving, and if he was up front, he could also hear the radio if they tried anything funny.

"Okay, we can do that, but I only want the three of us up there. I better not see anybody else."

"No problem. We don't need anybody else. I'll go let them know we're sending them to the back while we do business up front. When they start back here, you and Heather go up the other side."

As Colt walked away, Ray wondered if he could trust him. He seemed like he really wanted to help, and he probably just wanted to get this over with. It was only a minute or so until he saw the first passengers appear at the front of the cabin. When they were halfway down the aisle, he pushed Heather ahead of him. They moved up the other side. Some of them gave him contemptuous looks, but he didn't care.

When they reached the cockpit, Colt was resting with his feet propped on the instrument panel.

"Welcome to my office. It's been a long night, so I'm relaxing while I can. I was waiting until you got here to check on the progress."

He picked up the mic.

"This is Tri Con Triple One, what's the progress on the money?"

"Tri Con Triple One, they tell me it's being wired from Atlanta to a bank here on the island. After that, it will be transported by armored car to the airplane."

"Good, but don't let them approach the airplane until we say so."

"Roger, sir. I'll let you know when they get here."

"How about the fuel?"

"It's coming. We only have a five thousand-gallon truck, and he will have to make several trips to get you fueled."

He turned to Ray.

"How about this rinky-dink operation? These guys wouldn't know what to think about a real airport like Atlanta."

Ray smiled. "You got that right." He thought, *This guy is totally relaxed and unconcerned. I don't think he likes Tri Con any more than I do.*

Colt asked, "Have you had anything to eat? I'm starving."

"I could probably choke something down."

"Well, I don't know if Heather can cook with her hands tied, but if she can, I say let's go for it. I'd like a beer, but I guess I better have coffee if we're going flying again. What would you like to drink?"

"A beer would be great."

"Well, we've got to make a decision: either turn Heather loose, or I can get some of those girls from the back to fix breakfast. Heather looks pretty mean. I don't know if you can control her or not."

Ray didn't perceive the challenge that had been thrown at him, but he reacted as expected.

"I don't want any more people to watch, and I think I can control Heather."

"Well, let's be about it, man. I'm hungry."

Ray led Heather out the door and into the galley.

"I'm going to free your hands enough to do breakfast, but if you do anything stupid you'll be sorry, and so will your captain. He's being smart about this, and you should too."

He removed a pair of cutting pliers from his tool pouch and cut the tie wraps. After Heather rubbed her wrists and got the circulation going again, he placed new tie wraps on her wrists, but he left her hands in front of her and didn't pull the restraints as tight as before.

She asked, "What can I get you to drink while the meals are heating?"

"Where do you keep the beer?"

She pulled out a plastic bin in the bottom of the galley, and it was full of beer on ice. Ray popped the top on one and drank half of it in one pull. When the oven timer dinged, telling them the meals were hot, Ray was on his third beer. They took the trays into the cockpit and found Colt sucking on his oxygen mask. "This is great stuff to clear your head when you're tired. You want some?"

"No, maybe later."

Ray ate the food like an animal. Colt asked, "You want another one? Tri Con has plenty back there, and we shouldn't waste them. Heather, fix a couple more for us, would you?"

Heather walked out and put more meals in the oven, relieved that for the first time in hours she didn't have to smell Ray.

While they waited, Colt picked up the mike again.

"Hey tower, are we getting money today or what? We're tired of waiting."

"Tri Con Triple One, I understand the armored truck is on the way, and we should have you fueled by the time he gets here."

Colt turned to Ray.

"Check the fuel page and see how much we've got. You know how to do that, don't you?"

Ray pulled up the page on the screen. "Yeah, probably one more truck will do it."

Colt remarked, "These people are really slow. I never knew it would be easier to get a million dollars than a load of fuel."

Ray laughed, "Me either." He thought, *This guy is totally cool.*

Colt said, "You probably know more about this stuff than my first officer. Maybe you can fly copilot on the way to Damascus."

Ray puffed up and said, "I'll be glad to."

Colt punched some buttons on the flight management computer.

"What's wrong with this thing? It says Syria is not in the database."

Ray answered, "Yeah, it's in the Middle East database. You have to load the Middle East disk in the box to make it work."

"I never knew that. No one ever showed me how to load a disk."

"Of course not. A mechanic has to do it."

"Can you do it?"

"Sure, it's easy if you know what you're doing."

"Where's the disk?"

Ray stood up and went to the back of the cockpit. He opened a little door on the back wall, took out a box, and opened it. He pulled out a disk and held it up.

"This is it."

"Man, I never knew that was there. Can you really load it?"

"I told you it's easy."

"Well, load it up, man, so we'll be ready to go when the money truck shows up. Where does it plug in?"

"You can't do it here. The loading port is on the CPU in the forward accessory compartment."

"Well, we sure as heck can't go outside and climb up in there to load it."

"We don't have to."

Colt liked the way they were both using the word, "we."

"What do you mean we don't have to?"

"I can get into the forward accessory compartment without going outside."

"No way."

"Yes way. I'll show you."

Colt followed Ray out the cockpit door and watched him pull a square of carpet up near the galley. Ray opened a hatch in the floor and said, "There you go. Nothing to it."

Colt praised him.

"Man, you know some stuff. How long has that been there?"

"Since day one. It was built that way."

"Can we load the disk down there? How long will it take?"

Suddenly, Ray became wary.

"It only takes about five minutes, but I would have to do it. You don't know how."

Colt looked thoughtful and then said, "Yeah, I see the problem. If you go down there, it leaves us prisoners unguarded."

"You're right, that's the problem."

"Maybe I can get one of these Portuguese mechanics to do it for us. What do you think?"

"I think if we ask for a mechanic, we'll probably get a Portuguese FBI agent."

"I bet you're right. Man, you are way ahead of this game. I would have screwed that up for sure."

Ray puffed his chest up again. "I'm not going to blow it now."

Colt thought for a minute. "I don't blame you for not trusting anybody at this point, but I've got an idea. Do you have more of those tie wrap things?"

"Yeah, I keep a bunch of them all the time."

"Just to make sure nothing happens while you're down there loading the disk, how about if we secure Heather to a seat or something, and that way you'll know we're going to be here when you come back up. I mean, I'm not even sure you can do that with tie wraps, but it's an idea."

Ray unconsciously accepted another subliminal challenge.

"I think I can do that."

"Let's try it. Use the relief pilot's seat in the cockpit so I can keep an eye on her while I listen for the radio."

Five minutes later, Heather's hands and feet were tie wrapped to the seat, and she was looking at Colt like she wanted to choke him.

Colt said, "If anything important comes in on the radio, I'll let you know."

"Okay, this won't take long."

Ray went to the hole in the floor and stepped onto the ladder.

Colt asked, "Did you get the disk?"

"Oh yeah, I'll need that."

He went back to the cockpit and picked up the disk.

"Do I need to turn the computer off or anything?"

"Nah, just don't touch anything until I finish downstairs."

Any concerns that Colt had about a bomb were erased when he saw that Ray had left the voltage checker in the cockpit.

Ray disappeared like a rabbit down the hole. Colt hurried back to the cockpit and closed and locked the door. He picked up the mic and said, "Go, get out now."

He glanced up to see the four-left door open light illuminate and then reached into the back of the captain's seat pocket and removed the security kit. The kit contained several large tie wraps used to restrain passengers if necessary, but what Colt was interested in was the pliers used to cut the tie wraps. He quickly cut Heather's restraints and freed her. Next he opened the sliding window beside the captain's seat, removed the coiled nylon escape rope from the little door above it, and threw it out the window. He taught Heather how to put one leg out the window, then her upper body, and finally the other leg. He watched her slide down the rope into the waiting arms of the airport security forces. He was glad it was Heather and not Big Bertha. Colt followed next, and when he hit the ground, the security men guided them under the belly of the airplane and then rushed them to the rear. They ran between the main landing gear and past the big yellow emergency escape slide at the four-left door. The APU exhaust was roaring at the tail of the airplane, and there was a big bus waiting with the other crew and passengers already loaded aboard. As the bus drove away, Colt looked back and could see at least thirty men dressed in black fatigues and carrying rifles or machine guns. They were positioned strategically around and under the airplane, and several Humvees, with fifty caliber machine guns on top, were parked out of sight with their engines idling.

Colt found Glenn and Rick at the front of the bus. "Rick, you played the part of the tower controller pretty good."

"Thanks, boss. I was afraid he would figure out that you were talking on the interphone and not the radio."

"The only time he got a little suspicious was when I was talking to the real controller through the oxygen mask, but I bluffed my way through it. We should try out for an acting part."

"Yeah, but I want to be the hero next time," Rick said.

Heather said, "Can I play the hostage?"

"You need practice, Heather."

Colt looked around the bus and said, "I see our federal friends decided not to join us."

Glenn answered, "They said to tell you that they appreciated the option, but they were looking forward to meeting Mr. Slackman up close and personal after we were all safe."

Ray finished loading the disk, then removed it from the CPU and closed it up. With another problem solved, he was having happy thoughts of money and freedom. He had already decided to grow his beard back right away. He continually put his hand to his face to twist the hair in his fingers, but all he felt were the scabs where he had cut his skin shaving.

When he climbed out of the accessory compartment, the first alarm went off in his mind when he saw the cockpit door closed. The second and imminently larger alarm occurred when someone shouted, "Get down! Get down now! On the floor with your hands behind your back! Do it now!"

He turned just far enough to see a man in a dark suit with his feet spread and a Glock held in both hands pointing right at him. With no thoughts of money or freedom, he got on the floor with his hands behind him.

John Lehman kept the gun pointed at Ray's back until Joe Rand handcuffed him and patted him down. After that, Joe went to the one left door, disarmed it like Jenny had taught him, and opened it. He informed the men in black fatigues that the suspect was in custody, and they could bring the portable stairs to the door.

CHAPTER TWENTY-FIVE

The bus transporting the crew and passengers from Flight Triple One motored down the parallel taxiway and stopped at a large hangar with the huge doors standing open. They were all escorted to a table set up by customs and immigration officials, where it was discovered that no one had passports or even identification, rendering the process futile. The entire group was directed to folding chairs set up in the open hangar and provided with refreshments. After all they had experienced in the last few days, this was not much of a mountain to climb. They laughed and joked, and Colt entertained them. The officials spoke into their portable radios several times, and then informed them that the airplane was being towed to the hangar, and they would be able to retrieve their personal belongings. Much to the relief of the uniformed and confused officials, this would include passports.

They could see the Tri Con jet in the distance, and they watched as the emergency escape slide was detached and the escape rope was pulled back into the cockpit. A large tug pulled a tow bar down the taxiway to move the airplane once it was prepared. The morning temperature was comfortable, and a gentle breeze made their wait very pleasant. The runway was open for business again now that the Tri Con emergency was over, and airplanes were taking off and landing, providing a degree of entertainment.

Everyone relaxed, but it seemed that fate would not allow them to linger without drama. A police van with bars on the windows pulled up in front of the hangar and was followed momentarily by two ambulances. The three vehicles sat there with the engines running and red and blue lights flashing. Was it possible that there was yet another airport emergency in progress? Colt said, "If anyone has been injured while breaking the law, please step forward."

Even the Martin family smiled at his joke as they waited for whatever drama was to unfold. Someone pointed to one of the Humvees coming toward the hangar on the taxiway. The military vehicle, with its big machine gun on top, stopped near the police van, and the two FBI agents got out and exchanged credentials with the police officials. When everyone was properly introduced and vetted, the agents opened the Humvee door and two men in black fatigues escorted Ray Slackman out. He was handcuffed, and his feet were shackled. He shuffled along with short, choppy steps until he reached the police van where he was deposited into the back. His escorts climbed in and sat beside him on the bench. Before the door closed, Heather raised her right hand in greeting, even though her hands were still sore, and her middle finger was stiff and would not fold properly. Ray seemed to be unappreciative and agitated, but the two escorts smiled and appeared to be warm and understanding individuals. The two FBI agents came over and spoke briefly with Colt, then took a seat in the front of the van before it drove off with lights flashing.

Everyone expected the ambulances to follow the van, but they remained in place. Eventually they were forgotten as the group went back to their refreshments and discussions of what should happen to Ray. They were distracted once again when a huge tour bus pulled up and its air brakes hissed loudly as it stopped. The bus was brightly painted and had the words *Hotel do Caracol* on the sides. The doors opened and a uniformed gentleman stepped down and looked around. He saw Colt's uniform and approached him. He said in broken English, "Bom dia, are you Comandante Adams?"

Colt liked the sound of that and replied, "Yes, I am."

"Obrigado comandante, I am your concierge and here to transport your party to the Hotel do Caracol."

"Excellent. We will be delayed for a few minutes until we clear customs and immigration."

"I am at your service, comandante. We will wait."

"How far is it to the hotel?"

"A short trip to the town of Angra de Heroismo, comandante. It will be a pleasant ride to the south side of the island."

"We will require transportation to the docks at Praia da Vitoria this afternoon. Can you arrange that?"

"It is taken care of, comandante. The bus is at your disposal."

Colt was of the opinion that Tri Con management existed, for the most part, in delusions of reality, but this Harold Collins guy might be the exception.

The airplane was now moving toward the hangar, and everyone was ready to get this over with and move on. But for some reason, the tug stopped, and the jet sat out there motionless for no apparent reason. Colt thought they may have broken a tow bar, but the customs official came over to explain.

"Sir, there will be a short delay. There is a military flight inbound that will require the use of the ramp for a short time. As soon as he departs, we will bring your airplane here."

"Is there an emergency with the military flight?"

"I don't think so, sir. I was told it is a medical priority of some sort."

Colt explained the delay to the group and informed them that they would be taking the bus to the luxury hotel as soon as the formalities were concluded. No one seemed to mind. The emotional roller coaster had drained their desire or ability to complain.

The thump of helicopter blades interrupted all conversation, and as it got closer, everyone looked out to watch it. Colt had not considered that the priority aircraft might be a chopper. The big, gray machine approached along Runway Three-Three and then changed course to land on the ramp in front of the hangar. Colt recognized the British Sea King and knew it was the equivalent of the US Navy's Sea Stallion. The helicopter hovered briefly before touching down, and the words "*HMS Integrity*" were visible on its fuselage.

The fuel was chopped to the jet engine, and it began to whine to a stop. The rear doors opened, and the stairs unfolded. Two Royal Navy medics hopped out to confer with the ambulance attendants. A wheelchair was removed from the ambulance and rolled to the chopper door. The medics went back inside and returned shortly, with one of them holding a little girl's hand, and the other holding a bag of intravenous fluid high enough to continue the drip into her arm. The little girl wore a blue pair of sweatpants and a kid's souvenir sweatshirt with a picture of an aircraft carrier and the caption "*HMS Integrity.*" They led her to the wheelchair, gently sat her down, and then hung the bag on the pole attached to the back of the chair. She sat anxiously looking back inside the helicopter.

Colt said, "The British Navy must be having a tough time recruiting."

Several people wondered out loud why a ten-year-old girl would be on an aircraft carrier. The Martin grandchildren watched in awe and wished they could see an aircraft carrier and ride in a helicopter. The two medics left the girl with the ambulance attendants and went back inside while another wheelchair was rolled up to the door. The little girl looked around and saw the group of people at the hangar door. She quickly ignored the adults but returned the wave and smile of eight-year-old Elisha Martin before returning her nervous attention to the helicopter door.

It didn't take long for the group of weary travelers to lose interest in the helicopter, other than the fact that it was delaying their departure to the hotel. They went back to the refreshments and idle conversation. They were being entertained by the hotel concierge who was teaching the proper Portuguese pronunciation of bom dia (good day) and obrigado (thank you). No one noticed when the two medics returned to the helicopter door and assisted the heavyset female patient down the steps to the waiting wheelchair. She too was being given intravenous fluids, and the bag was hung on the wheelchair pole as with the little girl.

The chief immigration official on scene watched the process and mentally urged them on. He wanted to be done with this and get his personnel back to the terminal, where several international arrivals were due within the hour. The attendants began rolling the wheelchairs, side by side, toward the waiting ambulances, and the little girl leaned over to whisper something to the older lady. The immigration official, being married and having three daughters, instinctively concluded what that conversation was about. The patients, being female and consuming a steady flow of liquids while being subjected to the constant vibration of a helicopter ride, would logically be discussing the advantages of having landed on a civilized island with modern plumbing facilities. The older lady raised her arm like a wagon master in a western movie who intended to halt the entire pioneer westward migration. She spoke to the attendant pushing her chair, and he swiveled his head around as if she had informed him that they were surrounded by Apache. The wheelchairs pivoted in place and began rolling toward the hangar, which was the only structure in sight that might feature such a convenience.

The movement caught Jenny Kramer's attention, and she looked out at the approaching formation. It was as if she was attending the country club's annual fundraising ball and someone had showed up wearing the same identical dress. The lady in the wheelchair was wearing a Tri Con flight attendant uniform just like Jenny's, although it consisted of several more yards of sky blue material. They stared at each other and were speechless. A casual observer might have mistaken the scene for a silent movie set, because both their mouths were open and their lips were moving, but no audio was being produced. Had it actually been a silent movie, the hokey music would undoubtedly have been building to a melodramatic crescendo.

The impasse of sensory anemia and vocal paralysis was broken when little Elisha Martin screamed, "Nana!" She ran across the ramp at full speed, and the wheelchair attendant backed off as if the Apache had actually attacked. His apprehension was compounded when first Jenny and then the entire Martin family charged his position.

The reunion for Bertie and her family was tearful, joyful, and emotional, but for Mandy it was something totally different. Many of the people in the hangar had escaped the airplane with camera phones on their belt or in their pocket, and the entire event was well documented. In every photo of Bertie, Mandy could be seen clinging to her like a parasite.

By the time the initial excitement had passed, the airplane and everyone's passports had arrived. Bertie's family was cleared first, so they could accompany her to the Hospital Santo Espirito in Angra de Heroismo. Mr. Martin and Mandy accompanied Bertie in one ambulance, and the rest of the family was transported in the other. Before they left, Bertie took the time to explain to Jenny and Colt how she and Mandy had escaped the airplane. The ceiling and air conditioning equipment had collapsed into the galley and aisle and left the two of them trapped but unharmed by the door. She had tried to dig through the wreckage to help the passengers, but couldn't move the heavy debris. Ultimately, her only choice was to open the door and deploy the slide raft for their escape. She and Mandy had learned, while on the carrier, that almost everyone else was safe.

Much to the relief of the chief immigration official and the hotel concierge, everyone and their baggage were eventually loaded onto the tour bus with a great deal of festivity. When the bus finally drove away, the official was left standing on the ramp, mopping his brow with a handkerchief, and breathing diesel fumes. His portable radio beeped, and he was informed that he and his crew should return to the terminal posthaste, because over a hundred TV and print reporters were waiting to be cleared.

The excitement aboard the *Karuk* grew more intense by the hour as the morning passed. No one complained about the crowded conditions, and the crew did everything possible to make the passengers comfortable. Captain Maxwell arranged tours of the ship, including the engine room and the bridge, and all the kids had been given a turn at the helm. Some of them asked to fire the ship's cannon, which drew a huge laugh from Maxwell.

Early in the afternoon, Terceira came into view on the horizon, and everyone anxiously watched as it grew larger and more verdant. It took several more hours to approach the port. Two miles outside the mouth of the harbor, Captain Maxwell gave the command for all stop, and the harbormaster's boat came alongside. The Portuguese harbor pilot came aboard and made his way to the bridge to guide the ship to the pier.

Captain Maxwell assembled the Tri Con passengers and crew on the upper decks to keep them clear of the deck apes who would be scrambling around the main deck to secure the ship to the pier. The handicapped passengers were seated on the mess deck where they watched the action through the open hatches and portholes.

When the ship passed through the seawall that protected the harbor, they could see the huge crowd gathered to greet them.

Pattie could not remember when she had been so excited. She had tried to nap at the hotel, but it was impossible. A long shower and a nice lunch had helped pass the hours, but she had waited impatiently until it was time to board the bus for the trip to the port. She and Melissa took seats together when they left the hotel and listened to the concierge lecture about the history of the port and its commercial importance to the island. When they drove onto the quay, it seemed like Mardi Gras was in progress. There were at least ten tour buses angled together and parked in formation. Several of them were under contract to various news organizations, and two of them had transported high school bands to perform for the welcoming ceremony.

When the bus parked, a representative of the local police came on board to explain the plan that had been devised by the governor and the mayor. The families would be escorted to a roped-off VIP area, very near where the ship's gangway would be placed. There, they would wait with local officials for the arrival of the ship. Another area had been reserved for the high school bands, and yet another for the news media. The families were accommodated with folding chairs while they waited. The news media was extremely irritated that they were confined to their bullpen and couldn't interview the family members.

There was a flurry of activity in the bullpen when two taxi vans arrived, and Big Bertha and her family got out. The media had been alerted by reporters at the hospital that she and Mandy were being released. Bertie was still required to rest in the wheelchair, but the fluids were no longer necessary. Her oldest grandson chauffeured the wheelchair into the VIP area with Mandy sitting in her lap. They were greeted with hugs and kisses from everyone. Mandy's grandparents had been notified and were en route from Madrid to pick her up.

There was another stir in the crowd when the *Karuk* entered the harbor. Cameras began rolling and one of the bands cranked up with a Portuguese tune that no one recognized. The harbor pilot maneuvered the ship so that the starboard side was next to the quay. As they approached the mooring bollards, the engines were reversed and the ship was within twenty feet of the quay. The deck apes threw small lines to men on the pier, and they used them to haul the big hawser lines from the ship to be looped over the bollards. The ship's electric winches were then used to tighten the hawsers and snug the ship up to the quay. The family members were shouting to the crew on the gun deck and there were tears and laughter as they shouted back. Pattie and Charlie just waved and blew kisses.

Several deck apes began rigging the gangway, while others connected the shore power cable and fresh water lines. Mrs. Fowler pointed out Britt to Mrs. Johnson and then they began a flurry of whispering back and forth when Mrs. Johnson pointed out Tony, who was standing beside her. There was a brief lull after the gangway was secured while the handicapped were being prepared to disembark. Cameras began to roll and flashbulbs popped at the first sign of activity at the ship's rail, but it turned out to be just one man bounding down the gangway at full speed. At first the reporters thought it was a Navy enlisted man, because he was dressed in bellbottom dungarees and a blue work shirt, but then they saw the short pants, boots, and baggy shirt and decided he was part of the entertainment. So they continued filming. The guy had a nice opening trick as he tripped over a water hose and slid on his belly for six or eight feet, drawing a roar of laughter from the crowd, but after that, he faded fast. He got up and looked around wild-eyed like he didn't know where to go or what to do, and everybody lost interest as the first passengers appeared on deck and prepared to disembark.

The Tri Con crew had moved to the head of the gangway where, along with Captain Maxwell, they would say goodbye to their passengers. Britt and Tony were still side-by-side, which caused more whispering at the VIP ropes. When the passengers actually began coming down the gangway, the mayor rolled Bertie and Mandy to the bottom so they too could say goodbye.

All the survivors would be medically evaluated and caught up on their prescription drugs that had gone down with the airplane. After that they would have the option of hotel accommodations or transportation on Air Portugal to the destination of their choice. Once the handicapped were off the ship, the other passengers came down the gangway without assistance. They were escorted past the media bullpen, and only a few chose to stop and be interviewed. One of those was the old lady with the broken arm that Charlie had rescued. She gave him and the crew a glowing testimonial which, as far as anyone could tell, was never aired.

Colt, who was now in civilian clothes, blended in with the crowd and limped up to the bullpen to be interviewed also. The reporters crowded around him and stuck microphones in his face, whereupon he produced a card from his pocket proclaiming himself to be a deaf mute. After several minutes of frustrating hand signals and grunts, they lost interest and looked for more fruitful targets. The family that had pulled Pam from the airplane and cared for her in the raft received special hugs from each of the crew and was told that they would be honored with an exclusive ceremony at Tri Con headquarters at a time to be determined.

At last the crew came down the gangway as the band played what someone thought might be an off-key rendition of "America the Beautiful." It was most recognizable by the chorus, which was played by a solo tuba. Some of the reporters remarked that the deaf mute guy was the luckiest man on the quay.

Nancy and Pam came down the gangway first. Nancy used a pair of US Navy crutches due to her swollen ankle. They were greeted by their husbands, and after speaking to everyone and receiving hugs, they moved off to the bullpen to speak to the press. Neither of them really wanted to answer questions, but they had witnessed Allen Smallwood's headfirst slide into an imaginary second base on the quay, and they were determined that he get credit for his performance as a Tri Con executive. This information caused a feeding frenzy among the reporters, who had excellent footage of the sprawl, and the girls provided his title with the company and his purpose for being on the flight. When asked to spell his name, Pam said, "S-m-a-l-l-m-a-n."

Meanwhile, Alice Elon and Mary Dobson were greeted by their families and moved away to join Nancy and Pam on the bus. Candace Whitton and Shelia Graham came next, and Shelia had her hand behind her back. When they reached Bertie and Mandy, Shelia revealed her hand and the teddy bear that she had retrieved from the sea. Mandy squealed so loud that the emergency medical technicians ran over to tend to her. For the first time in days, she let go of Bertie and held the bear.

Britt Fowler and Tony Johnson came down the gangway hand in hand, to the great delight of their four parents. Formal introductions were made and informal speculation and encouragement began immediately. All four parents looked at

Mandy with her teddy bear and wondered if their prayers would soon be answered.

Molly Jackson walked onto the pier next, where her mother embraced her and cried tears of joy.

Robby waited at the top of the gangway while the two captains shook hands and said goodbye.

"Charlie, few men are ever given the opportunity to know the limits of their courage and ability. It's a privilege to know a man who has been tested and found worthy by all, in every respect. You, sir, have met the challenge with great success."

"I'm not sure success created from failure should be celebrated, Max, and I think anyone would have done the same under the circumstances."

"In that case, consider yourself first among equals, sir."

Robby slowly walked beside Charlie in case he needed help, but the captain refused assistance and moved along with an erratic cadence holding the rail. Patti met him halfway. He put his arm around her and leaned on her for support, just as he had been doing since they were teenagers. They joined Robby and Melissa on the pier, and Charlie stopped to look back at the *Karuk* and the sea beyond.

He somehow felt a kindred spirit with the seagulls gliding gracefully through the sunlit sky. Captain Charlie Wells thought, *Tri Con Eleven has reached its final destination; my passengers and crew have not.*

OTHER BOOKS BY HARRISON JONES

Tri Con Airlines has nine thousand pilots and they need more. When Tri Con hires eight new pilots and assigns them to a pilot class, they find the ground school and flight simulator challenge more than expected. The class is a mix of former military pilots and civilians with varying experience, including a former female flight attendant. Who can survive *The Pilot Class* and meet the challenge of flying the line as a Tri Con first officer. Personal relationships, a married flight attendant with an abusive husband, a major airline accident, and the federal government are all obstacles that stand in the way of *The Pilot Class*.

OTHER BOOKS BY HARRISON JONES

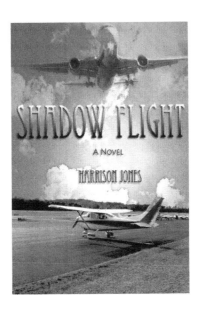

America's security may depend on a young flight instructor from rural south Texas. Kyle Bennett's charter flight disappears without a trace, along with a female student and the charter passenger. The mysterious disappearance cannot be solved despite the best efforts of the Civil Air Patrol, the Coast Guard and the FAA.

When a Tri Con captain, Bud Gibson, and one of the airline's mechanics, Matt Pierce, go missing, the two cases merge. A conspiracy to complete the 9-11 attack is underway and, the terrorists are sure they can defeat all of America's security measures. Only Kyle, Bud and Matt stand in their way.

About the Author

Author, Harrison Jones began his aviation career in 1967 when he was employed by a major airline as an aircraft mechanic. While working as a mechanic, he took flying lessons and obtained his commercial license with multi-engine and instrument ratings. Soon thereafter he became a flight instructor and taught flying for more than ten years. Along the way he was licensed to fly gliders and seaplanes. In 1972 he accepted a position with the airline as a pilot ground school instructor and taught aircraft systems until 1976 when he began flying the line as a pilot with the company.

As an airline transport pilot he was type rated in the DC-9, B-727, DC-8, MD-88, B-757, B-767 and the MD-11. He retired as an international captain with more than 20,000 hours in the cockpit, after extensive flying to Asia, Europe, South America and the Middle East.

His aviation career, along with a previous enlistment in the US Navy, lends credibility to his writing in *Equal Time Point* and his other novels, *The Pilot Class,* and, *Shadow Flight.* Realism and plausibility are major ingredients throughout the novels.

After being away from home for countless holidays, birthdays and other family celebrations, Harrison now lives in Georgia with his wife, Diane, and enjoys writing and spending time with his grandchildren with emphasis on the latter.

Harrison can be contacted at **www.harrisonjones.org**